IT MUST HAVE BEEN
THE MISTLETOE

www.**transworldbooks**.co.uk

IT MUST HAVE BEEN THE MISTLETOE

Judy Astley

BANTAM PRESS

LONDON • TORONTO • SYDNEY • AUCKLAND • JOHANNESBURG

TRANSWORLD PUBLISHERS
61–63 Uxbridge Road, London W5 5SA
A Random House Group Company
www.transworldbooks.co.uk

First published in Great Britain
in 2014 by Bantam Press
an imprint of Transworld Publishers

A CIP catalogue record for this book
is available from the British Library.

ISBN 9780593074404

Addresses for Random House Group Ltd companies outside the UK
can be found at: www.randomhouse.co.uk
The Random House Group Ltd Reg. No. 954009

The Random House Group Limited supports the Forest Stewardship
Council® (FSC®), the leading international forest-certification organisation.
Our books carrying the FSC label are printed on FSC®-certified paper. FSC
is the only forest-certification scheme supported by the leading
environmental organisations, including Greenpeace. Our paper
procurement policy can be found at
www.randomhouse.co.uk/environment

Typeset in 11/15pt Giovanni Book by Falcon Oast Graphic Art Ltd.
Printed and bound in Great Britain by
CPI Group (UK) Ltd, Croydon, CR0 4YY

2 4 6 8 10 9 7 5 3 1

ACKNOWLEDGEMENTS

A big thank you to Terence Blacker for permission to quote from his fabulous song, 'Sad Old Bastards with Guitars'.

And lots of thanks also to Janie and Mickey Wilson at www.chez-castillon.com for the most wonderful place to stay to do masses of writing in absolute peace (and also for the fun).

ONE

'It's *Christmaaas!*' bellowed Noddy Holder from the radio on Thea's kitchen window ledge as she opened the back door to let her brother Jimi in.

'Not yet it isn't, Noddy. *Waaay* too soon, matey!' Thea lunged for the off switch and cut Slade's exuberance into silence.

'Oh, don't switch it off, Tee. Who doesn't love that song?' Jimi reached out to turn it back on but Thea got hold of his long skinny wrist and stopped him.

'Oh, I know, I know, it's one of the best; the great annual classic and all that – but for later, yes? Since when did Christmas take up half the year? It's months away.' She didn't want to think about Christmas; not this year at all for preference, and even if she really had to, definitely not this soon.

Jimi shrugged. 'It's not that long. It's already November. I hope you're not turning into one of those ranting Christmas deniers, Tee. That's a real sign of age.'

'Cheeky sod. And anyway, what would that make you? You're years older than me. OK, you can keep the radio on – but *quietly*. There's coffee in the thingy so help yourself and I'll run upstairs and quickly dry my hair. I'll only be a few secs. It's very sweet of you to come and pick me up – saves me having to scrape the ice off my car windows and I hate having to do that. Are Rosie and Elmo with you?'

'Not Rosie – she's got a "headache".' Jimi made little quotation marks in the air with his fingers. 'You know how she is about Mum and Dad – thinks they're mad, irresponsible old hippies who should have taken up golf and good works by now.'

'Ha! She'd better not hold her breath waiting for that one.' Thea had a quick vision of their father with his customary Willie Nelson bandana but wearing a pink and yellow diamond-pattern golfing jumper, looking puzzled about where the ball he'd just hit had gone and wondering why he should even be bothered to go and look for it. The game wouldn't suit him; nothing that involved rules and a dress-code ever did.

'Exactly. I did tell her how they'd been very keen we should all be there, but she just closed her eyes and looked even more pained so I left her to it. But I've got Elmo; he's outside, iPadding. I asked him if he was coming in and he looked at me as if I'd just suggested he step out of the car and do a quick run to Brighton and back.'

'It's his age. Teenagers need all their energy for growing.'

'Do they? Heavens, if that's true he'll be seven feet tall by next summer. Anyway, go and finish your hair off, Thea, or Mum will blame us for the sinking Yorkshire puds and Dad will say it's our fault that he's somehow halfway down a wine bottle before anyone's even sat down.'

Thea raced up to her room and unwrapped her damp hair from its towel turban, shook it out and pulled a comb through it. Drying it would take a matter of minutes. In a furious *sod-you* moment, she'd had it cut quite short and spiky after Rich had left her, when she'd realized he'd gone for good. She'd half-hoped he'd come back to collect some forgotten item so she could get the satisfaction of watching him recoil from her new hair. He'd very much favoured a long-blonde look on a woman, having old-fashioned views about the notion of femininity. Well tough, she thought now as she blasted hot air at the fronds and pulled them into pleasing tufts. Before Christmas she must get some fun colour on it – coppery highlights among the blonde would give the tuftiness some definition. Or maybe some bright pink and a bit of scarlet. How Rich would have hated that . . .

She could still just hear the sound of the radio. Jimi was clattering about in the kitchen, probably having a second mug of coffee and going through her recycling

9

in search of a newspaper with a number puzzle in it that he hadn't already done. It felt very cheering to have someone else on the premises, as if Jimi somehow warmed the whole of this little house by a few degrees, even though he had only called in to give her a lift to their parents' home in south-west London for a big, whole-family Sunday lunch. Sudden solitary living when you've been sharing a home for the past three years with the man who had promised to be your happy-ever-after, plus his great big dog, was turning out to be a lonely old way to exist. Thea felt it especially at weekends, however much she went out to be defiantly social and however much bravado she tried to assume.

It seemed strange now, to think that on the odd occasions she used to have the place to herself, she'd relished the time alone, padding about in her pyjamas till lunchtime or lazing in the garden guilt-free with a book while Rich was away on work trips or at yet another dog show with his sister. And it wasn't as if Rich had ever been the rackety, crashing-about type even when he *was* there. Even his giant poodle Benji (Champion Heatherwood Disraeli Gears) had been a quiet sort, mostly to be found stretched out on the floor, easily mistaken for a fluffy orange rug.

It was just over two months now (OK, two months and three days) since Rich had solemnly announced his decision to leave, packed his stuff and gone, taking Benji, the hundreds of back-copies of *Your Dog* and

Poodle Variety magazines and a surprisingly small bag of clothes and personal possessions. This Sunday morning before Jimi arrived, the quiet had felt like something Thea could almost touch – a mute, lumpen presence that had sneaked into her home and settled, making itself felt in every room.

'Bloody Christmas,' she muttered as she finished fluffing her hair beneath the blast of the dryer. She felt unseasonably grumpy and her mood had been getting steadily worse since she'd spotted the first fat robins on cards in early September; at the same time, she was also cross with herself for feeling this way. She used to love the run-up to Christmas; loved the crowded shops and their glitter-filled windows, the fresh piny scent of the tree that took up too much space and moulted its needles all over the small sitting room, the mince pies she'd make with their delicious toffee-like trail of melted goo that had to be prised from the bottom of the tin while they were still skin-blisteringly hot. She'd even loved Rich's tradition of putting together a stocking full of treats for the dog. They would get their own card design printed up in early December – last year's had starred Benji wearing felt reindeer antlers, looking embarrassed. But this year she'd be buying her cards from a charity shop – and would Rich even send her one? Their years together surely qualified her to remain in his address book, even if she had given the ring back. She often wished she hadn't and had sold it instead –

11

the guttering at the back of the house needed fixing and the cash would probably have run to getting the kitchen painted in a fabulous, lively colour he'd have condemned as 'not sensible'. Oh well.

Slade on the radio had made way for the inevitable blast of Wizzard wishing it could be Christmas every day, and as Thea glanced out of the window, she could see Mrs Over-the-Road in her front garden, stringing lights up in her magnolia tree. Or rather, *Mr* Over-the-Road was doing the stringing. His wife was standing on the path, directing operations and breathing heavy gusts of frosty air as she shouted at her husband. A week ago, they'd put the Advent candle set in their sitting-room window, even though it would be ages till the lighting of the first one. Thea would bet serious money that by the following Sunday there'd also be a wreath of ivy and pine cones on their front door, and their pet Westie would be walked up the road to Tesco Metro wearing his little red and white Santa jacket.

Thea slicked a bit of serum through her hair then grabbed her make-up bag to take with her so she could apply some eyeshadow on the way, conscious not only of Jimi down in her kitchen but also of Elmo waiting in the car, surely getting cold by now. From the window she could see the toes of his huge trainered feet on the BMW's dashboard, twitching in time to something that would be blasting those delicate teenage eardrums. Was that another sign of age? Worrying about her nephew's fragile ears? Surely not – she hadn't even hit thirty-five yet, though it wouldn't be long.

As Thea and Jimi walked down the short path, Mrs Over-the-Road waved cheerily and called, 'Soon be here, won't it? Best time of the year, Christmas!' The Westie joined in, barking and bouncing as if equally excited and Thea smiled and waved back. At least Mrs OTR hadn't asked her about her plans for the holiday. She hadn't even given it a thought yet, other than wondering which part of the world she could escape to in order to let the whole event pass her by. If only, Thea thought, there was an option to cuddle up in a cave with a nice warm hibernating bear and not come out till Christmas was all over and the first snowdrops flowered. These November-to-January weeks for the newly single were – as Bette Davis had said about old age – no place for sissies.

'Christmas creeps up on you, doesn't it?' she said to Jimi. 'One minute they're sneaking cards in among the summer-sale stuff and big tins of chocolates by the supermarket check-outs, and the next you can't move for tinsel and crackers.' She could hear herself sounding wistful, only a breath away from pathetic. Rich – so damn sensible – would tell her to get a grip and he'd be right. But then Rich was no longer here, the sod. If he were, she wouldn't be feeling remotely feeble.

Jimi was looking at her, with a serious face on. Please don't ask me if I'm OK, she thought. Still, if he asked and her eyes went leaky as they still occasionally did, at least it was before her make-up had gone on, not after.

But all her brother said was, 'I don't know about creeping up, but Elmo gave me his present list in September, at the beginning of the school term.' He opened the car's back door. 'He said it was to give me plenty of time to save up. So thoughtful.' Jimi then asked, 'Would you rather sit in the front, Thea? The boy could move. *Should* move.'

'No, thanks, it's fine. Elmo needs the leg room far more than I do.' Thea climbed into the BMW and reached forward to ruffle Elmo's blond hair. 'Hi, boy.'

He half-turned and grinned at her, forgiving her the gesture that she always made, ever since a few years ago, when he'd mumbled that he hated people touching his hair. He'd decided she was the exception and she felt honoured. 'Lo, Thea. Y'OK?'

'M'OK,' she said. 'You?'

'M'OK too.'

Jimi started the car and, just as he pulled away from the kerb, he asked his sister, 'So what do you think it is with the old folks this time? It sounded ominous when Dad said he was rounding us all up because "We've got something to tell you all." That never sounds like good news, does it? Did you get anything out of Mum?'

'No. I did ask but she said to wait till today. It's anyone's guess. It could just be something simple, like they're off to Australia till the middle of January, maybe?' She hoped it would be something fun like that. A bit of her worried that one of them might be ill but her dad had sounded cheerful enough when he'd called to invite her over.

Jimi didn't sound convinced. 'I don't know. He seemed a bit over-excited, like a kid with a big bursty secret. I was wondering why he couldn't just say over the phone.'

'I thought that too – all madly mysterious. Also, the last time they had "something to tell us" it was he and Mum saying they'd decided they were splitting up. And yet that was more than a year ago now and they're still there, in the same house, just like always. Well, almost, apart from the separate rooms thing and them being competitive about telling us where they've been recently with their *own* friends . . .'

'That's true. Anyway, whatever it is, it can't be more of a stunner than that particular announcement, can it?'

'No, it can't. I remember it felt like a massive shock at the time. You don't expect that from two people who never argue about anything more serious than who gets first go at the Sudoku and who've been together for nearly forty years. But as you say, it turned out that nothing much changed.' Thea scrabbled through her make-up bag and pulled out a compact of eyeshadows and a brush. 'Perhaps they're thinking of – oh, I don't know – getting a cat? Taking up hang-gliding? They've been invited to be in a TV reality programme about amicable separations? Who knows! Whatever it is, we'll find out in about half an hour.'

'Sam, did you put Alfie's special cup in the bag? And some spare pants just in case? And where is Milly's owl? Please don't say it's still on her bed.' Emily could feel her voice getting shrill. She took a couple of deep breaths and tried to remember what they said in her yoga class about being gentle with the moment. With every moment. It wasn't working, not while she was trying to strap a reluctant four-year-old into his car seat. He could actually do it himself these days but she didn't trust him to get it quite right. If she left him to it, it would be the one time she drove into the back of a bus and Alfie would come hurtling through from behind and break both her neck and his own. She'd seen the adverts.

Sensing her tension, Alfie stiffened, sticking his podgy legs out straight in front and arching his back, pulling against the strap, ready to roar a protest. Shouldn't he have grown out of that sort of thing by now? He'd be starting full-time school in January. Emily moved to try to bend him and hit her head on the Golf's doorframe. 'Sodding *shit!*' she cursed. Alfie grinned up at her, relaxing at last and suddenly amenable, scraping some ancient dried-on biscuit from his seat belt and putting it in his mouth before she could stop him. Please don't let him be sick, she prayed.

'Daddy? Mummy said a bad word.' Sam, waiting in

the front passenger seat, turned to smile at seven-year-old Milly who was already tidily strapped in beside Alfie, twirling a mousy plait in her fingers and looking pleased with herself.

'I know she did, sweetie. I heard her. Naughty Mummy!' The two of them giggled like conspirators and Emily immediately wanted to slap them, which was against both the law and the essential spirit of mindfulness. Another deep breath. 'Sam? You didn't answer about the pants, cup and owl.'

'Did I need to? You'll have checked the bag twice over already. I know you.'

Emily climbed into the driving seat and switched the ignition on. 'Do I have to do *everything*?' she snarled. 'One thing. Just *one thing* I asked you to do.'

'Chill, Ems. It's sorted.' Sam leaned back and put a foot up on the dashboard. There would be scuffmarks, she thought. And would he be the one who wiped them off?

He yawned, and said with an air of exaggerated patience, 'Spare pants, cup and owl are all on board, along with the kids' wellies and mittens in case they want to go out and trash the garden. And why are you so uptight? We're only going to your parents'. They wouldn't give a flying one about a potential no-pants scenario. They've made being totally laid back into a complete art form.'

Emily caught him giving her a sideways look and

could feel him adding a silent 'unlike you' to his statement. She couldn't blame him for that. She was like a
twangy piece of wire these days and she hated feeling
like this. Rescue Remedy couldn't even touch it.

Emily carefully manoeuvred the car into the right
lane at the Chiswick roundabout. 'Did you check the
road situation?' she asked. 'Is Hammersmith Bridge
open today or are they still mending it?'

'Ah.' Sam started tapping at his phone. 'Hang on a sec.'

'I haven't got a sec, I've picked a lane now. Oh bugger,
I'll go the Kew Bridge way. Can't risk it. I *hate* being late.'
She did some more deep breathing and tried not to
flinch as a motorbike cut in across the front of the Golf.

Sam reached over to the centre panel and twiddled
the controls, putting his seat warmer on to the
maximum heat. Emily sighed.

'What now?' he said. 'Just because you don't feel the
cold.'

'Keeping the heat off saves fuel,' she stated, wishing
she hadn't said anything at all. They were only going a
few miles, so what difference did it make? All she
seemed to do these days was nag. She felt fraught so
much of the time, constantly sure that whatever she was
doing, there were other things she should be getting on
with. Did the children get enough vitamins? Had she
bought a present for whoever's party Milly was going to,
and wouldn't a proper super-parent keep several in a
cupboard, already wrapped? Were there notes or emails

from the school that she hadn't seen? All that was really Sam's responsibility but he was just so relaxed. It was so much easier in the week when she was at work. You knew where you were with numbers. Accountancy might be other people's idea of a boring job, but for her, the arranging of figures into a tidy order was soothing, safe and satisfying.

'Sorry,' she said as she slowed for the traffic lights at Mortlake. 'I'm just so . . .'

'Wound up?' Sam looked at her. He was smiling, looking fond. Was that an example of being passive-aggressive, she wondered, or was he just being nice? Whatever it was, it was confusing. If he'd been scowling at her she could have retaliated. Now she just turned her attention back to the road ahead as the heavy Sunday-lunch traffic inched forward. The blue Toyota in front had gone hazy. Oh, not tears – not now.

'You need to learn to let go a bit, Em,' Sam said softly, passing her a tissue from the box on the floor. 'I haven't completely screwed up on the home front, you know. The kids get fed, exercised and read to, don't they?'

'I know, I know,' Emily said, at last driving across the lights. 'It's just Christmas coming up and there's so much to do and I've got to clear the decks workwise because January is the busiest time . . .'

'I can do the Christmas stuff for you. I'll shop, get all the food, everything. Do the tree, get the cards. Just give me a list.'

'For you' and 'a list' – and that was what summed it up, didn't it? Emily felt her eyes filling again and dabbed at them carefully, not wanting her make-up to shift. Sam made a wonderful stay-at-home husband and had fewer than a couple of thousand words of amusing journalism to come up with per week, but even after two years of it he still needed *a list*. He was still doing the childcare *for her*.

'Mummeee. Are we nearly there yet? I need a wee,' Alfie called from behind Emily's seat.

'Yes, sweetie. We're here. Right *now*.' She turned the car off the road and in past the iron gates that had gone so rusty that they no longer even closed. The gravel skittered beneath the wheels and she stopped just short of her brother Jimi's BMW. She climbed out of the car and looked up at the house as she opened the Golf's back door. The windowframes all needed painting, and the windowboxes where her mother would have planted next spring's frilled purple and pink tulips looked as if they could crash to the ground any second, supported as they were at a dangerously lurching angle on the splintery ledges. But it was still the house she thought of as 'home', the haven – albeit now a bit shabby – she could feel comforted by.

Their own house was a constant work-in-progress, a building that was still only halfway to being the snug family nest she'd planned it to be. Would the tiles in the children's bathroom ever be grouted? Would the wind-blown garden fence-panels ever be replaced? Why were there two much-needed bookcases still flat in their packs? *Stop it,* she told herself as she helped Alfie down from the car. Things could be far worse. For a start, she wouldn't trade places with her sister, that was for sure. Who would want to be suddenly cast back into single-dom after all those years with someone, even though Thea had always been the one in the family who'd got all the gorgeousness genes. Where were the men of her age that would be any use? Single ones were either ditherers, serial shaggers or mummies' boys. Divorced ones had alimony and enough children already, thank you.

'OK – in you go, kids,' Sam said as Milly and Alfie celebrated their release from the car by running round and round the plum tree planted in the garden's central patch of scuffed grass.

Emily locked the car and took a deep breath. 'So now we'll find out what this big thing is that they have to tell us,' she said to Sam. 'I hope it isn't that they've decided to sell this place. They can't keep up with it much longer, it's obvious, but I'll be so sad if it goes.'

'Hmm,' Sam replied. 'But surely for them, moving might be a good thing? They must rattle around in here.'

'Yes, I know, but don't forget that according to them they're not even officially together any more, so they think they *need* plenty of room.'

He laughed. 'Oh, the irony. They split up and so they

need to stay together in this great big house. Mad, your parents. Tell me I'm wrong on that.'

Emily couldn't. She called the children away from where they'd crawled under the jungle of hydrangeas by the side wall and went up the steps. Thea opened the door and Emily hugged her, scenting from beyond the hallway the tempting aroma of a full-scale Sunday roast.

'Have they told you anything yet?' she whispered, peering past Thea to see if their mother was coming to greet them.

'No. No hint of anything different. I expect they're waiting till we're all here.'

Emily relaxed. 'You know what it'll be? They'll be wanting to ask us what we're all doing for Christmas.' Her sister's face fell and she wished she hadn't mentioned it.

'Sorry, Tee, I didn't mean . . . I shouldn't have . . .'

'No, no, you're OK,' Thea said flatly as they all headed for the kitchen, Emily's heels tap-tapping on the old tiled floor. 'And anyway, you're probably right. All it'll be is something about Christmas.'

TWO

Anna was almost having second thoughts. Almost, but not quite. She fired up the little blowtorch that she always imagined as a Barbie Doll's flame-thrower and carefully scorched the icing sugar on top of the lemon tart. As the sugar caramelized and browned, she wondered how it was going to be after the start of the new year, not to see Mike every single day. They would still be friends, they'd promised each other that; in fact, the very best of friends. How could they not be? Forty-five years of living with someone was at least half a good long lifetime, and you couldn't throw it all away just because there was a thrilling new path to take. Also, as she hadn't met him till she was nearly twenty you had to say it added up to more than the middle and best parts of her life, all things considered. You didn't give up on it lightly.

Was Mike feeling the same? Now they'd made their

big bold decision to go their separate ways in reality, not just apart-but-together, still sharing the house, as they'd been for over a year now, was Mike too having moments of wavering? She both hoped he was and that he wasn't. She had to hang on to the feeling that this was a bold and bright new adventure. It was a beginning far more than it was an ending. She mustn't think about what was over or have any regrets, because that was something else they'd promised each other.

She made a pattern of little hearts all over the top of the tart and watched as they blurred into shapeless splodges. It was all very well her and Mike being so cheerily positive about the arrangements they were making for the rest of their lives – but what on earth were the children going to say? And when did you stop thinking of them as 'the children'? When they hit forty (nearly there in Jimi's case)? Fifty? Never? The trouble was, they thought of her and Mike as parents first, 'people' second. They were going to see her and Mike's decision almost entirely from their own point of view, and it could get messy. Still they had to be told before the estate agent came and put up a *For Sale* sign by the gate. She'd know soon enough what the fall-out would be.

Anna could hear Thea in the hallway, letting Emily, Sam and the children in. Jimi was down the garden in Mike's studio, probably being asked about which storage warehouse would be the most reliable for his large stock of paintings and wondering why his father needed the information.

Time to face them all.

She switched off the blowtorch and put it on the worktop next to the toaster. All this 'stuff', she thought as she scooped a few old toast crumbs off the granite. She flicked them into the bin then stood back and, as if she were compiling an inventory, looked at the four pepper grinders, the lop-sided pot Emily had made in primary school which held at least two dozen wooden spoons and spatulas, the knife rack from which she only ever used two of the many knives, the mismatched heap of saucers that she used to put under plant pots, the metal basket of eggs from Win-up-the-Road's chickens. There were three woks and at least seven assorted-size colanders and sieves hanging from the hooks on the wall. Who needed that many?

She saw all this with the fresh and eager eyes of someone who would soon no longer be in possession of more than the essentials that would have to fit into a kitchen that was certain to be a lot smaller than this one. There was so much de-cluttering to be done; so much to get rid of to make way for the new start. It would be so liberating, no longer to be lumbered with all this excess kit. Recently she'd felt completely weighed down by it all. The house was massive – way too big for two people, even if they were occupying separate bedrooms and bathrooms. And the place was growing tired and shabby at the edges. It needed a lovely young family who had plenty of years ahead of them to update it and love it and make it sparkle again. That was what she wanted now too – somewhere light and new, without any dark, neglected corners, and where you didn't feel that, at any second, the ancient boiler was going to pack up or that the water tanks which had been in the loft for decades might give way in a big frost.

The back door opened and Mike came in. Jimi stayed outside having a sly cigarette, still cupping it into his hand and blowing smoke over the fence as if Anna was going to tell him off as she had in his teens. She did wish he didn't do it, but he'd been a grown-up for a long time now and, besides, he knew the risks.

'All ready?' Mike asked, opening the fridge and taking out a bottle of champagne. He smiled at her, his eyes shining and excited. He surely also looked at this Charlotte woman like that these days. Anna wasn't jealous – not at all. Even so, she didn't really want to dwell on it.

'All ready, though maybe we should leave the big announcement till pudding?' she said with a brightness that was not entirely genuine. 'In case they all kick off a bit.' Emily was the most likely to, when she thought about it: of the three of them, she was the most traditional. There were times when Anna was half-convinced she'd been swapped over in the hospital nursery soon after birth. Who would have thought that an artist and a textiles lecturer would produce a daughter who'd chosen to be an accountant? It reminded her of a Monty Python sketch in which a poet disparages his son's choice of career, with: 'You and your namby-pamby coal mining.'

'OK,' Mike agreed. 'Though as they already know we've got some big thing to tell them, they'll be hinting like crazy and pretty much bouncing on their chairs by then.' He laughed. 'Which is part of the fun, isn't it?' His laughter stopped abruptly. 'They won't think it's fun, though, will they? They might take some persuading. It'll be a shock.'

Anna had a sudden urge to take hold of his hand, to hug him, to snuggle up tight against the battered old purple Aran sweater that she had knitted for him about twenty years ago. This was going to be a big moment and they needed to face the assembled party properly united because for the others, if not for her and Mike, it might not be that easy.

It wasn't so much an elephant in the room as a big electric charge fizzing slightly in the background and waiting to go bang, Thea thought as she helped herself to another roast parsnip. The moment they'd all sat down, Jimi had asked what the big mystery was but Anna had brushed him off, saying just to relax, eat and hang on till pudding. It made conversation a bit brittle.

Everyone seemed to be talking (and eating) too fast, as if they'd get to the big reveal moment a lot quicker that way.

'How's work? School OK?' Mike asked Thea during one of the many slightly strained little breaks in conversation.

'Oh, school's great, always is, except the children are all completely hyper about Christmas. It's hard to get them to settle to anything now they've got the decorations up and the classroom is full of paper-chains and tinsel. I'm up to here in entertainment politics with the parents too. We're having a Yule celebration instead of a nativity play but there are three mothers who I'm sure have been training up their infants for the Mary and Jesus roles for years.'

'Awkward,' Jimi commented. 'But you can see their point – nativity costumes are so much easier to put together than sorting a Green Man outfit. You only need tea towels for headgear, a dolly and a toy lamb.'

'It's not the costumes they're fussing about, it's who gets the leading role,' Thea said. 'They all look completely puzzled by the idea that there might not be one.'

'Yes, but it's good to have something *not* nativity sometimes, because you need to embrace the multi-cultural aspect, don't you?' Emily put in. 'By the time children are eleven they should have some grounding in all the major festivals, not just one.'

'Embrace the pagan too? I'm all for that,' Anna said. 'Though I can see some parents might object.'

'You need a PhD in diplomacy skills to be a teacher, I think. I don't know how you do it, Thea. I'd be exhausted.' That was Sam. 'When I'm picking up Milly from school I see the same pushy mummies strutting on serious heels into the classroom almost daily to demand why little Tobias or Tabitha's genius is not being properly recognized. The nativity-play battle must be the least of it.' He then turned to Anna. 'So, in-laws, now we're on the Christmas theme: what are your plans for this year? Why don't all of you come to us this time?'

Thea saw him wince suddenly and guessed he'd been sharply kicked on the ankle by Emily, who was glaring across the table at him.

'Not run that one past you then, Em?' she murmured to her sister.

'Nope,' Emily said tightly. 'Not that I'm surprised. Typical Sam.'

'Christmas!' yelled Alfie. 'Father Christmas is bringing me a *bike*!'

'Is he, sweetie?' Anna said. 'You're a very lucky boy.'

'He might not be,' Emily hissed in Sam's direction. 'We thought perhaps *Santa* might leave bikes till next year.'

'But Daddy *said*!' Alfie was building up to a wail.

'Yes, I expect Daddy did.'

Thea felt sorry for the child. 'I think Father Christmas likes to bring surprises,' she told him, 'but always really,

really nice surprises. So whatever it is, I'm sure you'll love it.'

'He'd love a bike,' Milly growled.

'Oh God,' said Emily. 'Let's just wait and see, shall we? And will someone have that last potato so that I don't?' She tweaked at her dress, pulling it away from her stomach and frowning. Jimi reached across and took it from the dish, putting it straight into his mouth.

Alfie giggled. 'Mummy says that's naughty.'

'Mummy's right,' Jimi said. 'But it's not *badly* naughty.'

'Mummy is just trying to teach Alfie some manners. But self-discipline is all out of the window these days, isn't it? Like all the people who just won't even *look* at their accounts till the last possible day. Oh, I dread January! It's a nightmare, and all this last-minute tax-return panic could be avoided if everyone just had a *system*. How are accountants ever supposed to enjoy Christmas?' Emily rubbed her fingers briskly across her face and Thea got the impression her sister was about to cry. She'd always shed tears easily. Their mother had mostly ignored them unless there was actual blood or a limb looked badly angled or a pet had died. She'd shrug and say tears were the obvious youngest-child weapon against more articulate and stronger siblings.

'Not boo-hooing, are you, Em?' Jimi teased.

'Don't be ridiculous,' Emily mumbled, blinking hard.

'Oh, darling.' Anna reached out and took Emily's hand. 'You do sound so tense. I'm so sorry.' Thea saw her glance across at Mike, looking worried. He picked up a bottle and offered Emily a top-up of wine.

'No, thanks, Dad. Sam's driving home but I don't want any more.' She sighed and closed her eyes. 'I just want to know – actually, we all want to know – what it is you and Mum want to tell us. Are you ill?'

'Ill?' Mike repeated, looking puzzled. 'No, we're not ill. Not that we know, anyway. No more than any other old hippies of our age, I suppose. What made you think we might be?'

'Because you're being so secretive, all mysterious!' She was close to shouting.

'She's got a point, Dad. On the phone you sounded as if you had some seriously major thing going on,' Thea told him, then she joked: 'Have you had a massive lottery win? Aren't you taking the No Publicity element a bit far by not even telling *us*?'

'OK, look, let's clear all this lot away and get the lemon tart and the cheese and we'll tell you. It's nothing terrible, I promise.' Anna started collecting plates. 'I'm so sorry if you thought it was going to be. And it does involve Christmas too, so, Emily, please don't go thinking about having enough chairs and ordering a giant turkey. It'll all be fine, trust me.'

Jimi laughed. 'Hmm. Trust. We'll see . . .'

Thea stacked up a heap of dishes and followed her mother across the kitchen where she started rinsing plates and loading the dishwasher. She thought about

31

Rich for a second. He'd be standing beside her, his tall lanky body looming over her, reaching a hand in now and then like a swift-moving crab to reposition crockery from where she'd stacked it and doing it *his* way. He'd have palpitations if he could see her putting the spoons in the same compartment as the forks. She shoved a knife in with them at the same time as a kind of *sod you* gesture and had one of the few moments of sudden lightness of heart about not having him overseeing her every move. In retrospect, it had been pretty wearing at times. 'I just like everything to be organized properly,' he'd say if she came up with any small objection – or even an amused comment – about him arranging shampoos, conditioners and shower gels in height order in the bathroom cupboard. On one occasion when she'd just come in from work and had gone for a quick hello-I'm-home kiss, he'd put a hand up for her to wait, walked to the front door and straightened the mat after her incoming boot had skewed it an inch.

Jenny, who taught Year Four at the school, had suggested it was all about 'male brain architecture'. When Thea had looked it up on the internet, she couldn't argue with that interpretation, though it seemed to be just a polite and over-technical way of saying he was more than a bit obsessive. It explained a lot about why he and his poodle-breeder sister were so obsessed with pedigree and bloodlines. It was all about lists and order. Rich was never happier than when working through a dog's stud chart. No wonder he hadn't wanted children – and *that* was a piece of information he could have let her in on a couple of years earlier! Their lineage and ancestry would never have measured up to standards of perfection the way the pedigree of the ideal poodle puppy could.

Mike was carrying the big wooden platter of cheese and fruit back to the table. Thea felt a rush of love for him, her lovely, unkempt father who kept up his guitar-playing as if it were only a matter of time before he was called on to take over from Keith Richards in the Stones. He still played in a band with old friends and they were singing in local pubs most weeks, slotting themselves in comfortably between elderly folk singers who harked way back to pre-rock beatnik days and young, breathy girls in floral playsuits and wispy frocks, dreaming of fame and that elusive record deal.

'OK, so – Christmas,' Mike began as soon as they were under way with the lemon tart. 'I hope you'll all agree to this, because Anna and I specially want us all to be together this year.'

'Sounds a bit serious,' Jimi commented.

'Can we go outside and play?' Milly interrupted. 'I've stopped eating now.'

'Milly!' Emily gave her a warning look but Alfie joined in.

'And me. Don't like it,' he said, plonking his spoon down hard in the middle of the custardy topping.

'Emily, maybe they could just go out and play for a bit,' Anna suggested. 'It's nice and sunny and the swing is still up.'

'C'n I go too? Keep an eye on them and stuff?' Elmo had eaten his pudding and he quickly scooped up the remainder of Alfie's and wolfed that down too. 'Great pie,' he said to Anna. 'Ace lunch.'

The three of them raced off through the kitchen's French doors which they slammed shut after them.

'No coats, no wellies,' Emily muttered as they went, but she looked too exhausted to chase after them. Thea watched as Elmo walked down the concrete steps to the lawn in front of Alfie to make sure he'd catch him if he tripped. The care he was taking with his little cousin almost brought tears to her eyes.

Mike wasn't meeting anyone's eye as he started to speak; instead, Thea got the impression he was addressing the piece of oozy Camembert that he was cutting. 'You see, we had this idea. And if it's all right with you all, Anna and I thought it would be fun to go down to Cornwall. Anna's found a fabulous big place to rent, called Cove Manor. It's a kind of half-hotel, half-self-catering set-up and there's a cook and housekeeper on the premises who'll take care of shopping, cleaning and cooking evening meals as and when we want them to, though we can do the Christmas dinner between us and—'

'Cornwall?' Emily interrupted. 'What – all of us? But why?'

Mike shrugged. 'Why not Cornwall? Some sea air, walks, beaches – what's not to like?'

'And – well, we could make it a real event. A sort of celebration, of us. As a family.' Thea recognized a tone in her mother's voice that told her there wouldn't be any choice about joining in. 'In fact, this might sound a bit mad but I want us to put together a list of the things we'd all particularly enjoy doing. For me, I want a film night. There's a huge TV – perfect for us all to watch something together.'

'Got to be *The Great Escape*.' Jimi put his bid in. 'You can't have Christmas without watching Steve McQueen not quite making it over the wire.'

'Don't say that in front of Elmo,' Mike warned his son. 'He's probably never seen it. Nothing worse than spoiling the ending.'

'I didn't mean actual films,' Anna said. 'I meant all the old videos and home movies we've made over the years. We're getting them adapted into DVDs by a friend of Mike's friend – er, Charlotte.'

Thea noticed her hesitate over the name. This Charlotte was probably a singer. When she'd been growing up, her father had been madly enthusiastic on an almost weekly basis about someone he'd recently heard. A month later, he'd be on to someone else and have mentally deleted the previous one. Or maybe she was another painter.

'Anyway, *Charlotte* has got them all at the moment and they'll all be done soon.'

'Er, right,' Emily replied. 'So first of all it's like a fore-gone conclusion that we'll all agree to go, and also spend our time staring at home movies from before they met us, which should be hours of fun for the children and Rosie and Sam. *Not.*'

'They don't have to watch,' Mike said mildly. 'But it's just something we'd like. For us and for you, if you want.' He grinned. 'Now we're getting older we need reminding sometimes of how it was when we were young parents, coping with the kids the way you are now. Or not coping. There are a few battles royal on those old videos.'

'And we want a proper barbecue on the beach,' Anna added. 'Mike's keen to do one of those. That's his item on the wish list. You must all think about something you'd like to do as well.'

'A barbecue in December?' Jimi said. 'Are you completely mad? We'll freeze.'

'Probably,' Mike said, sounding perfectly happy with the possibility. 'We'll have a quiz night too. Anything but television and just slobbing out anyway. It'll be – y'know – *bonding.*'

'So this is – er, together?' Jimi asked. 'Like you two, Mum and Dad, you'll be together?'

Anna laughed. 'Yes, us two but mostly all of you. We wanted it to be a special family Christmas, but without the huge hassle for any one person who had to be in charge of it. Democracy at its best, you see. Don't you think it'll be brilliant? We can share the load. The children can do the tree together and we'll make mince pies and have a carol night and – I don't know, maybe games. Not computer ones, proper ones like a big Monopoly tournament, Scrabble, cards. Thea, you'll have time when the term ends, you could make a spreadsheet, a timetable kind of thing, couldn't you? Of activities?'

Jimi cut another tiny sliver of the lemon tart. Thea grinned across at him, knowing that he'd probably have another and another till there was barely a centimetre left of it. He put his finger to his lips and whispered, 'Shhh!'

'A spreadsheet?' Emily asked. 'Like a rota for chores?'

'Not chores, no. But, say, if everyone knows that on Boxing Day morning it's a beach walk and kite-flying, then there won't be any flaking about, no "what shall we do today" and spending half the day deciding it.'

'So, back to normal then?' Thea asked. 'Not any of this you and Dad doing your separate-lives thing any more?'

'Oh! Oh, that's fabulous!' Emily cheered up immediately. 'I'm so glad. I *knew* you didn't mean it about splitting up. Not that you really did, did you? You're still here.'

'Ah. Stick, slightly wrong end of.' Mike took hold of Anna's hand and Thea saw him squeeze it tight. 'Not exactly. Um, we wanted it to be a special Christmas

because we're going to make the separation a bit more
. . . separate.'

'We're getting a divorce,' Anna said quietly.

Emily gasped. 'But *why*? What's the point at—'

'Our age?' Mike gave his daughter a look. 'Because
when we decided last year that there's life beyond . . .
this, it was always going to turn out this way. Didn't you
realize that?'

'It's all completely amicable.' Anna put her arm round
Emily and hugged her. 'Honestly, your father and I will
still be *huge* friends. We'll see each other all the time. It'll
be the way they do it in Scandinavia – new partners
joining in, old spouses still seeing each other. Honestly,
not that much will change as far as you lot are
concerned.'

'New partners?' Jimi asked. 'Really? Wow. Didn't see
that coming.'

'Er, well, only possibly.' Mike looked a bit shifty.
'Nothing definite.'

'And why not?' Anna backed him up briskly. 'One's
batteries aren't yet totally flat.'

'Euw, Mum!' Thea said. 'Too much information.'

'So are we agreed on this Christmas thing?' Mike
asked.

'I guess so,' Emily said. 'The children will love it. I
think.' She still looked doubtful but made an attempt to
rally. 'And who doesn't love the seaside?'

'It's only a week. And the place is glorious; you'll love

it.' Anna got up and went to the kitchen dresser, rummaging in a drawer. 'I've got the Cove Manor brochure here. And there are more photos online that you can look at. It's massive – plenty of room to get together and to get away from each other for a bit of peace too.'

'And when you get back?' Thea asked tentatively. 'What happens then?'

'Oh. Well, I suppose this is as good a time as any to tell you,' Anna said, looking a bit downcast. 'We'll be putting this house on the market and finding some-where for each of us to live.'

And this time Emily really did burst into noisy tears. 'But this is *home*,' she wailed. 'You can't!'

'I'm sorry, darling,' Mike said softly, 'but even if we were staying together, it's way too big to keep up. It's time now to let this rambling old place go.'

THREE

It was the last day of term and the staff room was a shambles. The big central table, which usually held abandoned coffee mugs, biscuit crumbs and piles of books and papers, was now completely swamped by bottles (gifts from pupils' parents), packages and wrapping paper. It was a shame, Thea considered as she staggered, exhausted, into the room, that none of the bottles were open. After such a hectic final day with over-hyped and thoroughly excited children, they could all have done with at least a vat of wine. However, most of the staff had to drive home, and those who didn't were in a rush to get away to make a start on their own Christmases now the school one was over and done with. The carol service, the Yule play (big success, in spite of one of the elves being too late in asking to go for a wee) and the individual classroom parties had taken up most of the final week and there wasn't a single teacher who would be sorry to get home and simply flake out on a sofa for a couple of hours like a dog that's been run into the ground on an over-long walk.

Thea and Jenny were among the first to have dispatched their class-loads. They had done some essential tidying and were now packing up their cards and presents from the children and preparing for a quick getaway. Thea sniffed at one of her parcels. 'It smells delicious,' she said, 'and it's from that banker's daughter.' She shook it tentatively. 'Quite heavy, doesn't rattle. Might be a candle from Jo Malone.' Most of the rest would be chocolates, which were always welcome, but she'd take them to Cornwall to share with the rest of the family so she wouldn't come back for the spring term two dress sizes larger.

'It's so kind of them all to bother,' Jenny said, eyeing the label of one of her wine bottles. It featured a grinning, leaping kangaroo, suggesting a promise of risky jollity. 'I'm sure most of mine are more than a bit strapped for cash. Lucy Miller made me a bookmark out of cardboard from a cornflake packet. She's drawn a cat on it and coloured it all in and put some ribbon on it, but on the other side I can see the red part of the chicken's tail feathers. I could have cried. So sweet.'

'It is. I've had so many cards the children told me they'd made all by themselves, and they look so proud when they hand them over.' Thea had given each child a card and a puzzle book, and the evening before she'd made mince pies and cupcakes for them to have as a classroom treat after lunch, even though the sugar overload made them even more hyper. Her ears would ring for days from the sound of their squealing.

There would only be a few days between the end of term and the drive down to Cornwall, and Thea was in a panic about the activities spreadsheet that her mother had so blithely assumed she'd have all the time in the world to do. When to fit it in? There were parties to go to, friends to see, the usual round of Christmas hangovers. Tonight was possible: she might have time to give it a go between getting home and going out later because she was only going to the Over-the-Roads' and needn't stay all that long. Or maybe she could just scribble a quick list and run off a few copies? But somehow she didn't think she could cope with Emily's scorn if she did that.

'Looking forward to the big family get-together?' Jenny asked, as if reading her thoughts.

'Yes, sort of. But I've got a ton of stuff to do first. And I know I don't have a family to rush round and deal with.' Thea felt a little jolt of pain, saying this. 'But I definitely got landed with the organizing for the Christmas activity list because everyone knows that teachers walk out of the classroom every day at four o'clock and do nothing more than slob out on the sofa with wine, a giant pack of Pringles and *Pointless* on the telly, don't they?'

'Well, of course – what else is there to do?' Jenny agreed. 'We are such idlers, we barely deserve to be paid at all. When are you off for this clan gathering?'

'Next Tuesday. I haven't even thought what to take with me. I still have to shop for lots of presents, and this ridiculous timetable thing they want is hanging over me too. I've never known my parents want anything actually "organized" before. They've always been spontaneous sorts – you know, going with however the mood of the day takes them, or what the weather feels like. When we were little we always went for Devon beach holidays and just mooched about on the sand, digging and playing and collecting shells and things. Every now and then there'd be a trip to a wildlife park or something, but nothing decided way ahead. And certainly not before we'd even got there.'

'So this time, it'll be like, if it's Wednesday, it must be jigsaws, kind of thing?'

Thea looked at Jenny for a few moments and then spluttered with laughter. 'Jigsaws? Have you met my parents? It's far more likely to be a poker tournament, and fiercely played at that. I think Mum's stocking up on one last big family memory before they split up.' She sighed. 'It's all a bit sad. I still can't believe they mean to go through with a divorce. I've never met two people who seem such good mates.'

'Perhaps they won't,' Jenny suggested. 'Maybe they'll change their minds over Christmas.'

'I don't think so. They're treating it like some big adventure that we're all supposed to support them in. And besides . . .' She hesitated. 'They've – well, at least Dad has – hinted that there's someone else.'

Jenny's eyes went wide. 'You mean you'll maybe get a new young *stepmother*?'

'Aargh! Don't say that!' Thea laughed for a second and then when the idea really hit, she stopped abruptly. 'Now you've got me picturing my dad with someone even younger than me. Go away, thought – I can't even begin to want that in my brain!' She actually shook her head as if to dislodge the picture. Did you ever get to an age where the idea of your parents having a sex life was acceptable? Probably not. And certainly not a sex life with someone you might have been contemporary friends with.

'Sorry.' Jenny back-tracked rapidly. 'Of course it might be someone his own age. And . . . and it might not last. Is she coming for Christmas with you all?' The staff room was starting to fill with teachers, most of them sighing with relief at getting their little charges off their hands for a few weeks.

'Oh God, I hadn't even thought of that,' Thea replied. 'Nobody's said anything about extra people. Mum seemed to want just us, but who knows? The place is huge – it sleeps about sixteen apparently, so I suppose it's possible. I could ask, but I'm not sure I want to know the answer till I get there. That way, I can just take whatever the situation is and run with it. Best way.'

'Well, good luck anyway,' Jenny said, putting her coat on and gathering up her bags. 'I do hope it'll go well. Are you planning to be madly social before you pack up and leave?'

Thea smiled. 'Pretty much. I've said yes to everything in a spirit of *sod you* to Rich.'

'Good thinking. Back on the horse and all that, as it were. And have a really Happy Christmas, won't you?'

'Thanks, Jenny. Give the children a hug from me and you all have a brilliant time.'

Jenny hesitated just before she left the room. 'You will be OK, won't you? No moping, promise?'

'None at all. For one thing the family won't let me, and tonight I'm going to a party at the Over-the-Roads' so that'll keep me occupied for a few hours.'

'Good. So no brooding.' Jenny hugged her.

'No brooding, I promise.' It would be easier said than done, but she'd do her best, and if she didn't have too much tear-inducing fizzy wine she'd be fine.

Thea collected her haul of cards and presents together, said plenty of goodbyes and Happy Christmases to the rest of the staff and went out into the chill air to her car. It wasn't even three o'clock yet but it was already close to getting dark. Roll on spring, she thought as she drove out through the playground gates, carefully dodging the last stragglers of infants and parents. And in spite of what she'd said to Jenny, promising not to mope was one thing, but she'd have to fight quite hard not to give any thought to Rich and the lack of his big calm presence. But it helped that he'd sent a card and she'd hated it. It was a photo that featured Rich with his older sister Liz, whose house and dog-breeding business up near Chester he now shared. Benji was sitting in front of Rich and looking silly in a Santa hat that clashed with his apricot fur, and alongside Liz sat a large white poodle, its fur clipped into the extreme half-fluffed, half-bald show cut. Thea would pity this creature for the cold he must feel on the shaved parts of his body and legs, but she suspected he (a top champion of the breed) wasn't exactly allowed to frolic in the great outdoors much. Liz had one hand on her prize-winning poodle and another on Rich's shoulder, and you couldn't help seeing it as a gesture of claiming.

Thea had put the card on her kitchen dresser, making sure Liz and the white-fluff monstrosity were obscured by a card with a jolly robin on it. Surely it couldn't have been normal for Liz to have been so jealous of her brother's fiancée? What kind of weirdness was that? When Thea and Rich had told his family that they were engaged, Liz had privately told Thea that their relationship 'will never work'. And she'd sneered, 'Rich is a dog person, through and through, like all our family but you are quite obviously *cats*.'

Thea did not have a cat, hadn't had one since she was about thirteen and big ginger Barry, who'd been two years older than her, had quietly died while asleep in his favourite patch of sunshine under the wisteria – but she got the general idea. Liz also once said that she'd found a perfect dress to wear for their wedding – a green one. She didn't need to explain that green at a wedding was unlucky. An odd family.

It had taken a while, but that card was one more hand-hold up on that climbing wall to thinking she'd had a lucky escape from a lifetime of dog shows, puppies and the annual near-orgasmic excitement about Cruft's. In fact, and the thought lightened Thea's spirits quite a bit, once Christmas was over she would get herself a little cat. It would not be a fancy breed, would not require daily grooming or special food or mates chosen for their bloodline or have a pedigree that was up there with feline royalty. There were plenty of rescue mogs needing a warm home and a comfy lap to purr on.

Thea was in luck – there was a resident's parking space outside her house. She staggered up the path with her bags as Mr Over-the-Road was passing with the little Westie. 'You're coming tonight, aren't you, love?' he said. 'About seven thirty?'

'I'll be there – looking forward to it. Anything you'd like me to bring?' She dumped a few bags on the doorstep and put the key in the lock. She hoped the answer to her question would either be 'a bottle' or just no, otherwise she'd have to run down to the supermarket for some canapés that she could tinker with till they looked homemade. There was still the spreadsheet to tackle.

'No, darling, just your lovely self. There's a bit of mistletoe with your name on.'

It was too dark to see whether he was winking at her, but if she had to bet on it, she'd feel pretty safe to risk a tenner. Either way, at least she didn't have to go out for sausage rolls.

He was keen, Anna would say that for him. She hadn't really expected that someone twelve years younger than her would be so enthusiastic. It was very thrilling and of course hugely flattering, being adored by this delightful man, but even though it had been over a month now she was having trouble quite believing in it. It couldn't last, could it? She wasn't even sure she wanted it to as she certainly wasn't looking for another long-term partner, but for now it was just what she needed to launch her into the next stage in her life, the stage where she wouldn't be living with Mike any more.

She walked down the High Road, heading for the bookshop where she and Alec had first met as guests at the launch of a collection of poems written by one of her book-group friends. Over warm white wine and tepid mushroom vol-au-vents they'd bonded by having the giggles as Miriam (pushing eighty and with bright orange spiky hair, dressed in flowing purple which made Anna think of the Pope) read – in that intense, important way that poets so often do – a sonnet comparing a garden slug to a penis: *'the shaft thickens, glides and glistens, shifts its slickness on the moisted moss . . .'*

'. . . falls into beer trap, deflates and drowns.' Alec, who till that moment she'd never met, had whispered his own next line to her and she'd swiftly had to hide behind the science-fiction shelves and stifle an outburst of inappropriate laughter.

'Sorry,' he'd said, not remotely meaning it, as a few minutes later Miriam finished her reading to a polite blast of applause. 'I just couldn't resist.'

'No, please don't apologize,' Anna had said, still wiping tears of laughter from her eyes. 'It was very funny, and – er, probably poetically apt – the beer and so on . . .' She'd felt flustered then. Perhaps he hadn't meant to imply the thing about brewer's droop. But of course he had. He'd grinned at her: he had a very naughty sort of face and his eyes were full of laughter, something she later learned was very much a default setting.

'Another glass?' he'd offered, taking her empty one from her hand. And then later, there'd been shared chips and Prosecco at the bar across the road, neither of them fancying more to eat than that after overdoing party food at the launch.

'So how do you know the great poet Miriam?' he'd asked.

'From our book group. She's one of our more, shall we say, *opinionated* members. And you don't want to sit too close because when she's in full flow she's a great one for waving her arms around. We've had several wine-glass disasters and a messy vase of tulips accident. How about you? How do you know her?'

'She's my mother,' he told her. And they'd both laughed so ridiculously hard (the Prosecco effect?) that they ended up clinging to each other for support.

Anna was smiling at this recollection as she arrived at the bookshop. She stopped to look in the window and saw several books that would make such perfect Christmas presents that she felt thorough gratitude to whoever had arranged the window. You had to be so careful with books; this year it would be the height of tactlessness to, say, give Thea a selection of the romantic comedies she'd always liked till Rich went. And Emily, with her current mood of anxious gloom, would certainly not have her state of mind perked up by a dark and meaningful Scandinavian opus.

She went inside with a mental list already in her head, picked out what she wanted and made a heap of them on the counter.

'Have you got a good one for me?' Alec came up behind her and ran his fingers across the back of her neck, making her tingle.

'You'll have to wait and see what Santa brings you,' she said, putting a last book, a stunningly illustrated one about container gardening – Jimi's wife Rosie would love it – on the pile.

'Across to the usual place?' Alec suggested after she'd paid.

She nodded. He took the bag of books from her and clasped hold of her hand. His felt warm, in spite of the near-frosty air. She used to think anyone past teenage years looked utterly imbecilic holding hands on the street, but now she just found it rather romantic. And besides, the pavement was uneven and a bit slippery. She tried not to think this was even part of the reason for holding on to Alec. That way, the next stop would be a trusty cane and she hoped she had many years to go before that was the safest option.

The bar was screechily noisy with office Christmas parties but their usual table in the corner alcove was free. 'Tea or the usual?' Alec asked.

'Usual, please,' she told him. 'I'll get them.' And she went to the bar to order two glasses of champagne before he could protest at her paying. He seemed quite old-fashioned that way and she was surprised. Surely he'd grown up in an age where women's equality was well established, as opposed to Anna herself, who had been thoroughly involved in the early seventies' battle for it?

'So you're off to Cornwall at the weekend,' he said, after the waitress had come over with the drinks and two shot glasses full of Smarties. He sounded rather down about the idea.

'Yes. The big family Christmas. How about you? Seeing the children?'

'Well – on and off. Suki's taking them up to Cheshire to spend Christmas with her parents. I had them last year so it's only fair. I'll see them before they go and we'll do the presents and stuff at my flat. They'll stay over and we'll have crackers and a goose. Will teenagers like goose, do you think?'

Anna couldn't clearly remember how hers had been about food. Their teenage years were half their lifetimes away now. Alec's children were younger than her oldest grandchild. That had taken a bit of getting her head round. 'Well, I only really know one these days and he eats everything. It'll be fine.'

'Suppose so.' He didn't sound too sure.

'You won't be on your own for *actual* Christmas?' Anna asked.

He shrugged. 'I might go to my brother's. He's said I could if I've got nothing better to do.' He laughed. 'Not the most gracious invitation I've ever had, I'll admit.'

It didn't sound very merry. Anna thought for a minute. How terrible would it be, to add one more to the Cornwall party? Very terrible, probably. Terminally terrible. And so wrong. You didn't just impose a stranger on the family like that. And what about sleeping arrangements? She'd so far spent a few happy afternoons in bed with Alec and they had been very delightful times but it had been in his flat, in a darkened room. Her body was in good enough condition because of years of yoga, but all the same it was still the body of a woman who wouldn't see middle age again. She didn't want to be wandering about in full daylight in underwear, still less share a bathroom with a man again, even for a few days. Nor did she want to be conscious that her day-to-day knickers were what Elmo's friends would call granny-pants. But apart from those vanity questions, what about the family? You couldn't shock them by suddenly introducing an unexpected lover to the mix. No, she couldn't invite him. It wouldn't work. It wouldn't be fair on the others and especially not on Mike, even if he had got this ... Charlotte in his life. He certainly hadn't mentioned inviting *her*.

The two of them parted on the pavement, Alec to walk up to the tube station and Anna to catch a bus. He put his arms round her and kissed her, their accumulated years falling away so Anna felt they were just a pair of entwined teenagers.

'Euw, look at the olds.' A bunch of teens jostled beside them on the pavement. 'Get a room, *perlease*,' one of them called.

Anna and Alec ignored them. 'I won't see you for ages,' he murmured into her hair. 'Don't forget about me, will you?'

'Of course not,' she reassured him. 'It's not for long.

And if you get too lonely, I'm only a train ride away. Even if it is a five-hour one.'

'Really?' He stepped back and looked at her, all bright-eyed. 'Well, I might just take you up on that.'

Oh lordy, she thought minutes later as she zapped her Freedom Pass on the bus. After all her reasoning, what the hell had she just done? She would blame that second glass of fizz and hope he'd forget what she'd said.

After a hot bath, Thea would have been far happier on this last school work day to get into bed with a book and a mug of tea and snuggle deep into her duvet than to put on a slinky dress, full-scale make-up and killer heels and go out to a duty-party full of neighbours that she barely knew. On the other hand, if she didn't turn up, she wouldn't put it past the Over-the-Roads (she really should think of them as Robbie and June) to come and knock on the door to demand she stop being a party-pooper. They were very keen on neighbourly get-togethers, even if it was mostly to have a thoroughly pleasing grumble about some people's slapdash parking and some shocking wheelie-bin habits. So she made an effort, putting on a black crushed-velvet dress, a glittery necklace, silver lacy tights and a pair of not-too-high black patent shoes that were her favourites for parties where there would be a lot of standing around.

She and Jenny had agreed long ago in a staff-room

discussion that serious heels could be walked in quite easily over a good distance but could be strangely painful for simply standing about. You learned that the hard way, it now occurred to Thea as she flicked her hair into fronds. In her twenties, parties had been for dancing and running about and she hadn't given her footwear a thought. It was only on the more sedate, grown-up occasions that she seemed to go to now that she'd discovered this sneaky truth about heels. All the same, she was far too young to give them up, and she liked the extra height.

'Ah, you're here. Come in, come in!' Robbie opened his front door and welcomed her in with exuberance. Thea's arm brushed past the massive ornate wreath on the OTRs' front door, dislodging a satsuma that rolled and bumped its way down the path.

'Sorry,' she said.

'No problem, plenty more in the fruit bowl,' Robbie told her. 'No coat? You'll freeze, a little thin thing like you.' He took hold of her upper arm and gave it a rub. She hoped she'd only imagined his fingers were pressing against her breast. It must have been accidental and besides, he was definitely on the far side of a lot of mulled wine. There was almost a haze of it round him.

'Let me get you a drink,' Robbie said then, taking her hand and leading her through to the kitchen.

June noticed the hand-holding and raised an

eyebrow. 'She's a grown-up, Rob, she can walk without your help,' she warned her husband, grinning at Thea.

Thea wriggled her fingers free of his hot paw and accepted a steaming glass of wine. She took a sip. It was sweet and cloying, but wonderfully scented with cinnamon.

'It's the perfect taste of Christmas, isn't it?' June said. 'I do like to keep to the old traditions. You young people – if we left it to you lot they'd all die out. You haven't put up decorations, have you?'

Hmm . . . so June had been peering through her windows. She wouldn't think of it like that, though, more a vague looking-around while the Westie peed against the gatepost.

'No point this year,' Thea told her, 'because I'll be going away. Big family thing in Cornwall.'

'And where has that young man of yours been hiding lately? We haven't seen him and his lovely big dog for a while.'

'Ah. Er, Rich and I have split up.' Thea felt uncomfortable saying this. June made a sympathetic face that also managed to be full of curiosity as to what had gone wrong.

'Oh, that's a shame. So you won't be getting married after all then?'

Thea smiled. 'Seems not.'

'Such a pity. You'd make a lovely young bride.' Robbie, listening in, winked at her.

'Not *that* young,' Thea muttered.

'Of course you are, dear. And there's someone for everyone, that's what I think. So don't give up. Now – do you want me to keep an eye on the house for you while you're away? You could leave us a key.'

It was a kind offer but it meant Thea had to banish thoughts of Mr Over-the-Road rummaging through her knicker drawer. All the same, it probably made sense, though what she could do about any disasters he might report from three hundred miles away, she couldn't guess.

The party was full of couples: this was an observation that always seemed so obvious to the single and Thea joined a group talking about their children and about when and how to confess that Santa was really Daddy.

'Do you have children?' one of the bright young marrieds asked her.

'No,' she replied, 'but I'm a primary school teacher so I—'

'Ah, but that's not really the same, is it?' the woman cut in. 'You can't possibly know what they're like outside the classroom. What you see isn't even the half of it.' She seemed to find this amusing and her laugh was tinkly and sharp.

Thea didn't find it at all funny and felt hurt. She accepted a third glass of the sticky wine and wolfed down a few mince pies for ballast, wondering how soon she could politely make her excuses and go home to watch TV and wrap some presents. But just as she was getting to that possible moment, someone started playing June's piano and the room began to erupt in a rousing medley of Christmas songs. Robbie put an arm round her waist and firmly led her into the throng. Thea liked singing. She was a bit drunk by now and she joined in, deciding it was as good a way as any to forget about being the only partnerless guest, about the loss of that year's promise and plans and the fact that the bloody spreadsheet and list was still only half-formed in her computer. It was only when everyone started on the carols that she made a move to leave. There had always been something about them that made her feel tearful, even in the cheeriest of years, and the wine was likely to make her even more maudlin. The first line of 'Once in Royal . . .' and she'd be off.

'Thanks for a great evening,' she said to Robbie as she headed for the front door. 'I had such a good time.' And she had, she realized – apart from that woman's snippy remark.

'Our pleasure, my dear.' Robbie shuffled closer to her by the front door, showing no sign of intending to open it. She fumbled for the catch, at last managing to get it undone. Robbie was rather too close to her.

'So your boyfriend has buggered off then?' he remarked, which surprised her.

'Well yes, a while back. I was telling June. Why?'

To her surprise, he laughed and then lurched towards

her, his grey moustache twitching with excitement. 'Just making sure, because in that case, there's no one to punch me in the nose for this.' And he pushed her against the doorframe, waved a tiny twig of mistletoe over her and planted a sticky, cinnamon-flavoured kiss as close as he could guess to her lips.

'Merry Christmas, dear girl!' he bellowed as she shoved him away far more gently than she felt like doing, hauled the door open and bolted down the path, not turning to see him brandishing his mistletoe after her and shouting, 'And there's plenty more where that came from if your Christmas plans don't work out!'

She waved but didn't look back. Her original Christmas plans had fallen to pieces months before but she wasn't going to think about that now. Instead she ran straight upstairs, brushed all taste of the gloopy wine from her teeth, threw her velvet dress onto a chair in her room and fell into bed without taking her make-up off. Her dreams were full of plump tiny babies who lay silently watching as Santa placed stockings full of presents on the ends of their cots. And when she woke up in the 6 a.m. dark, the pillow was covered in stripes of mascara and her face was puffy from tears.

FOUR

'If you hadn't gone and promised them bikes, it would all be so much easier.' Emily was fuming over lists and trying to plan her packing. Work was backing up. Who would imagine there could be so many people who thought it cute and endearing that they couldn't organize their tax affairs till the very last minute? Hilarious. *Not.*

'We'll never get them in the Golf. In fact, if we don't hurry, we won't get them at all. Everyone's child wants a Christmas bike. Stocks will be low. We'll end up bike-less and it'll all be a disaster.'

Sam could have sorted this. *Should* have sorted this. Instead he was in his writing shed day and night, working on extra copy for New Year specials and apparently 'up to here' in it, as he claimed. She hadn't meant to be deliberately stealthy when she took a mug of coffee out to him that morning, but before he'd heard her approach she'd had time to see that he was engrossed in Facebook Scrabble on his computer and not writing about the Obituaries of the Year or his so-urgent piece on the possible line-up for the year's Sports Personality. It had made her furious. If he had time for Facebook, he had time for ordering the Christmas presents for the children. In fact, was it really too much to ask that he could even have got into the car and actually gone to the nearest cycle shop by now? There were enough of them in the area to cater for the many fit sorts round here with their state-of-the-art wheels and a taste for tight Lycra.

'I thought we'd wait and buy them when we get there.' Sam leaned against the kitchen worktop and stared out of the window at a squirrel that was raiding the hanging bird feeder.

'Shoo it away,' Emily said, rapping her nails on the glass. 'It's making a mess, dropping stuff everywhere.' The squirrel took no notice.

'It's as entitled to eat as the birds are. There's plenty to share,' Sam said, smiling as the little animal scrambled up to perch right on the top of the feeder, clutching a peanut between its paws.

'Sly things, squirrels. I don't like them. And what do you mean, Sam, buy them when we're there? How on earth can we do that?'

Sam rinsed the mug he'd been drinking from and put it in the sink. Would it hurt him to open the dishwasher? Emily flicked at the stretchy bracelet on her wrist, willing herself to be calm. Mindful. Stay mindful. *Breathe*.

'They do have shops in Cornwall, you know, Em. I thought we'd order from a local shop there and get the bikes delivered after we arrive. Simple and also obvious. Otherwise, even if we could get them in the car, which isn't likely, the children would see bike-shaped packages and know for sure what they're getting. Might as well keep the Santa mystery going, at least for Alfie. I'm sure Milly's had her suspicions for a year or two now.'

'I suppose we could ask Thea to drive the bikes back here after Christmas in her car,' Emily told him. 'There'll only be her in it. It's not as if she's got to drive a mountain of baggage and people, like we have. But OK, so where would you get these bikes from? Assuming we're not on some far rocky outcrop miles from anywhere?'

He shrugged and looked vague. 'Argos? A big Tesco? Same as any shops here? I'll go online and look up a cycle shop near where we're going. Truro, Penzance or something. Easy.' He opened the back door and gave her one of his best smiles as he went out to return to his shed. 'You see? Sorted. You can't say I'm not doing my bit.'

After he'd gone, Emily went and sat cross-legged on the big cream rug in the sitting room. She picked a little chunk of blue Playdough from the wool and kneaded it between her fingers to make it squishy and malleable again, rolled it into a smooth ball shape and put it on the coffee table – from which it immediately rolled off and vanished under the sofa. She sighed, deliberately emptying her lungs as far as she could, closed her eyes, circled her thumb and her middle finger together and took slow, deep breaths, trying to shut out the sound of children's footsteps thumping across the floor in Milly's room above her. After the tenth breath, she loosened her hands, stretched her arms high above her head and and put her index fingers to the sides of her nose, breathing in slowly through one nostril and out through the other and losing herself in the rhythm, feeling her body and spirit letting go of the stress of this strange Christmas which was very much *not* the sort she'd hoped for. So much for the silver and green décor scheme she'd decided on (last year's Christmas special *Livingetc*, kept for reference), the invitations she'd had to turn down, the drinks party she'd planned so the neighbours could admire her artistry and her canapés (a mixture of Delia and Ottolenghi). The breathing worked for several minutes but then some nearby scuffling and huffing sounds cut into her thoughts and she heard the door handle turning.

'What's Mum doing?' Alfie whispered to Milly.

'She's *mooing. Again*,' came the scathing reply.

'Are you sure you don't want to travel down with us? There's room in the car so long as you don't mind the reek of Lynx Peace. Elmo's taken to it in a big way. I think there might be a girl involved – not that he'd tell us. He's well into the grunt stage at the moment,' Jimi said to Thea on the phone.

'Thanks, that's sweet of you but I really want to take my own car,' she told him. 'I've got a huge amount of stuff because I put myself on the rota for the first lot of food shopping – I know it's partly catered but I thought I'd get the sort of extras that everybody suddenly wants but then won't find when they look in the cupboards. Crisps, crumpets, masses of tea bags, that Italian coffee Dad likes, the basics for making more mince pies and lots of party food – because everyone likes that over Christmas even if it's not officially a party.'

'Wine?' He sounded worried that it might have been left out. Jimi without wine was pretty much un-imaginable. If she had to do a portrait of him it would be with a large glass of red and a pile of Sudoku puzzles.

'Mum said she and Dad are bringing wine. And there are supermarkets a few miles away from the village. No need to panic that we'll run out.'

'Phew! Oh, and Rosie's bringing a box of our Christmas decorations, to add to the tree.'

'Really? I'd got Emily down for that.' Thea consulted her list. Definitely Emily. 'But that's OK, two lots will be even better. You can never have too many and if the place is as huge as it looks on the website, the right-size tree will probably need a ladder to get the fairy on top – so the more decs the merrier.'

Needing space for all the packing and the presents wasn't the only reason Thea wanted her own car with her. She had a feeling she was going to need it so as to make a few break-out trips from the family. Much as she loved them and was delighted to be spending time with them, this idea of constant all-together activity might well make her feel a bit claustrophobic. It would be good to have the means to get away. She might not actually need it if everything went brilliantly but it would be good to know that if she felt at all hemmed in or she needed a bit of space just to think, she had the means to whiz off for some quiet time alone to, say, St Ives to look at art galleries or to Land's End simply to stare at the waves crashing onto the rocks below the cliffs.

She and Rich had had a week in Cornwall only two years before. It had been spectacularly hot weather and they'd rented a cottage on the north coast, close to the Hayle estuary. They'd watched Benji hurtle along the endless dunes and roll in the sand till his fur was many shades of orange, and they'd eaten crab sandwiches on the beach. The sea was full of sleek surfers and exuberant body-boarders, and small children paddling in rock pools, where they caught little creatures and proudly presented them to their parents, who would quietly return them to the water a while later. Two small girls of about seven and nine whose parents were sitting close by had come to show Thea a starfish they'd found and she'd admired it, feeling flattered that they'd picked her out on their way to their own family.

'I must have some sort of teacher aura about me,' she said to Rich as the girls walked on with their treasure.

'You shouldn't have encouraged them,' he said, frowning. 'We could be anybody.'

She'd felt a bit sickened by this. Talk about spoiling the moment. 'They were just being friendly, Rich. What am I supposed to do, tell them to get lost?'

'Probably, yes,' he said, turning back to his book. 'For their own safety. And besides, we didn't come on holiday to have kids hanging around us. Don't you get enough of that at work?'

'I like children – it's why I do the job I've got. Don't you like them? At all? They're just *people*. Nothing to be scared of.'

Rich looked up and considered for a moment, squinting over the top of his sunglasses at her in the bright sun. 'Actually, I suppose I don't like them really, when I think about it.' He put his hand out and patted Benji's fluffy orange head. 'You know where you are with dogs. Children, not so much.'

As Thea now started loading the car in the pre-dawn dark, she thought about this conversation. Why had she ever thought it didn't matter? That he didn't really mean it? Probably because she couldn't believe anyone she was so close to could have such a lack of affection for his own species. She remembered thinking that of course it would be different when they had their own child, one hypothetical day in the future when (God willing) she was pregnant. Who wouldn't love their own baby, even if they didn't much like other people's? She should have realized that what her mother had said when Thea was going out with her first – and very moody – boyfriend at sixteen was actually true: you can't change a man. And if you think you need to, then you're with the wrong one.

The weather forecast was very much all doom and gloom and 'essential travel only' warnings. According to last night's TV, the entire west of the country could expect anything from gale-force winds and torrential rain to a thick blanket of snow by the evening, with more of the same over the whole of Christmas. Thea felt excited about the idea of snow – she'd never seen a white Christmas but she also knew it wasn't likely down in the far south-west. The description of Cove Manor promised log fires, in the plural, and Thea hoped fervently that these were in addition to phenomenally efficient central heating and not instead of. You could never trust big old houses not to be full of icy draughts and she'd been into Zara the day before and bought a gorgeous blue sparkly dress that went brilliantly with her new copper and pinky-purple highlights and was a look that wouldn't be improved by a cardigan.

She loaded the last bags into her Polo and slammed the boot shut just as June Over-the-Road came across to her, pulling the reluctant Westie on his lead. He looked quite bleary-eyed and a bit puzzled as if he'd been woken from a deep sleep. The hem of what was clearly a pink nightie was visible beneath June's coat and she was wearing sheepskin slippers. What on earth was she doing? It was only just after seven o'clock, midwinter dark and close to freezing. The dog blinked dozily in the light of the streetlamp and peed against the Polo's front wheel. Steam wafted up.

'Making an early start then. Very wise,' June said. 'I expect there'll be lots of traffic hold-ups.' She sounded rather pleased about this, as if she were inflicting a curse for a long and uncomfortable journey. Thea crossed her fingers for a moment, hoping it would be enough to ward off the bad luck.

'I want to get there in plenty of daylight,' she said. 'We've been told not to trust the Sat Nav so it's a matter of maps and luck.'

'You can't trust technology,' June sniffed. 'And there's a whole generation growing up who haven't a clue how to read a map.'

It was too early in the morning to argue the case. Thea ran through a very fast last-minute checklist in her head and opened her car door.

'Yes, you're probably right, though I expect they'd be able to do it if they needed to. Anyway – er, Happy Christmas, June. And Happy New Year too, because I won't be here for that either. Love to Robbie.'

'Hmm,' June said. 'You have a nice time too, dear, and perhaps you'll meet a nice man while you're away. Someone more your own age.' She patted Thea's arm. 'Someone *not* married.' And she turned and tugged on the Westie's lead and went back across the road, slippers slap-slapping on the tarmac.

Thea climbed into the Polo and switched on the engine. What on earth was June on about? Somebody – possibly even Robbie himself? – must have reported back to her about his bodged and clumsy attempt at a kiss at their party. Did June really think Thea was in hot pursuit of her husband? She looked back at her little house, whose spare key was safely with Jenny, and waved it goodbye for the holiday as she drove away towards the main road. Honestly, what was this? She was a single woman so must be chasing a man? *Anyone*'s man? Ugh – the thought of fancying Mr Over-the-Road, his sly pawing, his sticky moustache, his feeble twiglet of mistletoe, made her feel quite creeped out. Gross. She didn't know whether to laugh or cry.

'I suppose I'll have to get a car of my own now. Or you will,' Anna said to Mike as they sat in a barely moving traffic jam on the A303 by Stonehenge. 'There's a lot to think about with a divorce, isn't there? It's not just a matter of selling the house, divvying up the possessions and finding somewhere else to live with half the proceeds.'

Mike looked in the rearview mirror. There was a camper van coming up alongside with surfboards on the roof and young hippie-looking sorts in it. Funny how that look was still around all these decades on. That had been him, once. Same sort of van, though only Californians had gone in for surfing back in those days and his camper had been painted with swirly flowers, and had plastic roses and daffodils like a garland all along the front bumper.

'Remember when they used to give you a plastic flower as a freebie when you bought petrol?' he asked Anna.

'I do. Why did they ever think people would want them? Later it was wine glasses. At least they were useful.'

'I had them on the van when we first met,' he said, moving the car a bit in the traffic. 'Roses, daffodils and carnations.'

'They were horrible. They got filthy from stuck-on flies and road grime.'

Anna seemed in no mood for reminiscing. A hand came out from the van's passenger-side window as it pulled up alongside, holding a cigarette. Mike opened the window and sniffed. Ah yes, someone was smoking a joint; something else that took him right back to being young. Charlotte smoked a bit of weed now and then, but not the way he and his friends had done it, back in the far-off days when you rolled a big fat spliff, passed it round the assembled company and it was all something of a ritual with quiet, contemplative respect for the product, not unlike wine-tasting. Charlotte went in for skinny little roll-ups that stuck to her lips. She'd offered one to him last time he was at hers but he didn't fancy it, not after more than thirty years of going without. It would probably make him edgy, possibly affect the old potency level and he didn't want to muck about with that. He was surprised she smoked anything at all, with singing being her livelihood, but he wasn't going to come over like some old granddad and make a comment. It was her business and she was pushing forty-five so wasn't likely to tolerate a telling-off.

The camper van was crawling along next to Mike's Sierra now. Some kind of hip-hop music was blaring out, or was it house? If it wasn't blues or country or proper sixties' pop, he wouldn't know what it was. He raised his hand at the smoking passenger in a vague sort of comradeship gesture. The boy looked startled, closed the window and the driver accelerated quickly, neatly cutting in, in front of Mike. Two more lads on the back seats turned round and stared at him, and one of them picked up a red T-shirt and wrapped it round his head in mockery of Mike's own scarlet bandana. The van's occupants seemed to find it hilarious and their laughter was making it rock. He felt embarrassed, humiliated and uncomfortably old. Ageist little bastards, he thought, slowing and waving a fish-monger's van into the gap between him and the camper.

'This *is* a good idea, isn't it?' Anna asked as at last the traffic sped up past the ancient stones. The fields around them were pale and frosty. Grazing sheep looked grey and matted, and fat with next year's lambs. Circles of life, Mike thought, still feeling a bit maudlin.

'The Christmas thing? Yes,' he said, then, 'no. Hell, I don't know, Annie – we'll have to see how it turns out. Maybe we shouldn't have told them about the divorce.'

'Oh, bloody typical. It was your idea to tell them *before* Christmas, if you remember. "Let's be upfront about it, then it's out of the way," you said. *I* had my doubts. Still, too late now.'

'It is.' Mike could only agree. 'Sorry. Also, to be fair, telling them about the divorce was a bit of emotional blackmail to get them all to agree to come. I doubt Emily would have wanted to. She's an urban soul, that one.'

Anna reached across and squeezed his hand. 'It's OK. Nothing to be done about it now. I just think, you know, it could be strange. Awkward. Possibly for every-one. Rather like *Fawlty Towers* and "Don't mention the war".'

'We'll have to make sure it isn't awkward. We have to, because it's going to be the future normal, isn't it? It's the perfect chance for them to get used to the idea,' Mike said, reluctantly removing his hand from hers so he could change gear. He hoped she wouldn't think he didn't want her touching him at all. They hadn't got to that stage yet. With a little ouchy pang, he realized he hoped they never would. He reminded himself that they'd still be seeing each other, still be the greatest of friends. That was a given.

'So what will you get?' he asked.

'Get? Oh, are we back to the car? So you're keeping this one?' she said.

'Well, I just thought . . . But no, you can have it if you want. I really don't mind.' He was used to the Sierra, old and rather tatty though it now was, and he was the one who drove it the most. He liked having a substantial estate car for carrying his guitars and amps to gigs. He often got stuck with someone's drums too.

He stole a quick glance at Anna. She was smiling as she said, 'It's a bit of a – I don't know – staid sort of vehicle, isn't it? Sensible. Practical.'

'Thanks. You mean it's an old man's car.' He felt gloomy suddenly. Truth was, whichever way you looked at it, he *was* an old man – well, getting there, certainly by the standards of the generation below and not that far off even by his own. He didn't need his car to be reminding him of it, not when there were people like the camper-van boys making sure he knew where he stood in life's long, shuffling queue for the grave.

'What's wrong with practical?' he said, trying to rally.

'Nothing. But' – and she laughed, sounding as young as she had when he'd first met her and heard her giggling across the student union bar – 'I'm not going for staid and practical any more, not in my new life. I fancy a hot little Mini Cooper.'

Anna was looking exhilarated at the idea, smiling and excited and . . . happy. And he felt the same. Of course he did. After all, this was what they *both* wanted.

The light wasn't even starting to fade as it would have done by now in London. Thea was surprised. She'd forgotten that this far west, you got a bonus half-hour of light at the end of a day. She'd found the way through the village and out to Cove Manor easily enough and she now drove along a high track parallel to the sea and in through a pair of ancient stone gateposts that seemed to have lost a gate to support. After another fifty yards and round a bend, the house suddenly appeared. It was a long, three-storey Georgian building, pale stone and with many windows. Lights were on and smoke drifted from chimneys at each end of the house and also in the middle, which was a cheering sign. As she pulled up on the big gravel driveway across from the house where a sign indicated a parking area, Thea hoped those windows had heavy draught-proof curtains.

Opening the car door brought a blast of freezing wind. The scudding clouds were a deep, looming grey and she was sure that when her mother arrived she'd be scenting the air and declaring that she could smell snow. She'd always done that when they were little and it had seemed magical to them that she'd never been wrong. What Thea could smell was the sea – and she could hear it too, swooshing onto the rocks that from the website photos she knew were below the back of the house.

No one seemed to be around and for a second Thea wondered if she'd got the right place after all. Could there be more places called Cove Manor? Doubtful – the directions had been pretty clear. There was what looked like a converted stable block off to the side of the house; lights were shining in it and she could hear music (possibly Led Zeppelin; her dad would know for sure) so she started heading in that direction, but was met by a man approaching her.

'Hi! Find us all right? I'm Sean. Welcome.'

'Hello. I'm Thea. And yes, thanks – it was quite easy to find this place.' She quickly peeled off her glove to shake the hand he offered her. His skin was warm on hers. He was tallish and she recognized a typical Cornwall surfer look about his hair: sun-bleached streaks (comparatively dark now in the winter but would be searing blond in summer), a baggy grey over-sized hoody with a surf company logo on the front (she could hear Rich in her head, muttering that surely the man was too old to wear one. She told the voice to go away and stop being so ridiculous) and battered brown cowboy boots that looked as if they'd been hurriedly pulled on over frayed jeans. A creamy-coloured cat – Siamese? – had followed and was plaiting itself around his legs, giving her a hostile look from blue, slightly crossed, eyes.

'So it's just you? You drove here alone?' he asked, leading her towards the house.

'Just me. The rest of them all have . . .' *each other* were the obvious missing words here, but she let the sentence drop. He didn't seem to mind.

'OK, so I'll let you in and show you round before we unload your car and get you a drink. And you can bagsy whichever room you fancy.' As Sean unlocked the front door he turned and grinned at her. 'Getting here before the others has to have some perks, don't you think?'

The cat came into the house with them and jumped onto one of the two scarlet velvet chairs that were either side of a log fire in the hallway. 'This is Woody, by the way,' Sean told her, scooping up the cat which closed its eyes and rubbed its head against Sean's hand. 'He's a lilac Siamese and he gets everywhere. You'll probably find him joining in with you a lot of the time. I hope that's OK, but if you're not fond of cats I can make sure he stays over at the Stables where we live.'

Thea tentatively stroked the cat's ears and he purred at her. 'I love cats,' she said. 'I'd decided I'd get one once Christmas is over. He's gorgeous.'

'Excellent. To be honest, I'm not keen on people who can't like a cat,' he admitted. 'But don't tell anyone. It's probably not good for business here.'

'I won't tell. I promise.' Thea felt ridiculously pleased, as if she'd passed some kind of test. She must be tired, she thought. She wasn't usually this soppy.

Sean led her through the downstairs rooms, which were big and bright and more colourful than she'd expected. She'd assumed the house would be darker, that there would be much brown and muted chintz and dusty green carpet. Instead, the bigger of the two massive sitting rooms, each of which had a lavishly lit Christmas tree in an alcove, was painted a glorious bright pink and had an ashy parquet floor. The next room was pale turquoise with purple sofas. Fluffy cream rugs were everywhere.

'It's all so incredibly pretty,' she said, as Sean took her through to the kitchen which had a table at least four metres long and a huge white Aga.

'Thank you,' he said, turning to smile at her. 'We didn't want it to have some musty old country-house feel. People like it all a bit fresher, so we thought more *Livingetc* than *Homes & Gardens*. Though' – and he laughed – 'when we first came here it was so dilapidated we could have just left the shredded old curtains, peeled even more old wallpaper back from the damp and rot, and kept it as a kind of glorious ruin. *Très chic*, in some circles.'

'Not very cosy though,' she said. 'I think you'd have to be a seriously old-school aristocrat to go along with that.'

'Exactly. And they've probably got their own glorious ruins. They wouldn't want to take a holiday in another one.' He had very white teeth, she thought, or maybe it was that he had a leftover tan. 'Would you like me to take you upstairs now?' They were at the bottom of the stairs.

There was a moment's hesitation – she was still thinking about the tan and teeth thing, 'Upstairs? Oh – er, yes. Bedrooms.'

'Exactly. You're first here, you get first dibs.'

There were two floors of bedrooms, each with their own bathroom. She chose one at the end of the top floor which had a sloping roof. One of the windows looked out towards the converted stable block and the other towards the sea.

'Good choice,' he said, 'You've got the back staircase just round the corner in case you want to slide down to the kitchen for a midnight snack, and this room's got the biggest bath. You could have a party in it.'

'I'll keep that in mind,' she said, thinking about the last time she'd shared a bath with someone. It had been with a boyfriend at university and the bath hadn't been anywhere near big enough for anything more than being uncomfortable and bashing bits of body on taps.

It hadn't been Rich; he thought the idea was too weird. He liked sex to be something they did in bed, as it was 'easier'.

'OK – I'll go and get your bags from the car and bring them up here for you,' Sean said, and the two of them went back to the main stairs. There was someone else just coming into the hallway, another man.

'You up there, Sean?' he called. 'There's another car just pulled in.'

This man was about a decade older, with sleek greying hair. He was wearing old black cords and a lavender-coloured sweater that Thea guessed was cashmere.

'Thea, this is Paul. He's my partner in crime here. All the décor you were admiring is down to him,' Sean told her.

Oh, of course he was. Partner. Damn – wasn't it always the way? Thea was cross with herself for minding about this, but at the same time she felt a little extra notch had been reached on the recovery-from-Rich scale. She'd actually noticed at last that someone was attractive. She'd thought it would never happen. She hadn't even been looking for it to happen. Shame it had to be someone who was on the other bus, but it was a start.

There were noises and bustling from outside the door and Paul opened it wide to let Sam, Milly and Alfie crash through. Behind them she could just see Emily tottering on the gravel in her favourite Prada boots and hauling a case on wheels. 'Is the maiden aunt here yet?' she called, then stopped abruptly as she came in through the door. 'Oops, sorry, Tee. Just a joke.'

Sean was laughing. '"Maiden aunt"? Do those still exist?'

Thea fought against a severe sense-of-humour failure and put on a bright smile. 'Yes, they do. That is my *dear* sister Emily, and the maiden aunt she's talking about is – er, me.'

FIVE

'Well, whoever is doing the cooking is worth their weight.' Anna put her fork down, sat back and sighed with deep contentment. 'That was a lasagne to die for.'

'Let's hope not literally,' Rosie said.

'Always so optimistic, your mother,' Jimi whispered to Elmo. 'It's why I married her.'

Elmo glared at Rosie. 'Mum, don't say bad stuff. It was ace.'

'Better than mine?' she challenged. 'OK, don't answer that. I know it was. Better by a country mile. That's fine. In fact, everything's fine – I like it here.' She sounded surprised at her own statement. They all looked at her, Thea wondering if her sister-in-law half-expected applause.

'Yes, it's brilliant,' Sam said. 'Great choice, Anna.'

She smiled at him and handed him the wine bottle.

'For that, you deserve a top-up. Pass it round and we'll open another.'

Mike got up and pulled another bottle from the rack. 'Luckily that's one thing we made sure there'd be plenty of,' he said, wielding the corkscrew.

'So what do we have scheduled for tonight, Thea?' Sam asked. 'Are we on Monopoly-with-menaces or Dominoes-to-the-death?'

'You didn't really do a spreadsheet, did you?' Rosie looked incredulous. 'I mean, seriously? I thought it was a joke when Jimi told me.'

'Yes, I did. Mum insisted. I even laminated six copies to hang up in all your rooms so you won't have any excuses not to know what the schedule is.'

'You did *what*?' Emily stared at her.

'Not really, only joking about the laminating. And it's only a guideline, so for tonight—'

'Oh, I can't do anything tonight. You'll have to count me out,' Emily interrupted briskly. 'I have to get the children to bed. They're dropping on their feet and I still have a load of stuff to bring in.' She glanced sideways at Milly and Alfie who were lining up silvery bits of rejected onion round the edges of their plates. 'You know, some *things* are still *outside* in the *car*,' she hissed in a dramatic whisper in the direction of Sam.

Milly looked up from her onion remains. 'Christmas presents?'

'Not presents, silly. Santa does presents.'

'Yes, Mummy.' Milly rolled her eyes at Emily and flicked a bit of onion at her brother.

'It's OK, I hadn't got anything organized for tonight. I was going to say I thought we could just, you know . . .' Thea almost said 'chill' but was aware of Elmo looking at her as if he dreaded her using the word. Oh, teenagers, she thought, so sweetly transparent. 'We'll just do whatever we want, settle in and get the feel of the place, nothing communal. Me, I need to finish off writing cards so I can get them posted tomorrow.'

'They won't get there, you know,' Emily told her. 'The last day for posting was Monday.'

'They'll be fine,' Rosie contradicted her. 'No need to flap.' She yawned. 'Jimi, did you pack the Anadin? I can feel a head coming on.'

'Of course I packed it. Your head would fall off without that stuff and we don't want a mess on the carpets.' Rosie glared at him.

'Ah, well, the walk in the morning will blow your headache away,' Thea said. 'I thought we'd take the path from the back, through the gate here in the garden and go down to the beach and up the path on the other side and then back here for a help-yourself lunch. I'll put a copy of the activities list up.'

'Dear lord, is it all compulsory?' Rosie looked alarmed.

'Absolutely,' Mike teased. 'Otherwise you'll get no turkey.'

'An overrated fowl, in my opinion,' Rosie sniffed.

'That's not the point,' Anna said quietly. 'Just bear with us for a few days, Rosie. I'm sure you can manage that.'

'Yeah, Mum. You can.' Elmo looked upset. Thea felt sorry for him. In a way he was in a similar position to her, another one who was on his own here. She wanted to make sure he didn't get fed up or despondent, missing friends and then vanishing for hours with his computer to moan to his mates about being imprisoned in the deepest wilds with only his family for company and Minecraft to absorb him. At his age, she'd enjoyed being by herself but only in short bursts when she wanted to be, not alone among grown-ups with no choice about it. Perhaps Sean had a bike Elmo could borrow – she'd go over to the Stables and ask him in the morning.

'Tree!' Rosie suddenly exclaimed, slapping both hands hard on the table and making everyone jump. 'I can add our decorations to the trees tonight while you're all slaving over hot jigsaws or something.'

'But I was going to do that. I brought ours,' Emily said.

'Uh-oh – tree wars,' Sam said, grinning. 'The Battle of the Baubles. Bring it on.' Elmo splorted laughter.

'But I'm the one on Thea's list for decorations.' Emily was bordering on petulant.

'There are two trees,' Anna pointed out. 'Why not do

one each? Not that they need much – they've both got lots of shiny stuff on. Not enough, though. You can never have enough.'

'Good idea. Yes, a tree each.'

'And which one do all the presents go under?' Emily looked anxious.

'The one that's in the bigger sitting room, I'd have thought,' Jimi said.

The two women eyed each other.

'So it's just a matter of who does which,' Rosie said. 'I bagsy—'

'No, wait,' Thea interrupted. 'Flip a coin for it, then it's fair.' It was only a Christmas tree, she thought. Where was all this aggro coming from?

'I suppose that would be a good plan,' Emily conceded. Jimi pulled a pound coin from his pocket and flipped it.

'Heads,' Rosie said. It was tails.

'Best of three?' she said.

'No!' Emily declared.

'That was a joke, Em. It's fine.'

Thea was suddenly feeling the need for sleep. It had been a long drive with so much holiday traffic and the wind against her, and it had taken a good hour longer than she'd expected. She wanted to curl up in the lovely big bed upstairs, all alone with a book and some time to herself to think. What was Rich doing for Christmas? She wished she'd got to the stage of being completely uninterested but she hadn't quite yet. Maybe he'd gone skiing again this year. Possibly with his sister who had always said she'd love to do it. Liz had hinted more than once that the two of them should let her join them on their travels. Well, now she'd got Rich all to herself so . . . well, good luck to them, though it would surely not be that long before Rich found another girlfriend, and then Liz's possessive jealousy could be fired up again. She'd probably enjoy that: it did seem that some people run on love and affection and others on grudges and spite.

'Is this tree-decorating going to be a competition?' Sam said, looking sly. 'A prize for the best tree?'

'I think that's an absolutely terrible idea,' Mike said, looking mischievous and meaning the exact opposite. 'And completely against the spirit of this holiday.'

'A tree-off it is then,' Sam said. 'May the sprucest spruce win.'

It would have been hugely infuriating for the rest of the family, but for Mike it would be pretty convenient if the mobile signal to the house were a bit hit and miss. Lacking a signal altogether would actually be ideal, in fact. He supposed he could simply ignore all the texts and later claim that he hadn't received any from anyone, but he didn't want to offend Charlotte; she was a good sort and deserved better. Plymouth was quite a safe long distance from Cove Manor and she was working each evening and a few afternoons too, in the pantomime chorus at the Drake Theatre as a favour for a producer friend. She liked the idea of being out of London for a couple of months, she'd claimed, and besides, she fancied a view of the sea.

'We could meet halfway, on the wilds of Bodmin Moor or something,' she'd joked – at least he'd assumed she'd joked – when she'd heard that he would be down in Cornwall. 'I don't get much time off but there'd be just enough for . . .' She'd left the rest unsaid, and he hadn't prompted her to be more specific, possibly because meeting halfway for what she had in mind wouldn't be easy without a venue in which to get together. He didn't much fancy checking into a cheap motel for a few hours in an under-heated room, and as for a social preamble to activities, well, there wasn't a lot that was sexy about a menu where the high point was an all-day breakfast.

Now here she was texting every couple of hours, over-cheery messages full of exclamation marks and talking about trains from Plymouth and saying she could get to Truro easily enough. She must be keen: he knew from previous trips to Cornwall that 'easily enough' by train was actually close to two, slowly trundled hours. But, to be honest, was *he* keen? On seeing Charlotte on London territory, yes. Within reason. She was good, easy company. He liked that she seemed content with only seeing him now and then, nothing intense, no commitment. A gap of a couple of weeks didn't bother her at all – or hadn't so far. He loved her deep and wicked laugh and the fact that she wore stockings – never tights – full-time, not just occasionally as a mildly grudging dress-up favour. But here? When he was in the middle of the entire family? It would be plain wrong.

He quickly sent back a brief text saying all was hectic – luckily she couldn't see him sprawled comfortably on this huge purple sofa with his feet up on a squashy foot-stool, a glass of wine and his favourite acoustic guitar to hand – and that he hoped the job was going well and that they'd get together soon. Then he switched off the phone, feeling slightly bad about her. It couldn't be a lot of fun, being shacked up in a cheap B&B for the panto season, but she wouldn't be on her own. There were the rest of the cast, all equally far from home for Christmas, and Charlotte wasn't short of the skills required for making new friends. She'd be fine.

Thea stretched out under bluebell-scented bubbles in the bath and closed her eyes, then flashed them open immediately, suddenly convinced she would drift off to sleep and drown. Sean hadn't been wrong – this was a bath to hold parties in and she felt rather guilty about the amount of hot water she'd used. Rich had had a thing about it, tending to twitch if she said she was off for a bath as if she were being thoughtlessly profligate. He always took showers instead and for the shortest possible time, as if brevity in such matters was a sign of virtue. 'No need to waste the resources,' he'd say, and to be fair, you couldn't argue with that – well, not with him, anyway. She'd once snappily accused him of having his own metaphorical cable car for swiftest possible access to the moral high ground.

His attitude struck her now as depressingly joyless. He'd been a lot more fun when they'd first got together but, looking back, she wondered if he'd mainly thought of her as ticking all the boxes for good wife material rather than being someone he adored madly and couldn't bear to be without. He'd liked that she could cook, that she was buying her own house (thanks to Granny J who'd by-passed Anna and left her money to her grandchildren on the basis that they had more need of it), that she had a job that was 'sensible' and which, he'd once noted approvingly, came with a decent pension. The one thing he had never commented on in what she now recognized as an inventory of her suitability, was whether or not she had good child-bearing hips. As it turned out, this had definitely *not* featured on his list of requirements. Such a shame she hadn't been a champion standard poodle, all things considered. He'd have been hugely keen that she had at least a couple of litters of puppies.

Thea climbed out of the bath quickly before she went further down the path of thinking any more about Rich. He belonged to her past. A book and a good night's sleep were the immediate future and she didn't need to think more deeply than that. She brushed her hair, put moisturizer on her face and went back into the bedroom. As she reached out to pick up the white towelling robe she'd left on the bed, it suddenly moved. Something beneath it was making it shift and ripple. Her hand stayed in mid-air and her tummy did a nervous flip – till she remembered what Sean had said. Carefully, she moved the fabric aside and the long creamy body of Woody the cat rolled over voluptuously and purred. He narrowed his blue eyes, something she'd once read was a cat's equivalent of asking you out for dinner, though she suspected that in this case he was merely attempting to charm her into leaving him where he was. She was tempted, especially if she could get him to sleep across her feet and keep them warm, but – suppose he wanted to go out in the night? Suppose Sean and Paul woke in the early hours, realized he was missing and worried he'd been eaten by a fox? Though frankly she wouldn't fancy a fox's chances. For a Siamese, Woody wasn't a small cat – weren't they supposed to be skinny and slinky?

She put on her robe, tied it around her middle, shoved her feet into her cosy sheepskin boots, then picked up Woody, tucked him firmly under her arm and went to find this back staircase Sean had told her about. It wasn't easy, holding a cat, finding the light switches and negotiating unfamiliar, twisty stairs. Luckily the cat was still sleepy so he hung like a long floppy cushion, though he was more awake and grumpy by the time she got to the door and it was awkward holding him with one hand and dealing with the catch with the other. At last she managed it, but as she regained her two-handed hold on Woody he seemed to realize he was being evicted and got hold of her finger in his claws and clamped his teeth over it.

'Ouch, Woody. No need for that!' she said, trying to calm him by rubbing his ears. He wasn't having any of it and grabbed hold of her hand again, wrestling with it. She was outside now, in the cobbled courtyard, opposite the door of the stable block. Should she simply set the cat free or knock on the door? Lights were on and she could hear the muffled sounds of music. In the end Woody made his own decision and struggled out of her grip, jumping down and running across to the Stables' front door where he yowled loudly. Thea was just beginning to feel the chill of the night air and was about to go back in to bed when the Stables cottage door opened and Sean came out.

'Ah, it's the maiden aunt! Having a wander round?' he asked. 'Or are you running away?'

She pointed to Woody who was sitting looking innocent and peaceful on the doorstep.

'He was sleeping on my bed so I thought I'd better bring him back in case he wanted to, y'know – go out in the night.'

'Oh, right, thanks. Sorry about him – he does like to make himself at home wherever he can sneak in. I should do something about it, start locking him in before the day we get a screaming cat-phobic guest who'll sue us for a full refund and ten years' counselling.'

Thea licked at her bleeding fingers. 'Why not include him on the Cove Manor website,' she suggested, 'then they'll know what they're getting and they'll have the choice? It would be a bit unfair to imprison him if he's used to being free-range.'

'Hey, yes, good plan. What happened to your hand? It's bleeding. Come on in, I'll put something on it. Did Woody do that? Bad cat.'

She grinned at him. 'I think I'm lacking in cat-carrying skills,' she said. 'Once he woke up properly in my hands he decided he wasn't comfortable. Honestly, it's fine. I'll go back up and run it under the cold tap.'

'No, really, you need some antiseptic on that. Cats are pretty toxic. Come on in.'

Thea followed him inside, frankly curious to have a look around but also conscious that under the robe she was completely naked. She'd been too hot from the bath to want to put her nightie on immediately and anyway, she hadn't exactly had meeting someone and having a conversation in mind at the time. She quickly tied a firmer knot in the belt as Sean led her into a large kitchen and open-plan sitting room that was painted calamine-lotion pink and fitted, at the kitchen end, with cupboards made from what looked like driftwood. The door and drawer handles were in the shapes of silvery shells and starfish. Music – Joe Jackson – was playing from an Apple Mac on a desk. An untidy collection of paperwork was heaped on a big pine table along with cookery books that had Post-it notes sticking out to mark pages, and there was a trug full of sweet chestnuts, still in their shells. A pale green Aga (smaller than in the main house) heated the kitchen to maximum cosiness. On the window-ledge was a long planter with several pots of hyacinths which were in full bloom and filling the room with a heady scent. The rest of the room had rather well-worn leather sofas, shelves with masses of books, several brightly coloured naïve paintings and one wall hung with surfboards. There was a fire blazing in a woodburning stove.

'It's in here somewhere . . .' Sean said, opening a high cupboard and pulling out a first-aid box. 'You've got one in the kitchen over there too, of course. It's in the cupboard under the smaller sink.' He looked across at her and smiled. 'Come on, sit here,' he said, patting a long bench beside the table. 'Nurse Sean will see you now.'

He washed his hands then came and sat astride the bench, his thigh against hers, and he took her hand, gently cleaning the scratches with antiseptic lotion. He was so close to her that the scent of his hair conditioner overtook the hyacinths. His touches were soft and soothing and she realized it had been a while since she'd had attentive skin-to-skin contact with a good-looking man. She certainly didn't count the grotesque mauling from Robbie Over-the-Road.

'Cat scratches can easily go septic,' he said, looking up and smiling. His eyes were the colour of the flowers on the ledge and for a moment she couldn't quite reply. *I've got no knickers on*: the thought flashed across her mind as Sean stroked ointment into her cuts and then applied a plaster to the worst of it. But then she reminded herself that the knicker-thing wasn't relevant; of course, Sean wouldn't be remotely interested.

'Thanks so much. It's really kind of you to do this,' she said, starting to get up.

'Aw, don't go yet. You need something for the shock. Fancy a medicinal glass of wine? A cup of tea? Or are you really in a rush to get to bed?' He was looking at her in a teasing sort of way and she wasn't sure how to interpret it.

'Er, well, no, no great rush. A glass of wine would be good but' – she looked at the paperwork and the cookery books – 'aren't you busy? I don't want to interrupt.'

'Oh, that's Maria's stuff,' he said, taking glasses from a cupboard and wine from a large blue Smeg fridge. 'She's the one who cooks your evening meals. She organizes it back at her place in the village and she just wanted me to look over some of her recipe ideas. You'll see her in

94

the morning when she drops off tomorrow's supper.' He picked up a book, one of Rick Stein's. 'Though as you're the client, maybe I should let you loose on this.' He led her to a sofa close to the fire and quickly fluffed up some cushions before she sat down, with him beside her.

'Well, tonight's lasagne was fabulous, so if that's anything to go by, I think she's far better qualified than I would be,' Thea told him. She wondered where Paul was – there didn't seem to be any sign of him. Perhaps he was already asleep, or somewhere else at the other end of the building watching something Christmassy on TV.

'So are you a surfer or are they Paul's?' she asked, looking at the boards on the wall.

'Paul's? Ha! No chance. He thinks the sea is purely for looking at from a stylish deck through a glass of Pimm's. The boards are mine. I used to be a pro but it's a younger man's game. Was great while it lasted and I got to see a lot of the world.'

'A professional surfer? Wow!' Thea was impressed but not that surprised. If anyone wanted to draw a picture of a surfer, they'd probably come up with someone who looked a lot like Sean. 'I didn't know you could be a professional at it.'

'You get sponsorship deals, if you're good. And I was good,' he said, looking distant for a moment. 'But nothing's for ever. At least, not in sport.' Woody came in, jumped on the back of the sofa and settled himself down along the cushion as if keeping an eye on them. Sean reached back behind Thea's head to stroke the cat, who started to purr in her ear.

'So now you've got this place. You and Paul.'

He reached over for the bottle on the coffee table and topped up her glass. 'Yep. Finally got it sorted, I think. It was originally going to be a hotel but no one in their right mind wants the constant beck-and-call thing you get with hotel residents, or at least I didn't. It would drive me nuts. So for the last year it's been a regular holiday let for big parties of people, but after one hen group too many we came up with a kind of halfway idea. Self-catering, but with the option for evening meals, picnic lunches on request, that sort of thing, daily cleaners just for a bit of a tidy-up – whatever options the clients choose. It's not been going in that way for long. In fact' – and he hesitated – 'I probably shouldn't admit this but your family is the first to sample the new system. You're the guinea pigs.' He gave her a shy smile. 'Now you'll go straight back and tell them all we don't know what we're doing.'

She laughed. 'Of course I won't! Anyway, I owe you for the medical treatment. You can have my silence in exchange. Cove Manor is very sumptuous.'

He grinned. 'You're dying to know how we managed to afford to change it from the aristo ruin to designer glory, aren't you? Everyone looks at me and wonders that. How did the scruffy surf dude end up with *this*?'

Thea twiddled with the robe's belt, guiltily acknowledging that this was exactly what she'd wondered. 'The film business is the answer,' Sean went on. 'This place has been rented out as a location for everything, from Cornish historical dramas to porn for the Japanese market. It's worked bloody hard, this old house.'

'Well, you and Paul have done a fabulous job with it. We all love it.'

'Good to know,' Sean said. 'Make sure you tell me if anything's missing, anything more we could have done. I wasn't sure how far to go with making it Christmassy. Paul said everyone has their own ideas on that so in the end we just did the trees. There's one thing you could probably do with, though . . .' He looked at her speculatively.

'What's that?' she asked.

'Mistletoe. Got to have mistletoe at Christmas, haven't you? And I know just where to get some.'

'I don't suppose we'd get much use out of it!' Thea joked. 'My parents are divorcing, my sister and her husband are up to here in small children and my brother's wife Rosie seems to have a permanent headache.'

'Sounds like some of them need to do more kissing then. Sorry, that's not for me to comment,' he said, looking at her. 'And then, of course, there's you.'

'Me? Oh, I'm just . . .'

'. . . the maiden aunt, the family spinster. Yes, I know

– though from what I've read about them in old books they don't usually have bits of purple in their hair and look like teenage elves. And anyway, being unattached is all the more reason to have a massive bunch of the stuff in the house. You never know who'll turn up over the holiday.'

'I suppose there might be a passing postman, a lost stray rambler or something,' she said, putting on a comedy-glum face. She also put her empty glass back on the table. It was time to go before the wine went to her head and she fell asleep on this sofa in front of Sean's wonderful fire. 'Thanks for the wine and the medical attention,' she said, clambering out of the old sofa's depths while trying to keep her robe modestly closed.

'It's a two-man job, that's the thing,' Sean said as he followed her to the door.

'What is?'

'The mistletoe. I know where the best stuff is but I'll need someone to hold the ladder.'

'Is Paul a good ladder-holder?'

'*Paul?* Oh, bless you, I don't think so. Not if it means his fabulous Gucci shoes will be at risk of mud damage. But' – and he eyed her battered old sheepskin boots – 'if you're up for it, it could be fun?' He was looking terrifically eager, like a small boy planning an illicit adventure.

'Is it, er . . . ?'

'Legal?' He shrugged. 'Well, yeah, I think so. It's

wild-growing stuff, isn't it? So – how about tomorrow night, if you're not busy? Either before or after supper? Any time from four, once it's dark. It won't take long.'

Just before supper was the time assigned to show Anna's DVD of past family holidays and events. Thea could probably miss some of that – it wasn't as if she needed to see Emily's wedding all over again. Actually, being there on the day had been quite enough, given that Emily had made her wear strapless plum-coloured satin which needed underwear so tight it was practically scaffolding, and she'd spent the whole event barely breathing . . . but Emily was bound to make a fuss about her copping out. She wouldn't go so far as to say Thea was deliberately avoiding watching weddings but she'd probably think it. No, Thea decided, she'd join in, she'd watch and enjoy and – apart from the not-breathing thing – it *had* been a truly lovely day.

'OK, they want to eat early because of the children. I don't think anyone will miss me if I go out after, though. About seven thirty?'

Sean walked her across the freezing courtyard and opened the house door for her.

'Excellent. See you tomorrow then, maiden aunt. Sleep well.'

SIX

Anna stretched out like a big kiss-shape X under the duvet, relishing the luxury of so much space to herself. It still felt like a novelty, having a double bed with just her in it, after more than four decades of sharing her sleep with the big lumpy body of Mike. It wasn't that he'd been a snorer, particularly. Nothing much more than some forgivable sighs and harrumphs, but he was quite an unsettled sleeper, either too hot or too cold, forever turning over and back again while half-asleep, dragging the duvet this way or that, or flipping a pillow over and slapping it into shape as if completely unaware that there was someone else in the bed who might find that annoying.

The first few nights after they'd come to their arrangement about living independently, albeit in the same house, she'd been surprised to find she didn't miss his bed-presence at all. She'd imagined lying there having maudlin thoughts about how this was the way it would be if he'd died: that she'd spend the rest of her life feeling lonely on an excess of mattress, and why bring that loneliness on by insisting on it *now*? Instead, she'd had her new room – the big front bedroom which was actually larger than the one they'd shared for years but which they had rejected as their own because it overlooked the road rather than the peace of the back garden. She'd painted the walls a soft lavender-grey, made new curtains and gone mad on crisp new white bedlinen from the White Company sale. It had all felt like a treat, like a present. And it still did. She felt very lucky. Not many people could have such a convivial running down to a massively long marriage. In her head she could picture her own mother, tutting and shaking her head, reminding her to think about which side her bread was buttered and that independence only had so much going for it. But this wasn't about disliking each other, about losing touch. There was no rancour, no recrimination, just a warm and happy agreement that there would be more ahead in life for each of them than silent suppers on a tray while watching *Masterchef* (oh, the irony there) and an approaching old age of bickering in Tesco over which washing powder to get. Instead of the snippy claustrophobia that they'd noticed in so many other couples, they'd always be close and loving friends. It felt right. Definitely. All they needed to do was convince the children that this would work for everyone and that they'd still be one happy family.

Anna didn't need to look at the clock to know it was too early to get up yet but these days she rarely slept beyond 5.30. She switched on the light and picked up her iPad which warned that she only had 4 per cent battery left. She'd plugged its charger in the night before but had been too tired to realize the switch at the plug was off. There was maybe just enough time to have a very quick look at emails before it died. Her Hotmail account showed three messages from Alec and for the first time since they'd got together she felt a slight dread instead of the usual excitement about opening them. He'd have done his Christmas thing with his children the night before – she so hoped it went well and that he was about to tell her that they'd had a terrific time. She opened the first of them that he'd written while halfway through cooking the goose. All it said was, *Gallons of fat on this thing. Who knew?* Well, she did, but then she was many years older than him and had cooked geese several times. She wondered if he'd thought to roast the potatoes in the fat for maximum deliciousness and she also wondered if the tone of the mail was meant to be amusing or glum. Emails were sometimes so hard to interpret.

The second one had no ambiguity. *How can a great big fuck-off goose equal so little meat? Not that it mattered. The kids hated it. On my own now – call me if you get a chance but I expect you're in the middle of family fun.*

Not a good day then. She felt dreadfully sorry for him and slightly guilty. For the past couple of months they'd been seeing each other mostly when she felt in the mood for having someone to see a film with or fancied a companion for an exhibition or to have supper with while Mike was out doing his music or seeing bands. Alec had always been willing, even at a moment's notice, to come out with her. He was sounding lonely and fed up and here she was, too far away to be of any comfort when he could do with it.

Before she read his third email she sent a reply that underplayed her highly comfortable situation, saying the weather was gale-force and freezing (well, of course it was, it was late December), the house was massive (implying draughty rather than the snug and warm sanctuary that it really was), the family were a bit tense (slightly true – the her-and-Mike divorce was a thing that was Not Being Mentioned), and that she missed him. She added that she hoped he'd have a better time at his brother's and that there was very little that was better than cold goose sandwiches with quince jelly, washed down with a glass of delicious wine in front of a Christmas *Morecambe and Wise* special. The moment she pressed 'send' she wished she'd said something different. Christmas TV. On your own with a cold fowl sandwich. Could anything be bleaker than that? She was just about to open his third message when the iPad's memory gave way and the screen went blank.

She could hear thumpy footsteps on the staircase and the sound of children so, feeling the need for a cup of tea and a rethink about what to say to Alec later that could make her stupidly glib message any better, she left the iPad charging, got out of bed and headed for the kitchen.

It was dark when Thea woke and she thought it must still be the middle of the night but the clock beside her bed told her it was past 7.30. She climbed out of bed, wrapped her robe round her and went to the window to see if there was any sign of sunrise. There wasn't, but then she was facing west and it was all wrong for finding any silvery glow of dawn. She'd just have to trust there was one on its way, somewhere.

Below her, she could see the black edges of the garden sloping away down towards the lighter-black sea and she cracked open the window so she could hear it. A stronger wind had arrived in the night and the weather forecast had promised it would be a really cold one. The sea was crashing hard onto the beach below and she could taste salt on the freezing air. An oak tree on the edge of the slope was making groaning sounds and its long bare twigs were lashing about, creating whiplike silhouettes against a low moon that shone palely through racing clouds.

'Thea?' Her door opened a careful inch and the little anxious face of Milly appeared.

'Morning, sweetie,' Thea said, closing the window. 'Did you sleep well?'

'No. Alfie snores and he coughs,' Milly said, coming into the room and plonking herself straight into the middle of Thea's bed, pulling the duvet up to her chin. 'And when's breakfast? Daddy isn't awake yet. I went to Elmo's room but he told me to go away and threw a shoe at me. I'm *hungry*.'

'OK, give me a minute and I'll come down and get you something to eat. Do you know where the kitchen is? I'll meet you down there. Bring Alfie too.'

'I know where it is, but . . .' Milly's eyes went big. 'It's dark. And the stairs are scary.'

'We must leave some lights on for you tonight then,' Thea told her, hoping that was the right thing to say. Did Emily and Sam want Milly to feel free to wander this great big house by herself? Probably not. She quickly brushed her hair while Milly jumped out of bed and went into the bathroom to delve into Thea's make-up bag, starting to pull out blusher and eyeshadow. Alfie, cute in Batman pyjamas and clutching a toy rabbit with a well-sucked ear, came into the room in search of his sister and Thea managed to distract Milly from the delights of an open mascara wand with the promise of French toast. The three of them went downstairs.

'There's one thing we have to do first,' Thea told the children as they reached the hallway. 'And what do you think it is?'

'Go out and buy milk?' Milly guessed. 'Daddy's always having to do that. He forgets.'

'No, it's not milk. There's plenty of milk.' Thea took a hand of each of them and led them into the first sitting room and across to the window. 'It's the lights – we have to switch the Christmas-tree lights on, don't we?'

'That's so Santa can see where we are,' Alfie yawned, still sounding sleepy.

'No, it isn't.' Milly was scornful.

'Well, it might be,' Thea said, looking along the wall for the plug. Milly gave her a look.

Thea found the plug and switched on the lights, and Milly, in spite of her young cynicism, squealed excitedly, 'Look – that's *our* fairy on the top! From home!'

Emily had made quite an impact with the tree, Thea noted as she looked at Barbie-in-a-wedding-dress splayed wantonly open-legged across the top branch. Still, at least she was wearing knickers. Emily had added her exclusively silver, green and white hyper-tasteful colour scheme to the hotch-potch of multi-coloured decorations that had been there the day before. Thea was willing to bet she'd been in two minds whether to replace them completely, but Anna had been right – there really is no such thing as too much when it comes to jazzing up a Christmas tree. The effect was a crazy excess of shimmer and sparkle.

'It is yours! It's all very pretty, isn't it? Now shall we go and light up the other tree and then we can have breakfast?'

The tree that Rosie had decorated in the smaller sitting room was a cheery mixture of homemade cardboard angels with jolly crayonned faces, knitted robins and cotton wool glitter-spattered snowmen, all of which she must have kept from Elmo's infant-school days. To her surprise, Thea found this all a bit heart-rending and she had to fight back a tear. Each year, Jimi and Rosie must have collected and safely packed away these treasures which Elmo had proudly brought home for the tree. She did the same thing with her pupils, getting them to make decorations just before the end of the Christmas term, watching their pride in their efforts as they concentrated hard, making stars and snowmen and robins with movable wings and being liberal with the glitter, flecks of which would still be shining in classroom corners well into March. She would, she decided, help Milly and Alfie make something fun and Christmassy over the next couple of days. If she had to be stuck with the role of maiden aunt, she'd make sure she was a damn good one.

'Hungry,' Milly growled, reminding her what they were really all there for. She tugged on Thea's hand.

'OK, OK, into the kitchen then. Come on. You can beat the eggs for me.'

Breakfast was a long-drawn-out event as everyone had differing ideas about what time they wanted it and when. Elmo was last down, sloping dozily into the kitchen after most of them had finished and Thea was helping Anna to clear up.

Emily grinned at him. 'Good afternoon, Elmo,' she said, getting up from her chair and starting to load toast-crumbed plates into the dishwasher.

'Oh, leave him alone, Emily. The boy's on holiday,' Anna said. 'Elmo? Bacon sandwich?'

Elmo grunted and gave a slight nod.

'That means "Yes, please, and thank you for the kind offer, Gran",' Jimi translated.

'Oh, don't worry, I got it,' Anna said as she pulled a pack of bacon from the fridge. 'I've been fluent in teenage for years now. It's not something you forget.'

Elmo was halfway through his sandwich and most of the others had dispersed when the back door opened and a bulky red-haired woman in a scarlet coat and with a huge pink scarf came in, bringing a drift of icy air. She was carrying a large box and was followed by a young teenage girl equally bundled up against the cold in a fake-fur-trimmed parka and burdened by another plastic box.

'Hellooo!' the woman said to the assembled and slightly startled few left at the table. 'I'm Maria. You all settled in, then? I've brought you tonight's supper.'

Mike stood up and took the box from her. 'Hello, Maria. And if you're the one who cooked last night's lasagne, you're extremely welcome. It was delicious. Thank you so much.'

'My pleasure, darlin'. And also my job, of course.'

Thea took the girl's box from her, put it on the work-top and opened it. 'There's enough here to feed the five thousand!' she said, carefully taking out a huge dish, taped shut across the top. 'What have we got in here?'

'I've done you a chicken casserole in cider and a choice of vegetables to go with. Me, I'd go jacket potatoes as well, but it's up to you. Or there's a pack of rice and some of that quinny stuff I don't know how to pronounce because I know you up-London folks like that.' Her eyes sparkled as she said it and Thea laughed, recognizing a tease. The girl hunched further into her parka and backed away towards the door.

'Oh, and this is my daughter, Daisy. Say hello, Daisy.' The girl uttered a muffled 'Huh,' from the depths of her scarf and stared at the floor.

'She's not as shy as she looks,' Maria said, nodding across to the girl. 'And what's your name there, boy?' she asked Elmo.

He looked up from the last of his sandwich (crusts pulled off and left on the plate) and went a bit pink. 'Elmo,' he muttered. 'Hello.'

'You look about Daisy's age. Could be company for each other over the holiday, couldn't you? Gets a bit lonely out of school time here in the village for the young ones.'

Thea felt a twinge of sympathy as Daisy and Elmo shot terrified glances at each other and blushed to matching shades of puce.

'There's a table-tennis table set up out there in the games room, in that barn down the end of the stable block, did Sean and Paul tell you?' Maria continued cheerily, putting the last of the supplies in the fridge. 'Dartboard too. Keep you busy, that could. Right, I'll be off. I'll be back in the morning with Christmas Eve supplies. Sean says you want to do your own turkey and all the Christmas Day and Boxing Day food, is that right? I'd already done red cabbage and apples so I might as well bring that in the morning if you want it. My lot won't touch it, only sprouts and carrots.'

'Fantastic – yes, please. We've brought our own turkey; I did tell Sean,' Anna said.

Maria whisked her big boxes back out of the door and the two visitors left, but not before Thea had caught an exchange of curious glimpses between Elmo and Daisy. Good, she thought. Maybe he'd have someone to hang out with, if they could get over the bit where they didn't actually exchange a word.

'Maria's right – table tennis could keep us all busy,' Anna said. 'We should have a tournament.'

'But it's not on the schedule,' Jimi teased, looking at Thea.

'I can make room for it,' she said airily. 'There are several time slots waiting to be filled in.'

'Oh God, not more organized stuff.' Emily came back in at that moment. 'What time's the compulsory walk? I've got presents to wrap and Sam needs to pick up something in Falmouth.'

'In about half an hour, give or take. And no one's allowed to skive off,' Mike told her.

'Yes, sir.' Emily did a mock-salute, looking rebellious.

'There's a pub lunch on me at the end of it,' he added and she perked up.

'Ah, well, in that case I'll get the children ready. I'll have to wrap them up like little parcels. It's so cold out there.'

The path to the beach wasn't very long but it was winding and steep, and had a couple of places with alarmingly sheer drops. Thea took hold of Milly's hand at the worst bits, wondering if that was the right thing to do – or should she trust the instinctive sure-footedness of the child? She didn't want to make her fearful but couldn't bear to watch her skipping along while gazing out to sea, apparently oblivious of the path edge. Emily made Sam carry Alfie on his back, telling the boy that it was for fun, but Thea knew she was terrified he'd trip and fall and bounce bone-crunchingly off the rocks that jutted out through the deceptively soft-looking gorse and heather.

'He's not light, this lad,' Sam puffed as they went single-file down the track, leaning into the hillside so the wind wouldn't blow them to the sand below.

'Carrying him back up, that'll be your turn, Em. Equality rules and all that,' Sam half-turned to tell her.

'We're not coming back this way,' she said. 'And please keep your eyes on the path. I don't want you tripping, not when you're supposed to be keeping him safe.'

'I am, I am,' he said, laughing and jogging Alfie up and down till the little boy giggled.

They reached the bottom, the drift of shingle between the hillside and the sand, and Thea watched Emily take Alfie from Sam and hug him tight before she put him down on the ground.

'Thanks for watching out for Milly,' she said to Thea. 'I don't know what I'd do if . . .' and she blinked hard.

'She's fine, Em, very sure on her feet. You didn't need to worry so much.'

Emily turned on her, snappy. 'Oh, didn't I? Well, thanks for the advice. Come back to me on that when *you've* got childr—' She stopped suddenly and put her hand to her mouth. 'Oh, I'm so sorry, Tee. Really sorry. Ignore me, I'm just tense.' She put her arms out. 'Hug?'

Thea shook her head, took a deep breath and started walking off after the others, hugging her coat round her against the wind. 'It's OK, Emily, forget it,' she shouted back to her sister. 'And yes, you're right; what could I possibly know?' She strode off on her own towards the sea which was washing foam on to the sand. The shimmering wetness of the beach told her that the tide was going out. Good thing, she thought, otherwise she'd have been childishly tempted to do the angry drama-queen thing and go and stand in the shallows to wait for the rising water to knock her down and carry her off. Bloody Emily. Why didn't she *think*? And it wasn't as if she didn't know better.

Emily was peeling off the layers by the time they got to the village pub, tying her jacket round her waist and pushing up her sleeves. She felt restored and freshened by the blasts of cold air and from striding across the beach against the wind, but horribly guilty about what she'd so stupidly said to Thea. How could she have been so thoughtless? She, of all people: the one member of the family in whom Thea had confided all those months ago, a few weeks before Rich had left her. What must she think of her?

Thea had kept to herself as they walked, stamping along with her head down, slightly apart from the rest of them. Emily wanted to go to her and apologize again, but was afraid to broach the subject. If she left it, it would surely just drift away. It would have to – you couldn't have bad feeling at Christmas, it wasn't allowed. They had to keep up the good-spirits thing otherwise the whole family would want to know why. Things would be said, explanations demanded if anyone noticed the two of them avoiding each other. It would be fine. Later on, she would make it fine. She would.

The walk had been a circular one of about two miles – across the beach, up the other side, across the road and along a path through the woods. Jimi, who was there under protest and would have preferred to stay on the sofa in front of the fire, was carrying yesterday's newspaper folded at the crossword and would occasionally stop to write in an answer. Eventually he was trailing, followed at an even greater distance by Elmo, who slouched along with his hands up his sleeves and his hood up, having refused to wear a coat so as not to sacrifice any tiny fraction of cool.

'Do you *have* to?' Rosie said to Jimi. 'If I can manage this with my headache, you could at least show a bit of grace.'

'I'm stopping my brain from seizing up. You should try it some time – it would probably fix those heads of yours.'

'It's *tension*, not rot,' she said.

'Ah – thirteen across! Satellite dish!' was his reply.

Beneath the wind-rocked trees the small children kicked at soggy heaps of fallen leaves and Alfie rolled in something that smelled vile.

'Fox,' Anna, now they were in the pub, told Emily, who was sniffing at her boy's sleeve and trying to identify which bit to scrub at with a tissue. 'You won't get that smell off until you put it through the washing machine.'

'Oh, great. Well, at least it's warm in here. It can go under the table while we have lunch.'

'So long as you don't forget to pick it up,' Sam said.

'For heaven's sake, Sam.' Emily reared up. 'Do you really think I'd let Alfie walk back to the house with no coat in *this*?' The sky was going a bruisey shade of purple-grey, and some icy rain spattered against the pub windows, half-wet, half-snowy.

'OK, OK, no need to pick on me, Em. It's not my fault.'

'Sorry, sorry. Oh God, everything's *wrong*.' Emily's eyes welled up and Sam gave her a tissue from his pocket. Thea looked up at her from the far end of the big table they'd bagged, and smiled wanly. Well, that was a relief. Emily really wanted to go and hug her but that would possibly lead to a full-scale session of mutual sobbing so she gave her a small return smile and sat down, a fidgety child each side of her.

'I think someone's hungry,' Mike said tactfully, handing her a menu. 'Let's be quick and order – and hey, look, there's Maria working behind the bar.'

The pub was a light, roomy one with a pale wood floor, big windows and a view over the bay. It had been recently modernized and smelled of its new pale blue and white paint. Driftwood-framed pictures by a local artist were on the walls and a sail was hung across the ceiling. There were photos on the window-ledges of bands playing, and Mike went to have a look. Alongside the chalked-up menu was a list of up-coming events.

'I see there's plenty of music going on here,' he said to

Maria after he'd put the food and drinks order in. 'I could bring my guitar down.'

'You'd be very welcome,' Maria said. 'We could do with some new blood. We mostly get the same old chancers singing the same old stuff, and a few of the young ones thinking they're the next One Direction. Boxing Day's going to be a good one. You could come to that. Music starts at about seven that night. It's usually later, but there'll be a lot in that night.'

Anna drifted up and stood next to him. 'You'd better check with Thea first,' she said. 'It might clash with something.'

'Well, she did say she'd accept a degree of flexibility. Maybe we can all come up here instead?' Mike felt the phone buzz in his pocket. It would be Charlotte. Again.

'Back in a minute, just off to the bog,' he said to Anna, putting his pint of beer on the family table and loping off to the door in the corner. Once through it he pulled the phone out and sure enough, it was her.

Missing you babes. And surprise – unexpected time off. Got a lift down your way tomorrow. See if you can escape for a bit?

On Christmas Eve? What kind of pantomime production suddenly decides to let its cast go swanning off on the busiest night of the run?

Mike went down the corridor past the loo and found a door to a courtyard that had a smokers' shelter in it. The stuff that was now falling from the sky was more snow than rain. He hadn't expected that, not down here in the far south-west. Wasn't it usually a lot milder here than everywhere else? His fingers almost froze on the phone keypad as he clicked on Charlotte's name. Voicemail. Damn. He started leaving a message asking her what she was planning for the next day, making it vague from his point of view so that she wouldn't think he was actually inviting her down. She wouldn't expect that, of course – she hadn't even met his family – let alone imagine she'd be welcome to come and hang out with them on the night before Christmas.

'You OK, Dad?' Jimi came out, clutching a pack of cigarettes and a lighter. Mike, feeling like a caught-out schoolboy, quickly shoved his phone back in his pocket, his message only half-spoken and left up in the air.

'Fine, fine,' he mumbled. 'Just checking what the weather is doing. Wondering about going back for a car after lunch to come and pick up the little ones. This weather's a bit of a horror, isn't it?'

'Oh, they'll be OK.' Jimi inhaled deeply and grimaced. 'I hate these things. Going to quit, definitely. They just speed up the inevitable body rot.' He inhaled again and blew smoke upwards. It twirled away on the wind. 'The children won't mind the walk and it's not far. Alfie's kneeling up at the window all shiny-eyed at the snow and Milly is demanding a sledge.' He stubbed the cigarette out. 'Vile habit. Lucky it's my only real vice.'

Mike opened the door to go back in. 'Jimi? This was a good idea, wasn't it? Coming down here?'

Jimi looked at his father as if he didn't quite understand the question. 'Of course it was. It's just, you know, a little bit tense . . .?'

'I know. I wish we hadn't said anything about the divorce now.'

'I think we all do, Dad.'

SEVEN

'Did you get them?' Emily was hovering in the hallway as the Golf pulled up outside and Sam came in, looking tired. He brushed snow off his coat.

'I did. Two shiny new bikes stashed in the back of the car, boxed up for easy wrapping unless you just want to have them out of the packaging and propped up by the tree with a couple of big fancy ribbons on?'

'No, they're fine in the boxes. I've got plenty of paper. Unwrapping is the best bit.'

'Is it? Excellent. I wish you'd told me that a fifty-mile round trip and three hundred quid ago. I'd have just picked up some cardboard boxes from the village shop.'

Emily laughed. 'You know what I mean. Thanks, Sam, they'll be thrilled.'

Sam started gazing up at the ceiling.

'What are you doing?'

'Looking for mistletoe. For a minute there I thought you were going to kiss me but there isn't any so I suppose you won't.'

'Do you want me to?'

He shrugged. 'Only if you want to. Don't do it now, though, or I'll think you're only doing it because I mentioned it, not because it's what you want.'

Emily felt confused. She did quite want to kiss him but now he'd pretty much said definitely not to. How to get these things right, even after several years together? And why was he now analysing something that hadn't happened? She tried breathing slowly, remembering to be mindful of the moment. You were supposed to be mindful in a positive way, so going over something that was bound to make her feel down wouldn't be a useful thing – so maybe she should stop? She took his hand, hoping that he wasn't actually flinching at the gesture.

'Thea's got the children at the kitchen table, making paper angels to hang up,' she told him. 'She's so good with them. Come and see.'

'OK, but let me just tell you, in case this snow decides to settle, I got some cheap plastic sledges as well. Including one for Elmo.'

'Did you? That was thoughtful. I was hoping the snow would go away but now I mustn't wish that because they'll be disappointed if they can't use the sledges.'

There she went again, being negative. Or was she? She was putting the children first, which had to be good, surely?

Sam smiled. 'Well, it's definitely settling on the road-sides out there, but if it's all gone by morning, we can always haul the kids around on the sand. It'll be just as much fun for them.'

Sam went through to the kitchen to see what the children were up to and Emily went to the front door and had a quick look out. Did snow ever stop being a magical thing to watch? she wondered. Would there be a moment – perhaps a few years later on – where she'd look out of the window at it falling and get no thrill from it at all? She hoped not. She put a hand out beyond the porch and felt the soft icy drops landing on it. Snow always reminded her of fur, whereas rain made her think of leather. The flakes melted on her warm fingers and dripped to the ground. That was good. Snow falling was a beautiful thing but she didn't want it any deeper than the couple of inches it took to make everything look pretty. She was frightened of its power to cut off roads and villages and to make the world as she knew it stop functioning. That silent, white menace was actually chaos and she was terrified of chaos.

'Emily? Are you coming? Mum and Dad have got the DVD thing all set up and ready to go. We're supposed to all come and watch.' Thea went to stand beside her at the door. 'What are you doing? Oh wow, it's falling really fast!'

'I know. Suppose we get snowed in?'

'Oh, we won't be,' Thea replied. 'Or at least . . . well, we've got several days here yet so it wouldn't matter, would it? We definitely won't run out of food – there's tons of it.'

'But it could be weeks. What if it's weeks?'

'It won't be. It hardly ever snows at all this far south so it's not going to hang about, is it?' Thea was beside her in the fast-gathering dusk, watching the snow falling on the camellias. The bushes already had fat buds on them, some of them even breaking open and showing flushes of red. Short spikes of daffodils had also pushed up through the ground beneath, battling towards spring.

'I'm sorry about what I said on the beach, Thea,' Emily murmured.

'It's OK, you already said.'

'Yes, but—'

'No, really – it's fine. I'm over it.'

'Over what I said, or . . . ?'

'Both.'

'You're so good with children. Mine are lucky to have you.'

Thea laughed. 'Well, that's my job, isn't it? The role of the maiden aunt.' She closed the door and pushed her fingers through her damp hair.

'Oh, you won't always be one,' Emily assured her. 'There's someone out there with your name on him.'

'Hey, I'm not looking, I'm really not. And I love being an aunt, maiden or otherwise. It's fun, and when I've had enough I get to hand them back and revert to wine and irresponsibility. Come on, Em, let's go and be mortified by our on-film childhood.'

Rich would have hated this, Thea thought as she watched a shaky piece of home movie of her tenth birthday party. It was a circus theme and she was dressed as a ringmaster, annoying her friends with a riding crop in lieu of a whip. They shrieked and giggled as she got them to run round the garden pretending to be lions that she'd tamed. Rich would have started sighing and shifting about after the first five minutes and have found an excuse to leave the room after fifteen. 'Your family are always so *pleased* with themselves,' he'd once said on the way home from a barbecue in Mike and Anna's garden one Sunday the previous summer.

The comment had completely taken the edge off what had been a beautiful day. She'd been convinced he'd been enjoying it, cheerfully playing a loose form of garden cricket with everyone, having a long and commiserative conversation with Jimi about the downturn in fortunes of Manchester United and dozing comfortably on the swingseat under the cherry tree,

Benji asleep at his feet, after a garden lunch of Mike's homemade burgers and a fabulous pear tart. It had – at the time – felt like a pretty perfect summer afternoon, and then out he came with that mean little comment as Thea drove them both home.

'We get on OK, that's all. Is that so unusual in a family? And I haven't seen any of them for nearly a month. It's perfectly normal to like their company now and then, isn't it?' she'd asked, feeling very rattled. What he'd said had really hurt and she'd barely trusted herself to speak.

'Is it?' He'd seemed seriously puzzled. 'Don't most families go their separate ways once they're grown up? You lot still seem to have barely left home. You're always either seeing your parents or phoning them or going out to Emily's or off to your mum's for a chat. It's . . . I don't know . . . a bit infantile? My lot are quite happy with the odd visit in the year.'

'Apart from your sister,' Thea retaliated. 'She hasn't exactly let you go, has she?'

'That's different. It's all about the dogs. That's a shared interest as well as being her business.'

Thea had left it at that, not wanting to hear his reply to the question that was in her head: *will you feel like this about our children?*

'Oh bloody hell, look at my *hair*!' Rosie was pointing at herself on the screen, a bride at the register office wearing a 1940s-style pink- and flame-coloured floral tea-dress with her hair piled up in rolls at the side and one on the top. The style hadn't been entirely success-ful. 'I never went to that hairdresser again,' she said now. 'I knew as soon as I saw the wedding photos that she must really hate me.'

'You look better than me,' Jimi said, chortling at the sight of himself in an over-sized chalk-striped suit and a cream straw panama hat. 'What were we thinking of? What the hell made us go for a forties' theme?'

'Oh God, I'm *sooo* never getting married,' Elmo growled. He hid his eyes behind his hands. 'This is too random. When's food?'

Thea glanced across to where her parents were sitting close together on the big sofa. They were laughing at the film but also actually holding hands. She looked at Jimi and jerked her head in their direction. Her brother noticed and grinned at her, giving a discreet thumbs-up. How could they, with all this happy history between them, even think of splitting up for good?

'So – what's tonight's entertainment then, team leader?' Sam asked Thea as they started loading the dishwasher together after Maria's fabulous chicken casserole.

'Ah. Well, it's up to you. I think watching the second DVD might count as family overload, so – er, maybe you could all just make your own fun?'

'"Your"?' Anna chipped in as she rinsed a plate. 'You

make it sound as if you'll be elsewhere. Having an early night? Are you OK?'

Thea now wished she'd mentioned her appointment (obviously she couldn't call it a date, because it wasn't, really) with Sean earlier. Now it just looked as if she'd deliberately kept it a secret. Had she? Possibly. They'd only have teased her.

'Er, I'm just off out for a little while. Going out to get something with Sean. Not for long.'

That got their attention, especially the women. She sensed the eyes of Emily, Anna and Rosie on her and could feel herself going pink, though there was absolutely no reason to.

'What is it you're going to get?' Emily asked her.

Jimi gave a rather dirty laugh, and made little quote marks in the air. 'Some "fun"?' he said, giving Elmo a nudge. 'Way-hay!'

Elmo rolled his eyes at him. 'God, Dad – like stop?'

Thea laughed too. 'I don't think that kind of fun is very likely, do you?'

'I don't see why not,' Anna said, smiling at her.

'No, honestly, it's not an option. You can trust me on that.'

Thea backed out of the room quickly, deciding it wasn't for her to 'out' Sean if the others hadn't got the drift yet. His and Paul's relationship was their own business. Instead she went to her room, dug out her chunkiest sweater, her boots, a woolly hat, gloves and scarf and went down the back staircase and across the yard to knock on the Stables door. The air felt warmer, or maybe it was the layers of clothes she'd put on, and the snow that had previously settled was now dripping from the trees.

It was Paul who opened the door, wearing a black polo-neck sweater – cashmere? . . . and a chunky grey hand-knitted jacket over the top which somehow looked hugely expensive rather than homemade.

'Hello!' he said, looking rather surprised. 'Oh, and don't you look sweet, all wrapped up like a woolly elf! Is everything OK? No problems, I hope?'

'Oh hi! No, everything's fine. I just – er, is Sean there?' She felt for a moment as if she were asking a neighbouring mum if their child could come out to play. And 'elf'? OK, she wasn't very tall, but even so . . .

'Yes, he's here. Come on in.' He stepped back to let her into the kitchen and bellowed, 'Sean! There's a little elf-lady to see you!' in the direction of whatever was through the door on the far side of the sitting room. Woody came running through, miaowing at Thea and twirling his body against her legs.

'Sorry about Sean's cat,' Paul said. 'The damn thing's all over every visitor.'

'It's no problem, I like him.' She bent to stroke Woody and he rolled over on the floor, purring.

'Tart,' Paul said.

'I hope that refers to the cat.' Sean appeared, pulling on a beaten-up sheepskin jacket.

Paul chuckled. 'Of course it does. And you have to admit I've got a point. He'll roll over for anybody.'

'You've had dates like that, Paul.'

'Oh, I have, I have. Many of them. Back in the day, obviously.' He sighed and winked at Thea. 'Have a lovely time, you two, and be careful in the woods. Watch out for mantraps and murderers.'

'Mantraps?' Thea asked. 'Are they—'

'Only joking, Elf, they're safely illegal. There won't even be poachers, not in this weather. There's nothing to poach in the middle of winter and anyway they'll all be keeping warm down the pub. Go on, get yourselves going before the snow comes back.' And Paul chivvied them out of the door.

Thea walked with Sean to the far side of the stable block where a gleaming little silver Mercedes convertible was parked next to a grubby and ancient Land Rover. She didn't need to ask which one was Sean's. They climbed into the Land Rover and he set off down the driveway, the engine chugging and spluttering for the first few hundred yards.

'He's pretty funny, Paul, isn't he?' Thea said.

Sean hesitated for a moment before replying. 'He can be. But don't ever flick mud on his jacket or he'll turn on you like a tiger. I slopped a teeny drop of olive oil on his sleeve once and you'd think I'd shot his sister. And he can shop for Britain, that one. He was online just now, checking out man-bags at eight hundred pounds a go. Ridiculous, especially as he won't actually buy one. He'll go all envious and sniffy and tell me you can get the same thing at Kempton market for about a score.'

Thea laughed. 'This doesn't seem the kind of area for men with fancy city bags – not that I'd know.' She stopped, not wishing to sound as if she were criticizing or mocking. She wasn't, but she didn't want Sean to get the wrong idea.

'Yes – rural south Cornwall, the epicentre of the metrosexual male. Doesn't really work, does it? Fishermen in wellies, farmers in – well, more wellies – and Paul with his blue suede Jermyn Street loafers and a Mulberry knock-off man-bag. Yep. Can see it. Luckily he has another life that properly accommodates his tastes, up in that big London.'

'So he doesn't live down here full-time?'

'Hell, no. Can you imagine that? He'd wither on the vine. Business-wise, now the décor is all done, he's very much the sleeping partner.'

Well yes, she'd gathered that. 'So – er, where is it we're going?' she asked as the lanes grew more narrow and low-lying twigs clattered against the Land Rover's roof. The ground was getting rougher too and the ladder was clanging about in the back.

'Nearly there. It's the edge of an old estate. Lots of lovely mixed woodland with a fair selection of mistletoe. I've already checked out the best bits but I needed back-up. Only an idiot would go shinning up trees and ladders in the dark with no one else there. And yes, I am an idiot to do this at all, but even I have a bit of a grip on self-preservation.'

'I could have bought mistletoe before I left home but there was such a lot to remember.'

'You'd only get a measly little twig for a tenner, even on the markets, which wouldn't rate a half-decent snog. We can do better than that. A *lot* better.'

As they turned off the road and passed between a pair of old stone gateposts – not the main estate entrance, Thea assumed – Sean turned the headlights off and slowed right down, passing a big lily-covered lake on the right and a looming shrubbery on the left.

'This *is* illegal, isn't it?' Thea whispered. 'You said it wasn't.'

She caught him glancing at her, his eyes gleaming in the dark. 'I didn't exactly say that, only something close enough to it. But really, it's rather like poaching rabbits. Not exactly legal if you don't ask permission first, but in the long run you're doing the landowner a favour. Don't worry, you won't spend Christmas in the nick. OK – here we are.'

Sean turned the car down a narrow track through a gateway, circled the car round in a small clearing and switched off the engine.

'Is that for a quick getaway?' Thea asked, wondering why he'd turned it round.

He looked at her, smiling. She felt she was being

teased but didn't mind. 'It is. Because unless we're quick, old Lord Thingummy and his faithful band of retainers will be after us with a selection of ancient axes and an entrenching tool.'

'Like Uncle Matthew in *The Pursuit of Love*,' she said, laughing.

'Exactly like him. Except we're not The Hun, as he called them and it's not the war. But the gist will be the same.'

Thea felt nervous as she dropped down from the car seat onto muddy ground.

'Actually,' he said, 'no entrenching tools. I only turned the car round so that I can shine the lights on the right bit of the chosen tree.' He pointed. 'That fine oak there. Look up at the top – it's covered in mistletoe. It'll thank us for this when it can breathe more easily.'

Thea watched as he pulled on a pair of gloves and opened the back doors to unload the ladder. 'What can I do to help?' she said in a loud whisper, scared of making a noise. She peered in through the car's door at a jumble of tools, ropes and paint cans. Sean rummaged about and took out a pair of secateurs which he gave to her. 'You can hold these,' he said, turning back and pulling out the ladder with a great deal of metal clattering. Thea shivered.

'Are you cold? I shouldn't have dragged you out from the fireside, should I? This isn't what you signed up for, is it?' He actually looked worried. Did he imagine she'd be asking for a refund?

'No, honestly I'm not cold, just a little nervous, that's all. And you didn't drag me away. I'm really enjoying this.' And she was – this was the most silly, exhilarating fun she'd had in ages. She smiled at him and he stood with the ladder leaning against him, looking at her.

'You really do look like an elf,' he said. 'I think it's the way those silly fronds of your hair are sticking up at the front. I like this pinkish one.' He flicked at one of them and she ducked, giggling, tripping on a fallen branch and almost falling. 'Sorry!' He grabbed her arm. 'I am an idiot.'

'No, you're not. You're completely nuts and you're fun, but you're not an idiot.'

'Phew. Relief. Right, now I'll get the ladder up.'

He'd done this before, she thought, watching as he expertly set up the ladder after checking the ground for the right stable spot. 'OK, hang on to it and don't let go,' he instructed. 'This thing is a bit flimsy.'

'Now you tell me,' she said as he went up the first few rungs.

He looked down and grinned at her. 'I didn't tell you I don't like heights either, but needs must. You can't say I don't go the extra mile for my house-guests.' And he vanished in the darkness of the lower branches while Thea counted the steps as the ladder shook under her hands.

All was still for several minutes before there came a loud whooshing sound, a rush of wind through the leaves, a 'Jeez! *Fuck!*' from above – and Thea was convinced that at any second Sean would be hurtling to the ground. As she stared upwards, the pale shape of a barn owl swooped past. She held her breath but all seemed well and a couple of minutes later there were rhythmic clunks on the ladder and Sean came down again, clutching the biggest bunch of mistletoe she'd ever seen.

'Wow, it's massive!' she breathed. 'I'm impressed!'

'Yeah, they all say that,' he chuckled, then, 'Oops, sorry, inappropriate – forgive me.'

'I had no idea what you were implying,' she teased. 'After all, I am a mere maiden aunt.'

'Ah yes, I'd forgotten. Here, hold this, Miss Innocent, while I get the ladder down.' He handed over the mistletoe and she held it gingerly, afraid to crush its mass of berries. 'And please don't, whatever you do, drop it.'

'I'll do my best, but—'

'No, really.' He looked serious. 'If you drop it, all its powers will vanish into the ground.'

'You believe all that pagan stuff?'

'Of course I do. I'm Cornish. Mistletoe has powers for friendship and fertility. Don't want to take a risk with either of those, do we?'

'No, we don't,' she agreed, carefully carrying the mistletoe to the car as Sean stowed the ladder in the back.

'Did you see that bloody owl?' he said as they drove through the estate gates. 'Thought it was going to take my head off. It must have been sitting inches from where I snipped off that mistletoe.'

'I saw it – fabulous bird. We don't get a lot of those in West London, though it did give me a scary moment too – it sounded as if you were going to fall off the ladder.'

'What would you have done?' he asked.

'Left you there, taken the car and pretended I'd never been out, I expect.'

He laughed. 'Are you sure you haven't got form? I should have checked your references. You're on parole from a long GBH stretch, aren't you? I knew it.'

'Bang to rights. They've only let me out for Christmas.'

'Will you show me your ankle tag?'

'Certainly not,' she said. 'I'm not that sort of girl.'

'But are you the sort who'd like to celebrate our successful mission with a quick drink down at the Fish?'

His request surprised her; she'd assumed they were heading straight back but it was still early and she didn't much want to go back and have the rest of them questioning her. 'OK, yes, that would be great. First round's on me, though, as a thank you for the mistletoe.'

'It's a deal,' he said, speeding up a bit now they were back on a proper road. Sleet was falling again as, just minutes later, they climbed out of the car in the pub car park. Thea wrapped her arms round her body and huffed clouds of steam into the night air.

'There'll be proper snow tomorrow,' Sean said, looking up at the sky as they went into the hugely welcoming warmth of the pub. 'It'll be an incredibly rare white Christmas.'

The pub, the Fisherman's Arms, was the same one that Thea and the family had had lunch in. It seemed like days ago somehow, even though it was only a few hours, and the rest of the family seemed half a world away rather than little more than half a mile. At the bar she bought a half of shandy for Sean and a glass of the pub's Christmas special mulled wine for herself and took them to a corner table where Sean had bagged a cushioned bench close to a log fire.

'I've never seen a white Christmas,' Thea told him as she peeled off her coat, hat and scarf and plonked them down on the bench between them.

'Me neither,' he said, gathering up her clothes and moving them to the far side of him. He shuffled closer to her. 'I'm more used to Christmases on hot beaches. I've been one of those really annoying people who calls up the family in the UK far too early in the morning from Australia and brags about having a barbie on the beach.'

'Was that when you were surfing?'

'That's it. Contests on the circuit in winter in the southern hemisphere.'

'Sounds idyllic,' she said, sighing. 'No fog, no sleet, no half the day in darkness.'

'It was OK for a few years. But you realize two things quite quickly: you're never going to be World Champion while there are Americans and Aussies in possession of surfboards, and second, that you really do miss home and family and even the bleak weather like mad. I used to get off the plane at Heathrow and sniff at the cold air like a dog scenting a cooked sausage.'

'What are you doing on Christmas Day?' she asked, suddenly having a mad thought that he might like to join her and the family. After all, it *was* his house they were in.

'Going to Paul's. His family are from round here.'

Of course he was going to be with Paul – where else would he be? For a moment there, she'd forgotten about the two of them. It had almost begun to feel as if she was with someone she might . . . no, ridiculous to think like that. Wasn't it always the way though? There had to be a catch.

Later, Sean drove them back to Cove Manor and parked behind the Stables again. The Mercedes had gone.

'Paul's out,' she said, then felt rather silly. It didn't need saying if the car wasn't there and also, what had it to do with her?

'He'll be back at the parental gaff,' Sean said. 'He's keen on its proper carpets and the lack of a cat.'

'Oh right, I see.' She didn't really, but it wasn't for her to question without looking intrusively nosy. She clambered out of the car and Sean opened the back door and carefully lifted out the mistletoe.

'Are you going in through the front door or back? I'll carry this for you, if you like. And I'll come over in the morning and hang it up for you.'

'Back door, I think. I'll put it in my room and surprise them with this in the morning.'

'OK. Let me escort you to your door then.'

The two of them walked over the cobbles, Sean holding her hand which she assumed was because the ground was slippery. She opened the door and turned to say goodnight when a question came to mind. 'Why did you ask me to come and hold the ladder and not one of the others? My brother Jimi would have gone with you.'

He considered for a moment, 'Well, the truth is . . .' and he hesitated, 'you're a lot prettier than Jimi.' He scuffed his foot on the ground like a caught-out schoolboy.

'Oh. Right. Um . . . well, that's very sweet of you to say.' She felt confused. This almost felt like flirting. Wasn't that the equivalent of her flirting with a girl?

'We should test this,' Sean said, holding out the mistletoe.

'Oh yes, we should. Thanks for a lovely evening, Sean, and goodnight.' She leaned forward to kiss his cheek but his mouth seemed to land very close to hers. She kissed him briefly and stepped back. Awkward. 'Sorry!' she said, laughing. He was smiling at her, looking as if he was enjoying her discomfort.

'Hey, don't be sorry. Here,' he said, handing her the mistletoe, 'I'll see you in the morning. Nine thirty sharp, you and me and a hammer.'

'I'll look forward to it,' she told him, going in through the door.

'Sweet dreams, Elf,' he said, turning away towards the Stables block.

'And to you, Sean. And thanks.'

EIGHT

Oh God, Alec! Anna came out of the shower, glowy and warm, and suddenly remembered what it was she should have done yesterday. She'd assumed it was something to do with Christmas and as she shampooed her hair she'd quickly run through the presents she'd bought, checking she hadn't left someone out. But Alec – oh, the guilt. She'd forgotten all about him, which was completely horrible of her. The iPad had been left on its charger all day and night and she hadn't even bothered to read the third of his emails.

Now, as she rushed to the still-charging iPad to read it she almost dreaded looking, sure that by now he'd have sent either a hurt message or a furious one. She wouldn't blame him. The truth was that she'd had a lovely evening, watching the second of the DVDs that Mike had got his ... friend Charlotte to help put together and she'd pretty much forgotten the existence of anyone outside Cove Manor. She hoped that Alec had recovered from what had sounded very much like a not-ideal day with his children. How sad that it didn't go well. But perhaps it was only the goose they hadn't liked, and everything else had been brilliant.

Email number three from him was a relief. He sounded cheerier because he and the children had parted on good terms and they'd loved their presents. Phew. She vaguely started concocting an apologetic reply as she skimmed through a few more messages, mostly from retailers she'd bought things from in the past, offering her unmissable bargains in the New Year sales, and then she clicked on the most recent one – sent that morning about an hour before. Goodness, Alec was an early riser.

. . . *so as my brother's gone to Ireland, I'm taking up your offer. Train arrives Truro at 2.30. Can't wait to see you.*

What the hell was he playing at? Those last throw-away words she'd said to him that day – did he really take them as a proper invitation? Maybe he wasn't coming to stay with *her*. Perhaps he had other friends in Cornwall. It was a big county, after all, with lots of people in it. Thousands. Hundreds of thousands. This thought didn't help.

Anna felt shaky. She put on her dressing gown and padded along the corridor to the room at the far end and knocked. Mike's sleepy voice answered and she went in. He had his lamp on and was reading last week's

Private Eye. He looked younger, she thought, in the lamp's soft orangey glow. She'd almost forgotten what a sweet just-woken face he had.

'After more than forty years, I don't think you need to knock, Annie,' he said, pulling back the duvet and patting the mattress. 'What's up? You look worried.'

She climbed into bed beside him and hauled the duvet up to her chin. 'I am,' she said. There was no point pretending she wasn't.

'What about? It's all going well so far, isn't it?'

'It is. That's what I'm worried about. That it might not after this afternoon.'

'Oh. How did you know?' He looked at her, puzzled. 'I haven't said anything yet.'

'Know what?'

He was silent for a minute. 'Ah. I thought you meant bloody Charlotte. She only wants to come and see me – this afternoon. I tried to put her off but I only said half of what I wanted to say and she'd taken it as an invitation before I got to tell her that no, it wasn't at all a good idea. Sorry. I'll just go and have a quick drink with her in a pub somewhere and send her back to Plymouth with her mate.'

Anna felt thoroughly confused. 'I didn't know about any of this, Mike. What's "bloody Charlotte" doing in Plymouth, for heaven's sake?'

'*Snow White*.'

Anna spluttered a laugh. 'Yeah, right.'

'No really, working in pantomime. Or at least she was. They don't usually end a run before Christmas Eve, do they?'

'No. of course not. That and New Year's Eve are the absolute sell-out shows.' So Charlotte was coming. Oh, the joy. But at least that was only for a few hours, unlike Alec.

'So if you didn't know, then what's bugging you?'

'Someone I've – er, been seeing just now and then. I said something stupid about being only a train-ride away and he's – well, he's got on a train.'

Mike laughed. 'Oh no. That's hilarious! He's not coming to *stay*, is he? What will the children think?'

'It's not funny, Mike! This trip is supposed to be about . . .'

'. . . about getting used to the idea that we're still going to be absolutely fine as a family even when we're divorced? Well, exactly. But I guess this is how it will be and what they'll have to get used to. Us being with other people at some point. It'll be a chance for them to see how civilized and so on the arrangement can be. All one big happy extended family. Isn't that what we're aiming for?'

'Yes, but not *yet*,' Anna said. 'And not – well, not Alec. And not *here*. Also, not permanently. Not like . . .'

'Us?' he said softly, taking her hand.

'Yes. Not like us. Old-us. He's mostly just a friend.' Did Mike wince at the word 'mostly'? She hoped not.

This wasn't about causing him pain; she absolutely hated the idea of doing that. And besides, he'd got Charlotte, hadn't he? Anna couldn't help feeling a teeny bit prickly about that, but she could hardly complain: this really was the so-amicable future they'd been practising for this past year. She just wished it hadn't suddenly crept up and pounced on her like this.

'Well, seeing as it looks like a fait accompli,' Mike said thoughtfully, 'I suppose there is still a room spare, next to this one. Unless, of course . . .' He gave her a questioning look.

'Oh God no, don't even think of it. I couldn't. Not *here*. Can you imagine what the children would say?'

'I can. Though they're hardly "children", and why they think there's an age cut-off point for all that malarkey, I really don't know.'

'Leaving them all out of it, though, Mike, it would be just plain bad manners.'

'Agreed.' She thought he looked quite relieved.

'And embarrassing,' she added.

'Yep.'

'And inconsiderate.'

'To . . . ?'

'To you, of course, Mike.'

'Thank you.' There was a silence for a few minutes. She wondered what he was thinking. Anna wanted to hug Mike for his generous practicality but it would feel strange to be that close again, in bed, especially after this particular conversation. They hadn't even sat in a bed together for over a year now and bodily contact outside one was limited to hugs and the odd comforting cuddle, fully clothed and usually in the kitchen. She wondered if deep down the fact that she'd been seeing someone was painful for him. But then he rallied.

'So, hey, what's one more joining the party? It's Christmas – you have to take in a stray or two. Is this Alec a joiner-inner, do you think?'

'I really don't know if he's a good mixer. But if he wants to stay here he'll bloody well have to be. Oh God, why did he have to do this? Who'd want to invade someone else's big family party? He must have known I couldn't refuse at this point, that I could hardly be callous enough to tell him to get off at Exeter and catch a train straight back to London or book him into some lonely B&B, even assuming there'd be one that was open or had room.'

'He sounds a bit solitary, poor bastard. Doesn't he have family?'

'Divorced. He was going to stay with a brother for Christmas but it was a very loose arrangement and the brother's gone away. His mother's being jolly on a cruise. I know her – she's Muriel from my book group.'

Mike turned to look at her, startled. 'He's your friend's *son*? How old is he? A teenager?' He was laughing at her. And well he might, she thought, given the situation.

Anna walloped his arm. 'No! Muriel's our oldest

144

member. But – OK, he's a few years younger than I am. I bet Charlotte's no pensioner either, so don't have a go at me.'

'I'm not! I'm impressed, that's all. So we'll take him in and look after him, but what do we tell the others? Let's have a bet on which one is the first to come out with the words, "Mum's toyboy." My money's on Jimi.'

'Mine's on Emily,' Anna said. 'And she won't be saying it so much as spitting it.'

Thea knew she was being an idiot. It was eight in the morning and here she was in front of the mirror, carefully fronding up her hair and putting on make-up before she'd even had breakfast, and why? Because she didn't want to look sleep-raddled when Sean came over to hang the mistletoe. It was ridiculous, she told her reflection; utterly pointless. Like he'd notice or care? It wasn't very much make-up, true, and as she applied just enough mascara to look as if she wasn't actually wearing any, she did remember reading some irony piece about how many hours it took to get a natural look. She told herself she'd be doing this anyway, regardless of Sean, because feeling as good as you could manage to about how you look was well known to go a long way to lightening any gloom you might be feeling.

Christmas Eve. In spite of herself she couldn't help wondering what Rich would be doing now. He was probably out with Benji for an early walk, striding along a bridlepath in the crackling frost, chucking the dog's ball for him and dodging the Cheshire pony club children out on a Christmas hack. What *was* good was that she didn't at all wish he were actually here. If she was feeling a bit on-her-own, it wasn't because she wanted him staying here with her and the family. It just wouldn't have worked. If he got tetchy after a few hours of a family lunch, then after two days holed up with the lot of them, and several more days ahead, he'd have started to grumble. By now he'd have withdrawn to their room and his computer and opted out of any joining-in. At meals he'd have been fine at first and then have faded into a mildly moody silence. One by one the others would have started asking Thea, quietly and away from everyone else, if he was all right, and she'd have ended up being defensive about him, caught in the middle between hinting to him on the quiet that he might make more of an effort and reassuring the others that all was well. It was actually hugely relaxing not to have him around.

The mistletoe had spent the night in her bath. The others hadn't seen it yet. When she was ready and all her non-make-up had been applied, she went and picked up the huge bunch and carried it carefully down the main staircase. She could hear the others in the kitchen, breakfast noisily and cheerfully under way.

'Morning, everyone!' she said, pushing the door open

with her bum and half-backing in. 'Look what I got for us last night.'

'Wow, awesome!' Elmo said. 'Where'd you nick it from?'

'Elmo!' Rosie said, but looked at Thea, eyebrows raised.

Thea gave her nephew a sly grin and he said, 'Respec',' to her and they exchanged a high five. For a moment she regretted not suggesting he came with them the night before, but it hadn't crossed her mind.

'Oh, it – er, came from some woods that Sean knows. He thought it was something missing from our Christmas decorations so we went and got it. He's coming over in a while to put it up in the hall for us.'

'Not that we need it,' Emily said. 'It's only – y'know, us.'

'Oh, don't be like that, Em,' Jimi told her, 'not after Tee's been to all the trouble of getting it. And anyway, who knows who'll turn up?'

Thea noticed Mike and Anna exchanging looks. 'Passing strangers?' she suggested, looking at them.

Anna coughed. 'Um, actually – sorry about this, everyone, but – er, some wires got crossed back home and we are actually having an addition to the party. As from this afternoon.' She fiddled with her teaspoon, turning it over and back on the table. 'It was completely by accident.'

'What was?' Thea asked. 'Is someone coming?'

'Yes,' Mike said, 'a friend of your mother's. Son of one of her book group.'

Anna smiled at Mike. Thea wondered why she looked so relieved.

'He hasn't got anywhere else to be so he's kind of' – she shrugged – 'kind of coming here.'

'But why?' Emily asked, looking at her mother with deep suspicion. 'Why is he coming all the way from London just to stay with a friend of his mum's? Is he a kid? That will be nice for Elmo.' She slightly cheered up at the thought. Elmo didn't look so sure and his face expressed a grim suspicion that someone might be foisted on him.

'No, he's a grown-up, about ten years older than you. And as I said,' Anna continued, 'it was entirely my fault. I mentioned in a stupidly flippant way that we were only a train-ride away if his arrangements fell through and I never dreamed he'd take me up on it.'

'Well, that's fantastic, isn't it?' Sam said, rubbing his hands and grinning. 'Evens up the numbers a bit.'

'What numbers?' Emily asked.

'In-laws and out-laws, as Rosie and I have been known to call ourselves.'

'True,' Rosie said with a grin. 'Sorry, nothing bad meant.'

'Another body in the house is fine by me, but can you get him to pick up a *Guardian* on the way? They don't have it at the village shop and there's a jumbo

Christmas puzzle to do,' Jimi said. 'Thea – are you OK with this passing stranger idea?'

'Course it's fine. It's not as if we don't have enough room or food.'

'Exactly,' Anna said. 'He's going in the room next to Mike. Phew – so glad nobody minds. I've sorted the bedlinen and so on with Maria. There's a cupboardful of the stuff, apparently.'

'Maybe that mistletoe will come in handy, after all,' Jimi said, looking at Thea. They *all* looked at Thea. She could feel a blush creeping up as well as a horrible bit of suspicion. Was this really an accidental 'visit'?

'Don't even think about it. What I really *don't* want for Christmas is a kind of blind date.'

Anna handed her a mug of tea. 'It's OK, darling. I absolutely promise, it is absolutely *not*.'

'So what are you all doing today?' Sean asked Thea as he carried the stepladder in through the front door. 'I saw Elmo in the barn and he told me all about your printed-out schedule. I hope there are some rebels and lots of arguments about it. Or is everyone trying to be the class pet and keeping to the list?'

'It's turned out to be a very flexible arrangement but what's actually listed is that later this afternoon it's the children's carol service at the village church so I think most of us are going to that. And this morning I'll get the little ones to help me make more mince pies, if anyone can manage any more.'

'It would be a sad sort who couldn't, don't you reckon?' Sean said, looking at the beams in the ceiling. 'Will you save a few for me?'

'Of course I will.'

'Come over to the Stables with them after the church thing?' he asked. 'I can offer you better mulled wine than the stuff at the pub.'

'OK, sounds a fair swap.'

'So where do you think for the mistletoe? About here?' He pointed to a beam directly in line with the front door.

Sean was standing close beside her and she could smell a peppery shower lotion that she recognized. It was one she'd once brought home for Rich but he'd taken a sniff and said it was 'a bit girly'. She'd ended up using it all herself. Sean had washed his hair since the night before too – it looked a bit baby-birdish. It was all she could do to stop herself reaching up and touching it. He probably wouldn't actually mind – maybe they could compare conditioners.

'Your hair looks so cute and fluffy,' she blurted out before she could stop herself. He looked at her in silence and she presumed he was thinking what a completely ridiculous thing she'd just come out with. He wouldn't be wrong.

'So does yours.' He reached out and ran his fingers

gently through the front tufts of hers. 'As soft as Woody's tummy,' he murmured.

She felt muddled again and a bit thumpy inside. This was like the slightly embarrassing mistletoe moment the night before. Did he enjoy near-flirting with women? It seemed he did. Presumably if you were gay it didn't count as anything more than a bit of banter. It was all very confusing, especially as he probably didn't know for sure that she knew about him and Paul.

'Oo er – what's happening here then?' Rosie came out from the sitting room, carrying a couple of empty coffee mugs. 'You two testing out the mistletoe? Might as well get in the spirit of things.' She went through the door to the kitchen, smirking at them as she vanished.

'OK, to work.' Thea stepped away from him. The moment was fractured and Sean set the ladder up. Thea handed him the hammer, the nail and then the heavy orb of mistletoe and the two of them stepped back to admire it.

'You can almost hit your head on it,' she said. 'Don't you want a piece of it for your own place? There's more than enough for a bunch for the Stables.'

He laughed. 'Over there? Who am I going to kiss over there? I don't much fancy the postie, Maria would slap me and her daughter is about ten years too young.'

'Well, there's . . . Paul?'

'Ha! True. Though not at the moment – he's off at the ancestral pile. And even then, I think he'd be pretty amazed if I started getting romantic under a pagan sprig after all these years.'

Thea laughed. 'Oh, tell me about it. I know what that's like. Or, at least, I used to.' The laughter vanished abruptly and she felt a rush of sadness. It wasn't for Rich – it was for, what? Possibilities? An awful sense of a potential lone future? She mustn't think like that. Who knew what might happen later. A whole clean, shiny new year was about to start, after all, and when it arrived she was going to make the thorough best of it, even if it meant signing up for a bit of online dating.

Sean folded the ladder and leaned it against the wall, then came back to where she stood beneath the massive mistletoe. 'Well, it's his loss. Unless it's hers, of course. I don't know you that well yet, do I?' he said, putting an arm round her and giving her a gentle hug. He kissed her softly, close to her mouth but not on it, as the night before. Then he opened the door on the cold, grey day and said, as if nothing had happened, 'It's going to snow, did you know that? Heavy stuff expected later today.'

'Yes, you told me so last night, and this morning it was on the news. It feels unreal.'

'Christmas always does,' he said as he went. 'Have a good day and I'll see you around five thirty-ish. And if you don't make it I'll trudge through the drifts to make sure you're OK.'

'All the way from the stable block? Right across the yard?'

'Yep, all that way.'

'Thank you. I'll appreciate that.'

'Part of the job, Elf; part of the job.'

The clouds were low and almost purple. It looked as if the sky was about to burst from its burden of snow, and the day had gone still and silent waiting for it to tumble to the earth. All that could be heard was the sound of Mike in the next room, playing 'Tambourine Man' on his guitar. Emily felt jittery. All the others were so excited about the prospect of a white Christmas and she was secretly dreading it. She told herself it was ridiculous. After all, what was the worst that could happen? That the steep road between the village and the main road to – well, to 'civilization' – would be blocked for a couple of days. They'd be fine. For heaven's sake, it wasn't as if she were a farmer with a flock of hugely pregnant sheep to worry about.

Elmo was in the big sitting room, standing beside the Christmas tree and gazing out of the window.

'I used to do that,' she said, going to stand beside him. 'I'd watch for hours on a day like this, willing the first flakes to fall. I'd go all glassy-eyed, imagining I was seeing them when sometimes it was just flecks of dust.'

'Sam got me an actual *sledge*,' Elmo said to her. 'That's like, *so* good.'

'Looks like you'll get to use it,' she said as a flurry of fat flakes began to drift down.

'*So* cool,' he sighed. 'That slope on the other side of the beach will be *awesome*.'

Emily stared through the window at the feathery flakes and thought about those worst-case scenarios she tended too often to dwell on. *Think of the good. Think of the good*, she told herself. She pictured Elmo and Milly and Alfie out on their sledges, faces pink, the deserted snowy beach echoing with their laughter, the three of them hurtling down the slope, shrieking, falling off – and no, *not* getting hurt or breaking a limb but rolling joyfully in the snow, getting up again and hauling their sledges back up for another go. It would be all right. It really would. But for now, while the little ones were busy in the kitchen with Thea and Anna, making mince pies and icing the Christmas cake, she had time to go up and finish wrapping their presents. She'd try not to think of yet another worst-case possibility – that she might run out of Sellotape.

It was a good thing Anna was out, Mike thought. She'd gone to Truro to do some last-minute food shopping and to meet this sodding Alec person. With luck, Charlotte would have been and gone before Anna got back and the two women's paths wouldn't cross.

Mike opted out of lunch, telling the others an edited version of the truth – that he was going to chat to the landlord about playing a few songs at the open mic session on Boxing Day evening – and walked up the lane to meet Charlotte at the pub. Her pantomime friend was dropping her off and he'd decided that lunch and a drink on neutral premises would be the most tactful option all round. After all, nobody needed to know more than they needed to know.

'Be careful, Dad,' Emily said as he left. 'The snow's starting to settle. Call us when you're on your way back so we know to go looking if you don't get back in good time.'

'It's not even half a mile, Em,' he said, wondering why she was always the worrier. Accountancy was perfect for her and brilliant for her clients – she'd never risk approving unchecked figures or be blasé over their VAT being a few pounds out.

'I know. I'm just being sensible, that's all. Suppose you slid over and nobody knew you were lying in a ditch, freezing to death? You read about it happening.'

'I'll call, I promise.' He patted his pocket. 'Phone charged and ready to rock.'

He pulled on a pair of ancient hand-knitted gloves that Anna's mother had given him decades before, and stepped out into the cold. He'd hardly worn them over all the years, probably through some macho belief that men don't 'do' woolly gloves. Perhaps it was a sign of age or of becoming grown up (at last) enough to think that taking care of your circulation was a sensible idea.

It really was snowing quite hard now and he felt a twinge of worry for Anna who had to make the journey back from Truro. Never mind him slipping over into a ditch, what about her driving the old Sierra along these last few miles of twisty, narrow lanes? Halfway to the pub he stopped under a tree and tried to phone her. His call went straight to her voicemail (presumably no signal her end) and he left a message, saying he hoped she was all right and to let him know when she was back so that he wouldn't keep worrying about her. She'd probably find that pretty funny. For most of the past year they'd been coming and going to their separate social events without giving the other one too much thought beyond a later conversation as to whether the film/play/exhibition/gig had been a good one. Certainly they hadn't stayed awake at night waiting for the door to slam or for footsteps on the stairs. Perhaps they should have done, he now considered as he plodded on towards the welcoming lights of the Fisherman's Arms. But as they'd reminded each other in a spirit of new independence: neither of them were teenagers, neither was each other's parent.

Mike pushed open the door of the pub in a mood of mild pessimism. He both hoped Charlotte would have arrived already, in which case they could get the whole lunch over with as fast as possible, and also that she hadn't arrived. Maybe she'd changed her mind and any second now he'd get a *Sorry, darling* text citing weather conditions and wishing him a Happy Christmas. In which case he'd chat to the bar staff about music, have a slow pint and a sandwich and see if someone fancied a game of darts, if playing the game against up-country strangers wasn't contrary to local tradition.

There she was. Charlotte was perched on a bar stool in a white fun-fur coat and a pink and purple striped scarf that was long enough to please an old Dr Who. She was halfway down a large glass of red wine, some of which had added to the outside line of her lipstick, and as she looked up and waved to him he wished he could turn and run out and slither straight back to Cove Manor.

'Darling!' Charlotte squealed at Mike as he crossed to the bar. She leaped off the stool as nimbly as if she weighed half as much as she did and clasped him to her. He inhaled a mixture of warm, strong perfume and a mildly doggish scent from the coat as if a damp spaniel had recently slept on it.

'Isn't this amazing? To get together so far from home? Such luck that Ivan was driving this way.'

'Wasn't it. How are you?' Mike ordered another red wine for her ('better make it another big one') and a pint of Doom Bar for himself, hoping the name wasn't prophetic, then he led her to a corner table by the far window where the rest of the pub could be reasonably sheltered from the volume of her voice.

'I've been better, darling, frankly,' she said, taking a large glug of wine. 'Truth is, I've been fired. Surplus to requirements, it seems, though why they couldn't tell me this at rehearsal stage, I've no idea. They've paid me and Ivan off for the next two weeks but it comes down to the bloody dancers having reasonable singing voices and taking over from us to save costs. So here I am.'

'Sorry about the gig, Charlie. But never mind, surely it means you can get back to London for Christmas?'

'Ha! You'd think. It was too late to book a seat on a Christmas Eve train, darling, and they won't let you on without a reservation at this time of the year. So I thought I might as well stay put. I'm supposed to be staying with Ivan and his mum, but . . .' She looked out of the window at the fast-falling snow and shrugged. 'Well, who knows if he'll make it back to collect me? I mean, look at it out there. And he's only got a Mini. He's going to call in an hour, let me know.'

Mike felt as if he were missing a vital point here. Then his foot struck something under the table and he saw that she had with her a fair-sized blue suitcase, sitting by her side like a good dog. This wasn't looking promising. The deal had been, she'd said, 'a quick drink', not 'I'm moving in with you'. She surely couldn't expect that, could she? With his entire family? This was beginning to look like Anna's bloody Alec situation all over again.

'Oh, the snow isn't that bad,' Mike said, trying to sound breezy. 'It'll probably have melted by the time we've had lunch.' He looked at the stuff falling outside, willing the temperature to rise just enough degrees to turn it to rain.

'Do you think so? Well, let's see.' Charlotte rubbed a hand on his thigh. 'After all, there could be worse things than you rescuing me from being marooned in this terrible snow, don't you think?' She opened her green eyes wide and pouted at him. 'And I'd be so *very* grateful.'

NINE

'Ah, that's beautiful. Just how a Christmas cake should look,' Thea told Milly and Alfie. She'd made a big batch of royal icing and the children had taken a spatula each and splattered the cake's marzipan topping with icing much in the manner of Jackson Pollock constructing a painting. But with Thea's help and patience, and a lot of scooping of misplaced dollops from the worktop to the cake (and from the wall and floor to the bin), they'd finally got it done. Milly had been particularly good at flicking up the icing to make the cake's surface look as if someone had been playing in the snow.

'Let me do the robins?' Alfie asked, opening the box of cake decorations that Anna had brought with her.

'OK, you do the robins and Milly can put the little trees on.' The decorations were ancient. Thea handled them carefully, remembering them from her own childhood. It didn't seem that long since she too had been standing on a kitchen chair, carefully placing the plaster snowman in the centre of a roughly iced cake.

'You have the patience of a saint, Tee,' Sam said as he handed her a mug of tea. 'If that had been me there'd have been a good loud tantrum and at least three bouts of tears by now. And the children wouldn't have been much better either.'

Thea laughed. 'It's only a matter of giving them each something to do at the same time, so it's as fair as it can be. Children tend not to argue with "fair". They get it.'

'You're keeping us well supplied with comfort food. I've had about four of those mince pies you made this morning. Don't tell Emily, though, she thinks I'm—'

'Thinks you're what?' Emily came into the kitchen carrying the children's coats. She draped them over the Aga rail.

'Thinks I'm getting porky.' Sam patted his middle.

'I didn't say that,' Emily said, eying the bit of him he'd patted.

'You didn't need to, darling. You just give me those eyebrows-up looks sometimes when I have second helpings.'

'Do I?' Emily looked upset. 'Sorry. I don't mean to.'

'But I'm allowed to eat as much as I like over

Christmas, aren't I?' Sam asked. 'If I promise to do a New Year diet?'

'I already said. You're fine as you are. You don't have to go on a diet.'

'See?' Thea said to him. 'Permission granted.'

'Unless you think you should, obviously.' Emily gave Thea a sly grin and laid the children's mittens and scarves on top of the Aga, above the coats. She sent Milly and Alfie to wash their hands as it was getting close to the time they all had to leave for the Crib service at the village church.

'Right.' Sam looked glum. 'Well, that's me told.'

Just then Jimi came in with Rosie. 'Told what?' he enquired.

'Apparently I'm fat.'

'Bollocks.'

'No, tummy.' Sam patted his front again.

'Oh, ha ha. Listen, while we're all in here, what do we think about this Alec bloke rocking up?'

Thea put the cake on a plate and a mesh cover over the top then placed it on a shelf in the larder.

'It's a bit weird, isn't it?' Emily said. 'Has Mum mentioned him before?' They all looked at Thea.

'Hey, what makes you think I'd know?'

'You're the senior daughter,' Emily said. 'And you talked to her about Rich, so . . .'

'I didn't though, not really. There wasn't much point, seeing as she didn't ever take to him. I told her it was over, she hugged me and just about managed not to say, "Phew" and "Oh good" and that was about it. She's never said anything about an Alec.'

'That's probably because it's no big deal.' Rosie shrugged. 'She said he was a friend's son, so that'll be all there is to it. We'll be nice to him.' She gave Emily a stern look. 'Won't we? All of us.'

'Of course we will. Why wouldn't we be? It can't be the most comfortable thing, going to stay for Christmas with a bunch of strangers.'

Sam said, 'I think I'd just have stayed at home. Telly's good, you can catch up on box-sets and eat fried-egg sandwiches if you want.'

'Perhaps he *lerves* her,' Jimi suggested.

'What?' Emily's eyebrows went up. 'What, *Mum*?'

'Why not Mum? She's still a cool woman.'

'But she's *Mum*.'

'Yeah, and your point is?' Jimi wasn't going to let it go.

Thea looked at the clock. They really should get off if they were going to make the carol service. Where were the parents? Was Mike really still down at the pub? How long did it take to sort out a couple of slots at a music night?

'Well, the "why not" is because – well, isn't she a bit . . .' Emily was struggling here.

'Past All That Nonsense?' Sam teased, putting on a prim voice. 'She's been looking particularly well lately, so maybe she's got lucky. Free spirit, your mum. And soon to be divorced as well.'

'"Got lucky"? Oh, don't be so ridiculous, Sam!' Emily looked furious. 'They're not breaking up because of *other people*.'

'I didn't say they were. I was just saying—'

'Well, don't. Come on, let's get these children into their coats. I don't want us to end up crammed into a pew at the back. They won't be able to see what's going on. Will someone phone Dad? Perhaps he could meet us at the church – if, of course, he's not too busy chatting up some young bar girl and *getting lucky* like Mum.'

Anna sat in the car trying to concentrate on reading the paper. She couldn't take in a single word. Not even the double-page spread about the expected extreme weather conditions in the far south-west of England and the usual photos of Gatwick chaos for the Christmas getaway. Instead she listened to the service of Nine Lessons and Carols from King's College, Cambridge, on the radio and really wished she was hearing it back at the house with the others, pre-cooking the vol-au-vent cases ready for their parsnip and sorrel fillings the next day and helping the children choose a carrot to leave out for Santa's reindeer.

She thought about how on earth it was going to be, introducing Alec to Mike. Alec was well aware of the score, knew that Mike was still (on paper) Anna's husband, and yet he seemed to have no qualms about coming to stay with them all. It was her own fault, she decided, for having so breezily claimed that she was a free woman. Though come to think of it, he hadn't ever actually asked if she was. She'd volunteered the information the first time they'd gone out for dinner together and he'd told her about his difficult divorce. She'd been sympathetic and it had probably been tactless to tell him that she and Mike were so cheerfully and good-naturedly separated.

'But you live in the same house still?' He'd been surprised. Most people would be, to be fair.

'Well, yes, why not?' She'd been defensive. As far as she could remember, he hadn't answered that but had asked instead if they should have another bottle.

The train wasn't late. She was surprised – given the snow that must have surely been heavier further north and east – that it had got further than Exeter. It wasn't too bad in Truro, far lighter than where they were staying and she hoped it would have stopped by the time she and Alec got back. Having to dig the car out of a drift would just about be the perfect extra treat for the afternoon.

She climbed out of the car, rubbing her back as it was aching from the wait, and walked across the station forecourt where a gaudily painted wooden sleigh was parked among the waiting taxis, flashing scarlet lights and blasting out American-accented carols. A short fat

Santa with a slightly menacing stare shook a Rotary Club tin at her and she put a couple of pounds in, then went through the little waiting room to the platform where the train stood whirring and revving as if impatient to get on with its last trip till after Boxing Day. That was another thing, she thought with some trepidation. If things all went wrong at Cove Manor, there would be no get-out for Alec, trainwise, because that was it till after Boxing Day – and even then there'd be a reduced service. They were all stuck with each other for the duration.

On the platform, passengers struggling with luggage and bags full of wrapped presents were being welcomed by friends and family. Some clutched mistletoe and reunited lovers kissed and hugged and laughed. And then suddenly there was Alec, hauling a wheeled case and wearing a huge black coat and a Manchester United scarf. He was carrying an elaborately wrapped bouquet of flowers she couldn't yet see, which poked out of a Harrods carrier bag with something big and round in it.

'Anna!' he called, only a few feet from her. '*Soo* good to see you!' It was a tight hug and she tried not to interpret this as having a certain amount of needy desperation about it. People got depressed at Christmas. Wasn't it known to be the worst time of year for suicide? She realized how little she knew of him, really. The best option would be to assume all was well unless he said otherwise, in which case whatever issue came up could be talked through and dealt with as cheerily as possible. There was no point being pessimistic.

'Great to see you too, Alec. The car is just out the front. What was the snow like on the way down?'

'Hardly any in London. I think it's all down here.'

'So, the complete opposite to usual then. It's usually Kent, isn't it?'

'Global warming, maybe?'

They were talking about the weather like a couple of strangers, she thought as they went outside and got into the car.

'I brought cheese,' Alec said, once they were in the car. He held up the Harrods bag.

Anna started to giggle. She tried to stop but couldn't and had to scrabble in her bag for tissues to wipe her eyes.

'What's so hilarious? What's wrong with cheese?'

'Nothing wrong, just that you said it so seriously and it sounded so funny! It's Christmas and you tell me you bring cheese. You sounded like one of the Three Wise Men offering a gift. I love it.'

'Cheese is good then. That's a relief. It's Stilton,' Alec said, starting to smile a bit.

'Stilton is very OK, thank you. And it's far more use than myrrh.'

'Do your family know I'm coming?' Alec asked as Anna drove up the hill out of Truro.

Strange question, she thought. Surely he hadn't imagined she'd just turn up with him as if she'd found him in Sainsbury's? 'Yes, of course. I told them all this morning.'

'What about your husband?'

'Mike? He's fine.'

Alec sounded a bit worried. Strange he hadn't had these doubts before he left. Still, too late now. All would be well. The season to be jolly and all that.

'Listen, it's a wonderful house, the family are all in good form and there's nothing to worry about. Trust me, you are very welcome.'

It sounded convincing enough, she thought. It was only for a few days and they'd all get by on Christmas spirit. And if that ran out, there was always the other sort: they were well stocked up on gin.

Mike was going to miss the carol service. He didn't particularly mind – he'd been to many of the same over his lifetime and he doubted there'd be anything new at this one. But he did like singing carols. There was something comfortingly uplifting about them, their changelessness. It was a sort of annual anchoring to a collective goodwill. If he were of a whimsical bent, he'd say it gave you hope, at least till you read the first post-Christmas headlines and the mood was shot down by whichever new atrocity had happened out there in the world.

What he *did* mind was missing the service because of Charlotte. He'd managed to dissuade her from a fourth glass of wine by promising there'd be plenty more back at the house later. Because now *she* was going to be at the house. Staying. How had it come to this?

'Ivan just called and he says he's very sorry,' Charlotte told Mike as he came back from the loo. She waved her phone at him as if it were likely to speak and add its own apology and a back-up confirmation of this news. 'Apparently the Mini got as far as his parents' but it won't get up the hill out of there again. So he's stuck.'

He's not the only one, Mike thought. What on earth was he going to do with her?

'I suppose they might be able to find me a room here at the pub,' she said, doing a downcast face. 'Just a small one, in a corner. I don't need anything much.'

'It won't come to that,' Mike reassured her, as he knew he was meant to. 'Obviously you must come and stay with us.'

'Really?' Her face lit right up, rather too fast, Mike thought. He felt outmanoeuvred. What was she up to? Had she actually made any arrangement with this Ivan? Possibly not. Though why she'd want to gatecrash his family Christmas, he had no idea. She'd never before shown much sign of wanting a relationship that was either exclusive or permanent. It had been one of the things he most liked about her. If she wanted to move them as a couple on to a new level, there were more subtle ways. And ways that surely could wait till the New Year.

'Won't your wife mind? I mean, I know you're not officially together, but . . .'

Yes, she would mind, was Mike's honest opinion but he kept it to herself. And besides, with this Alec person about to descend on them, Anna was hardly in a position to complain. Sleeping arrangements might be tricky, though. It would take some thinking through. With Alec on the premises, all eight rooms would be occupied. The thought that Anna might then consider it logical, after all, to have Alec sharing her room was one Mike felt horribly uncomfortable about. Why had he ever thought he wouldn't? This divorce business didn't seem to be as simple as the two of them had blithely imagined.

'I'm only small, I can sleep on a little sofa somewhere out of the way,' Charlotte said, flickering her eyelashes at him.

Small wouldn't be how Mike would describe her, but again, he kept that thought to himself.

She put her foot out and rubbed it against his. 'Or we could . . .'

'No, I don't think we could.' Mike was firm on that. 'Not tactful. Bad manners, even. But it'll be all right. Anna has a friend staying, so why not me? Goose, sauce, gander – all that.'

He started to cheer up. This could be fun, bringing this loud, blowsy guest into their midst. If she calmed down a bit on the gestures of affection and managed to keep her hands to herself and not embarrass them all (OK, to be honest, he meant *him*), she might well be the life and soul. He'd maybe ask Thea to schedule in a music hour that evening. Charlotte had a hell of a voice and the two of them, with him on guitar, sounded pretty damn good together. And they could do the session at the pub too, Boxing Day evening.

The bar was now almost empty and he realized they'd been there way too long. 'Hey, look at the time. We'd better get back. It might be an idea if you're already there when the others get back from the carol service. That way, it's a sort of fait accompli. Grab your coat, honey, you've pulled.'

Charlotte giggled. 'Is your car outside?'

'Car? No, Anna's got it. But it's only about half a mile, not far.'

Charlotte looked at her feet. The heels on her boots weren't as high as some shoes he'd seen her totter about in but they were pretty spindly. 'As Kirsty MacColl so brilliantly put it: "In these shoes? I don't think so".'

'Ah. Don't you have anything more sensible?' He glanced at the blue case.

'More sensible? Darling, I thought you knew me better than that. I can walk perfectly well in these but the snow will *ruin* them and they weren't cheap. Prada sale.'

Some negotiation with the bar staff followed and ten minutes later, the two of them were out in the snow, Charlotte's legs up to the knee neatly tied into black bin bags with string criss-crossed all the way up, like, Mike thought, a pair of ribboned espadrilles that Anna had once owned.

'I'll have to do high steps like a show pony,' she sniggered and staggered a bit as they started out down the lane. 'But look at everything.' She waved her arm, encompassing the snowy view, and almost slipped over, then hung on to Mike who was towing the case. 'This snow and the view and the country stuff. It's all so *purrty*.'

Oh dear lord, he thought. What the hell were the others going to make of her?

The snow had stopped but as Jimi pointed out on the way to the church, the sky was still full of it. The air was calm and silent, broken only by the occasional powdery whoosh of snow falling from overhead branches.

'It'll start again soon and it'll be halfway up the hedge in the morning,' Emily said, trailing her gloved finger along a drystone wall.

'Cool,' Elmo said. 'Sledgin'.'

The little ones were already on theirs, being pulled

along by Sam and Jimi. 'Faster!' Milly demanded every few minutes and Sam ran up the lane with her, stopping till the others caught up. Alfie was more cautious, Thea noticed, holding on tight to the sides of the sledge and looking nervous about the chance of falling off whereas Milly loved to hurtle along, fearless and un-caring when it bounced over stones hidden beneath the snow.

What would a child of mine have been like? Thea suddenly wondered. Brave or scared? Reckless or careful? She watched a robin hopping along a fallen oak, leaving tiny, perfect tracks, and she tried hard to con-centrate on watching it. Then Milly shrieked as she fell off the sledge and rolled in the snow, laughing. The robin flew away and Emily started a telling-off and a warning about getting too cold and wet and spoiling her coat. Thea couldn't interrupt and tell her it didn't matter: under-mining a mother was beyond the remit of the fondest aunt. But she did sympathize with Milly, who went into a sulk and now trudged along, pulling the sledge rather than riding on it, and staying well away from her mother. Thea caught up with her and offered to pull the sledge for her. The child looked up at her, eyes a bit teary, and she took hold of her hand.

The church was filling up fast. 'Lots of fathers,' Rosie pointed out. 'Probably been sent to get the kids out of the way. A woman's work, and all that. Where is feminism?'

'If it's got any sense, it's at home, lying on the sofa

with a mince pie and watching *Kind Hearts and Coronets*,' Jimi said.

'Are you kidding? It's probably up to here in turkey giblets and wishing its mother-in-law wouldn't keep saying, "Oh, I wouldn't do it like *that*".'

The church was tiny and lit by candles. A crib that must have been used for a good fifty years had been set up below the pulpit, and as children arrived they were each handed a toy animal and told to take care of it for later because these were going to be put on the crib to be with the Baby Jesus. Milly had a sheep and Alfie was given a donkey. Thea looked at Emily, who made a worried face. 'And they expect to get them *back*?' she whispered.

'It'll be fine, don't worry so much.' If Thea could give her sister one perfect gift for Christmas, it would be a less doomy outlook. She'd got everything she could possibly want, hadn't she? Why waste the joy by looking for so many downsides. Here, surrounded by small children, Thea felt much as she did at work: how lucky were these parents.

She felt in her pocket to check she'd got tissues because, sure enough, as the solo choirboy sang the first notes of 'Once in Royal David's City', she felt her tear ducts prickling.

There were footprints in the snow all leading outwards, not back, so that meant they were all still out; that was the upside. But the Sierra was in the driveway – parked at an angle that suggested a bit of a slide on the ice – so Anna was here, presumably with this Alec person, and that was a bit of a downside. Mike could have done with putting off the tricky Charlotte-meet-my-wife moment a bit longer.

'We're here,' he said, opening the door and realizing his statement was ludicrous.

'I thought we might be. The key and door thing was a bit of a giveaway.' Charlotte had slurred a bit on 'was' and Mike could see she was quite drunk. Perhaps that glass of wine she'd been drinking when he arrived hadn't actually been the first.

'Anna? Are you here?' he called from the hallway, hoping fervently that Charlotte wouldn't look up and see that massive mad bunch of mistletoe. The last thing he wanted was for Anna to come out and find them in a clinch. She'd never believe it wasn't his fault.

'In the kitchen!' Anna called. 'Er, Alec's arrived.'

Mike pulled Charlotte after him towards the kitchen. Might as well get this over with.

Anna was stuffing the turkey. Alec was sitting at the table with a mince pie and a beer. He stood up as Mike came in.

'Oh!' Anna said in surprise as she turned to greet him. 'I assume you're—'

'Charlotte. Charlotte, this is Anna,' Mike said, adding, 'My wife.'

'I can't shake hands, sorry,' Anna said. 'I'm covered in stuffing.' She looked at Mike, who felt a blast of hostility. 'And this is Alec. Alec, this is Mike. My soon-to-be-ex-husband.'

Charlotte giggled. 'My mother would say this is all *terribly modern*.'

'And will you be seeing her this Christmas?' Anna asked with a certain crispness. Mike felt nervous. Anna's tone didn't bode well.

'I doubt it, unless I get run over by a bus. She's probably on a cloud somewhere, enjoying a spliff with Elvis Presley. She won't want to be interrupted by me.'

'Oh. Sorry.'

'Er, bit awkward, Annie.' Mike started peeling off his scarf. 'Thing is, Charlotte's been let down by the friend she was supposed to be visiting, so she hasn't got any-where to stay. I thought perhaps as . . .' He looked across at Alec, who took a large gulp of beer in the manner of someone who suddenly needs courage.

'So I said she could stay here. After all,' Mike laughed abruptly, 'what's one more?'

'It's fine,' Anna said, her tone sharp and precise.

'Really? Oh, you are *sooo* kind!' Charlotte hurtled forwards and flung her arms round Anna. 'I know we're going to get on brilliantly. Now,' she turned to Mike, 'show me our room, darling? And where is the loo? I'm desperate.'

'I'll show you where the downstairs loo is,' Alec

volunteered, giving Mike a nervy look. 'It's through here.'

'"Our" room?' Anna shoved a spoonful of stuffing very forcefully into the turkey and Mike winced.

'No, not "our" room. Definitely not. I never even suggested it.'

'I bet *she* did, though. And why has she got bin bags on her feet?'

'Prada boots. Snow,' he said, shrugging.

Anna glanced up, her eyes (at last) amused. 'Oh, *Prada boots*. Well, excuse me for asking. At least there's a rack of spare wellies she can take her pick from in the boot room. Practical, if not Prada.'

'Look, I'm sorry. There wasn't anything else I could do. I could hardly leave her there all alone at the pub, could I?'

'She'd have got by,' Anna said grimly. 'That sort always do.'

'Your Alec seems a bit wet,' Mike retaliated. 'And young.'

'He is both,' Anna agreed. 'But that's all right. We can't all be blowsy and raucous.'

'She's OK when you get to know her,' Mike said.

'So where is she going to sleep, if not with you? There's only one spare bed and that's in Elmo's room. We can hardly inflict her on him.'

'Maybe we could inflict your Alec? No – not a good idea, come to think about it. Definitely not fair on Elmo and probably illegal or something. That just leaves one option, realistically.'

'Does it?' Anna started layering rashers of bacon across the top of the turkey, slapping them on briskly. Mike wished he too had something to do. Anna seemed to have the upper hand while she was occupied.

'Yes. I could move into your room. Charlotte can have mine. Simple.'

At last she stopped decorating the turkey and turned to face him. 'Simple? Hardly. We don't do that any more, remember?'

'We wouldn't be "doing" anything. Oh, come on, Annie, it's just a room-share, nothing more.'

'Definitely nothing more – you've got that in one. I've got used to my space. I don't see why I should have to give it up just because you've imported your . . . floozie to spread her substantial self out all over the place.'

'OK, I'll sleep with her then,' Mike said, shrugging. 'Seeing as you're practically insisting on it.'

Anna rinsed her hands under the tap and turned to look at him, silent for a few considering moments. 'Ah. Well, when you put it like that . . .' she said at last. 'Maybe you coming in with me is the most practical solution, bar you sleeping on the sofa which would make the place all untidy. And it looks like we're stuck with the bloody woman now. But as you said, it's just a room-share. Definitely nothing more.'

'Nothing more, I promise.' He grinned at her. 'I've probably forgotten how to anyway. After nearly a year.'

Charlotte and Alec came back in and Anna said in a half-whisper to Mike while looking at Charlotte, 'A year? Now that I very much doubt.'

TEN

'So who *is* she?' Emily cornered Thea in the sitting room and pointed towards the kitchen from which the sound of shrieky laughter was coming.

Thea shrugged. 'Friend of Dad's, is all I know. She's the one who sorted out putting the old home movies onto DVD.'

'But does that mean she gets to stay for Christmas? How come?'

'No idea, other than that she got marooned by the snow when she was supposed to be staying with a mate. But there are plenty of us here so she's quite diluted. She seems fun.' Thea felt quite cheered by Charlotte's presence. She appeared so resolutely unfazed by the situation, so completely taking for granted that you made the very jolliest best of a mishap. It made such a change from the rest of the family, who were deter-minedly *not* talking about the impending divorce but whispering in corners about their parents and their intentions. Much as she and Emily were doing right now. On the other hand, who were they to confront their parents about their personal lives? It would be excruciating enough the other way round, but who'd want to ask their pension-age parents *what on earth they thought they were playing at*, as if they were under-age teenagers?

'Dad's surely not been sleeping with her,' Emily said. 'Do you think he has? And Mum with that Alec person? Please tell me no.' Her face was showing absolute horror at the idea.

'Well, they might have been. I expect so. They're all grown-ups and – as they keep telling us – free,' Thea replied. 'But it's not really for us to speculate, is it? Their own business and all that. And anyway, does it matter?'

'Oh, Tee, sometimes you're just so damn annoying. Why can't we speculate? These are our parents – of course it matters. It would be gross. Surely you don't want them to just—'

'Have a good time? Yes, I do want them to. And what's gross about it? They're the ones who've decided life's too short not to, and they should know, so why not let them get on with it?'

'I wasn't going to say anything about them having a good time but, come on, Thea, there are some things I think we *really* don't want in our faces, aren't there?

I was going to say they need their heads banging together and that we mustn't give up on them getting back together. Can you imagine what it'll be like? They'll each be living alone and being stubbornly lonely but pretending they're not. And then suddenly they'll be ten years older and wishing they'd never split up, but one of them will be with someone else by then and the other won't. We'll be whizzing back and forth between the two of them, and we'll all get together on birthdays and make out everything's just the same, but it won't be, however much they pretend it's all so civilized and Scandinavian, as if that makes a difference. And now they've brought in a couple of bloody *strangers* – and that is going to distract them from the big family-bonding thing that we're all supposed to be here for. I think they've done it on purpose. I bet they planned this the whole time. They wanted us to meet their new people and decided this was the way to do it. Sneaky.'

Thea felt weary, tired from all the cooking and the emotional carol service, the trudging through snow (on the way back mostly carrying Alfie) and from simply being relentlessly *upbeat*. It was like trying to keep a reluctant fire lit in her head the whole time, one that was supposed to warm her spirits and stop her thinking about what might have been. But the closer they came to Christmas Day, the harder it was not to think about what should have been happening instead of giving her full attention to this strange house-party. She told herself to get a grip – there was nothing she could change.

'Oh, come on, Em, it's not the end of the world. And it's only for a few days. Can't you just make the best of it? Everyone else is. Let's just play nicely.'

'Mummy?' Alfie came into the room carrying his Christmas stocking. 'Can we hang our stockings up now? Is it time?'

'After tea, sweetie. You and Milly are having yours in a minute and then it's storytime and early bed.'

'Ohhh!' Alfie protested, stamping his foot. 'I want to do it *now*. And so does Milly.' His face went into pre-wailing expression, starting to crumple.

Emily frowned. 'But we always do it just before bed. You know that, silly.' Alfie pouted and slumped down on the fireside rug, hugging the red felt stocking close to him. He was heading for a major sulk.

Thea felt irritated. What difference did an hour or so make?

'Oh, let them hang them up, Em,' she snapped, 'if it makes them happy. I mean, why not?'

'Because this is how *we* do it, Thea,' Emily said. 'But of course now you've gone and said it, I suppose they'll have to, won't they? Otherwise there'll be tears. And we don't want that at Christmas, do we?'

'Sorry, Emily. Tell you what, I'll just butt right out of it. I really thought it wouldn't matter. Am I allowed to take Alfie into the kitchen to get a mince pie to leave out for Santa, or is that interfering as well?' She was being horrid and she knew it. Alfie gazed up at his mother and then at Thea, big-eyed and confused. Thea felt ashamed. She had no excuse apart from sheer envy. Emily, though – did she ever stop to think just how lucky she was? Why did she so rarely seem to celebrate the utter delight of her fabulous children? She seemed to find it all such hard work and so difficult simply to enjoy them. But then what would Thea know? As that neighbour at the Over-the-Roads' party had so kindly pointed out, she might be a teacher spending hours every day with small children, but it wasn't (apparently) anything remotely comparable to being a mother.

'No. Just leave it, Tee. I'll get Milly and Sam and we'll do the stockings and the mince pie and carrot ritual all together. As a family. While we still can, before Sam and I go nuts and end up as barking as Mum and Dad are,' Emily snarled at Thea. 'And frankly, *you* need to lighten up. I saw you going all weedy teary at the carol service.' She smirked at Thea. 'Sam would say he knows what *you* need.'

'Would he? Oh, thanks for that, Emily. Is that how you sort everything out in your house? A good seeing-to? Well, fucking lucky *you*.'

She stamped out of the room and into the kitchen where Charlotte, wearing three tied-together tea towels as an apron, was cutting crosses into the bases of sprouts and singing a jazzy version of 'Away in a

Manger'. She had a large glass of red wine on the work-top beside her.

'Hello, petal, I hope I'm doing this right,' she said, waving the knife at Thea. 'I'm just trying to be useful, work my passage kind-of-thing.'

'Looks fine to me. That's quite a mountain of them you've got there. Do you want some help?' Thea felt shaky. Was Emily right? *Had* she been moping? She'd tried hard not to.

'Oh no, I'll do it. I don't mind. When you live on your own it's great now and then to be part of a big party. Especially as it's so unexpected.' She grinned at Thea. 'I've had a couple of your mince pies – just to soak up the wine – and pretty damn fab they are too.'

'That's what I've come for,' Thea said, fervently hoping there were enough left. 'I'm just nipping out to see someone with them.'

Charlotte's eyes sparkled. 'Ooh, a man?'

'Yes, a man.'

'Where did you find one round here? The one I fancy is apparently going to be sleeping with his wife. I might need to make other arrangements.' She winked at Thea.

Thea laughed, enjoying Charlotte's up-front frank-ness. She also wished Emily had heard. It would be wicked fun to see her appalled face.

'Well, you wouldn't have any better luck with the one I'm seeing. Sadly for me, he's on the other bus.'

Charlotte put down the knife and gave Thea a

sympathy hug. 'Oh, darling, isn't it always the way, and if a gorgeous thing like you can't turn him . . . Still, always some little hiccup. But never mind, have a lovely time anyway. And you can't beat a nice gay man friend; every girl needs one. It's like a brother without the added hassle of family. Oops! I shouldn't have said that, should I? Not now that I'm in the middle of yours.'

'It's OK, I know what you mean and you're not wrong.' Thea picked up the cake tin of mince pies from the larder and was relieved to find it didn't weigh as little as she'd dreaded. She didn't much want to make any more, not after six batches of the damn things. She would if she had to, but felt she was in danger of turning into one. She took out ten and put them in a Tupperware box then collected a bottle of champagne from the fridge. She wasn't convinced – after the run-in with Emily – that mulled wine and the possibility of the alcohol having evaporated in the heating process would quite hit the spot.

'I only realized when I was on the train,' Alec said to Anna, 'that daffodils weren't the best choice of flowers. They'll have come from down here, been sent up to there and now I've brought them back again.'

There were masses of them, just beginning to open, the earliest ones with the subtle scent and the very short but sweet life. Anna arranged them in a vase on the console table in the hallway high enough up so that

Alfie wouldn't reach them. She liked them – they didn't smell of cat pee like the Paperwhites always seemed to.

'They haven't suffered from their travels,' she told him, 'and it was so sweet of you. I love to have flowers in the house over Christmas. It makes me feel all happy that spring won't be long.' She thought for a minute about home and how she would miss the best of her Christmas-flowering hyacinths that she'd left behind on the kitchen window-ledge. There was always a moment when they started to go over and the scent went from gloriously overpowering to slightly decaying. She'd probably arrive home in time for that stage and they'd have to be banished to the terrace to complete their decline. She'd almost brought them with her but had forgotten them in the mêlée of packing the car and arguing with Mike about whether to take the A303 route or the M4.

Anna was conscious that she and Alec seemed to be skirting around one another. It all felt a bit awkward and she wished she knew how not to make it so. Anything more intimate than the brief hello kiss at the station had to be out of the question here among her family. He couldn't expect anything different, surely? She was one person when she was back in London and out alone with him and with no one else to answer to, but quite another here in the middle of her closest people. It was going to be a tricky few days, trying to be all things to everyone and probably failing at every turn.

Thank goodness for Thea's list. She had found a Trivial Pursuit box in a cupboard and, as no one had come up with a better selection of quiz questions than the *Guardian*'s Quiz of the Year – and Sam had filled in most of those already – they were supposed to be playing that later after supper. It was old-fashioned and a bit daft, and probably most of them would rather slob out and watch vintage comedy repeats on TV while getting quietly sloshed, but if they divided everyone up into three teams it should be kind of . . . bonding. That was what they were all supposed to be here for, after all. Though nobody had anticipated bonding with a pair of interlopers as well.

The massive clump of mistletoe couldn't help but be directly over the head of anyone who was pretty much anywhere in the hallway, and right now, with the wall lamps on, it was casting several spooky circular shadows of itself across the wood floor as if to give any kiss-ditherers a nudge. You can't get away from the damn stuff, Anna thought slightly crossly. Its size made it seem bossy. She was half-inclined to take the kitchen scissors to it in the night when everyone was asleep, to stand on a chair and cut it back to a less brazen size. It was hanging there being too seductively vast, demanding attention. And even if she and Alec weren't going to give it the satisfaction of some serious snogging, she'd bet any money that Charlotte would be planning to.

'You know what? We should get out there and make a

snowman,' Alec suggested, peering through the window. 'It would be wrong to be given all this snow and then find it's melted away by morning and no one's been out and played in it.'

'I have a feeling there'll be plenty of it still,' Anna said. 'According to the radio, there's a lot more to come. They've even got it on the Isles of Scilly and that's practically unheard of. I can't remember the last white Christmas I saw.' She could, actually. She was just getting into her teens at the time but she was pretty sure it was the year before Alec was born, so she decided not to draw attention to the age gap.

'Come on, let's go and look.' Alec opened the door and a gust of freezing air blew flakes of snow in and set the mistletoe swaying above them.

He took her hand and they stepped out under the porch roof. She didn't much want her hand held, not here. And if she was going to make a snowman she didn't wish it to be with just him; the children would love to join in and she'd want them to.

'We'll need boots,' Anna said, putting off the moment but at the same time thinking how mumsily sensible she was sounding. If she were back home, out alone with him, she'd probably be skipping about in the snow with her face to the sky, letting the flakes fall on her tongue. But even then, she probably wouldn't be racing outside to the icy wetness in flimsy scarlet ballet flats.

'There's a boot room here, just behind the larder, with

a shelf of wellington boots in every size, so in the morning we could all come out and build something out here. Even Charlotte,' she said with a grin, picturing her as she'd first met her with her bin bags over her feet. A snowball fight, that's what they really needed. Some good old-fashioned, tension-busting violence. It would make them all feel better. She'd add it to Thea's list of things to do in the morning.

'You've brought champagne as well as the mince pies?' Sean looked surprised as Thea offered him the bottle.

'Sorry. I felt the need in case your wine was a bit light-weight.' She explained, 'I've had a bit of a run-in with my sister. But I'd love to try your mulled wine first. It smells fabulous.' And it did – the scent of cloves and cinnamon filled the room.

He led her through the kitchen to the sofas and she sat down, settling into the cushions and feeling tensions seep away as the warmth of the big log fire blazed at her. Woody jumped onto her lap and purred, narrowing his blue squinty eyes as she stroked his back. He settled and squirmed against her thighs, leaving a feathering of pale fur on her black jeans. Sean arranged the mince pies on a plate and put them on the coffee table in front of her.

'Families, eh? Can't live with them. Can't live . . . with them.' He ladled the warmed wine into a glass. 'Here, try this. Let me know – honestly – what you think.'

Thea took a slow sip. It was tangy and soothing and nothing like the thin, slightly bitter one she'd had at her neighbours' party, nor thick and cloying and low on alcohol like the one at the pub.

'Oh wow, that's gorgeous.' She sighed, having a bit more. She mustn't have too much, she warned herself; there was still supper to get through. Maria had left them some sea bass and Anna had delicious-sounding plans for it.

'New people have joined you, I see,' Sean said.

'Ah. Yes. The unexpected extras.'

'What – they just landed themselves on you?' He was laughing. 'They are friends of yours, though?'

She gave him a short version of who was who and he frowned, concentrating to take in the details while munching a mince pie.

'So they weren't invited – they just rocked up? These pies are fabulous, by the way. Eat your heart out, Delia, Nigella and Co.'

'Well, not quite, but actually, yeah, that's not so far out. Definitely in Charlotte's case,' she said, leaning back and closing her eyes.

'Aw, you look so sleepy, poor Elf,' Sean said. 'It must be pretty knackering, dealing with that lot. Why don't you stay over here for the whole evening and let them all get on with it over there? You can stagger back later and say you got stuck in a snowdrift or a blizzard or something. I could roll you in the snow for dramatic credibility.'

She opened her eyes. His face was surprisingly close to hers and she wanted, very suddenly, to put her arms round him, to rest her head against his warm body and simply *be* for a few minutes. She resisted. She had to – or he'd think she was completely loopy and that her Gaydar had tripped a switch.

'Tempting, but I can't just bail out on them all on Christmas Eve.'

'Would they put you on the naughty step?'

'Probably. And they'd ask a lot of questions.'

He laughed at that. 'I can imagine. The youngest in the family always cops it, long after they're grown up. It's like they're forever about to ask if you've finished your homework before you're allowed to watch TV.'

'I'm not the youngest, though, Emily is. She's only a couple of years younger but she's the family baby. Apart from her own children, that is, obviously.'

'Is she? I thought she looked older than you. She looks . . .'

He foundered for a moment and then together they both said, 'Cross.'

'So true,' Thea said ruefully. 'She's always worrying and thinking everything's a disaster. Maybe it takes it out of you. Gives you lines or something. Or it's the nights up with babies. That'll be it.'

'But is it a disaster?' He got up and put another couple

of logs on the fire. Sparks crackled and Woody jumped down from Thea and went to lie closer to the flames, his tummy facing the blaze.

'For her? No. She's pretty damn lucky, y'know. Lovely husband, top job, house, children. It should be the full package.' Thea suddenly felt she'd been disloyal. It must be the wine. She'd almost finished her glass and was feeling welded to the sofa and all soft and mellow. 'She definitely does appreciate her luck, somewhere inside. I just wish she didn't look on the downside all the time. But it's pretty freaking annoying if you're actually going through a massive personal downside of your own and she's fussing about the ribbon on Milly's plait coming undone as if it is the end of the world.'

She drank the last of her wine and wriggled herself more upright so she could get out of the squashy depths of the sofa. 'I really should be getting back,' she told him.

He made a disappointed face. 'Shame. Sure I can't tempt you to stay for a bit longer? I've got sausages.'

'Blissful idea, and thanks for the thought, but I really can't. And anyway, aren't you supposed to be with Paul?'

'Not till tomorrow. I thought I'd do the professional thing and stay on the premises in case the hiring party in the house – that's you lot – have any problems due to the snow.'

Thea giggled, realizing the wine had been quite

strong. 'Well, it's still outside the building so I don't think it'll turn out to be that much of a problem, will it?'

'Power cuts are a possibility – snow on the lines, all that. This is Cornwall, after all – none of your underground cables here. So I'm on duty tonight to do the manly bit with candles and torches should the worst happen. They're in a box in the room where all the boots are, by the way, just behind the larder. I might as well tell you. Power-cut kit – torches, matches, candles, all there.'

'Thank you. Sorry to screw up your Christmas arrangements. Please send apologies to Paul.'

'It's not the only reason I stayed.'

'Oh?' She wished she didn't keep forgetting he was gay. Why did he have to look at her as if she was even more delicious than the mince pies? It was so disconcerting and completely out of order.

'No. It's the surfing, tomorrow morning. We all do it. Christmas Day is a given, down in the cove.'

'What? You're going in the sea in this weather? Won't you *die*?'

'But I'm in the sea pretty much every day,' Sean pointed out. 'It was my job, don't forget. The only months you really feel the cold out there are February and March. The sea takes a long time to chill right down from the summer. And the summer was a pretty good one, wasn't it, this year?'

Thea thought back. Not so good for her, not after what happened and with Rich leaving and all. Weatherwise, she'd barely noticed. She wished she had – a beautiful summer deserved better than to be ignored and endured with misery.

'Hey, you look sad, Elf,' Sean said, taking her hand. 'Why don't you skip down to the beach with me now and we'll check out the waves for tomorrow? It'll blow the glooms away.'

Thea checked her watch. She was on washing-up duty later and wasn't needed for any cooking so she had time, just. It seemed a mad idea but he was probably right. A few blasts of fresh air would clear Emily and her comments from her head.

'OK, let's do it,' she said, standing up. The warmth in the room made her head spin. Or maybe it was the wine. She pulled her coat on, wondering if he'd mind if she went back to her room for a scarf.

'Hang on, I'll get you some more wrappings.' He must have read her mind and after a few minutes came back with a hand-knitted scarlet bobble hat and a tartan cashmere scarf, both of which he put on her as if she were a child, carefully pulling out the front fronds of her hair from the hat and tweaking them into shape. 'The front bits look like Tin-Tin,' he said, laughing at her.

'Oh, thanks – a small boy. My favourite look!' she said, blushing, which was more from enjoying the soft touch of his hands on her hair than from real embarrassment.

'Trust me, Thea, you don't look anything like a boy.'

Sean picked up a bag from the kitchen and the two of them set off through the snow along the path to the beach. Woody trotted alongside, picking his feet high up and occasionally grabbing at the snow as if fighting it. The night was now clear and bright. The snow had stopped falling, and more and more stars were visible as the clouds began to clear. It was hellishly cold but Thea still had the remnants of the warmth from Sean's log fire and the mulled wine. It was exhilarating to be out, striding down the path. Sean took hold of her hand on the sheerest bits of the path and she was grateful. It was a tricky enough descent in daytime, let alone on snow and in the dark, but at least with the whiteness she could see the ground. Without it, she'd have been terrified of tumbling the twenty feet to the shore.

'Wow, look – snow even on the actual *beach*,' she said as they got to the bottom. There wasn't that much of it and it petered out a few yards away towards the sea, but all the same, it was a sight she'd never seen before, and in the soft glow from the moon it looked as if a white volcano had erupted on the hillside and poured great tongues of pale lava across the shore.

Woody was still picking his way through the snow, occasionally stopping to wash a paw.

'He doesn't like it, does he? He must have freezing

paws,' Thea commented as she watched him. 'Or does he like the taste, do you think?'

'I guess it's just water. I wonder if cats know never to eat yellow snow?'

Thea laughed out loud. 'You can't tell a cat anything. They know it all.'

'Cat gods,' Sean said, putting the bag down beside a rock and starting to gather some snow together. 'Come on, help me roll a big ball of it. We'll make something – got to be done, hasn't it?'

Together they rolled and rolled a ball of snow along the beach and back till it was as high as Thea's shoulder. Then they rolled another and put it on top and added some pointy snow ears. Thea found pebbles for eyes and sticks for whiskers, and Sean shaped a tail at the back.

'There you go, Woody,' he said when they were breathless and pink from the effort. 'That's for you.'

The cat took a look at it, turned and trotted away back up the path, distracted by a sound from high above them.

'We're being watched,' Sean murmured, pointing up towards Cove Manor. Out on the dark back porch, away from the lights of the sitting room, two cigarette ends glowed in the dark.

'Hmm, that's probably Jimi having a sneaky cig. He still feels he has to slide out to smoke in dark corners in case Mum and Dad tell him off, like a teenager. Wonder who he's with?' And when a blast of laughter cut through the quiet: 'Ah, that'll be Charlotte. No mistaking that laugh.'

'Good sign – they're all getting on,' Sean said.

'Hope so.'

'Hey, I brought this for us.' Sean cleared snow from the rock and spread out a large bin bag on it. 'Sorry about this,' he said, pulling her down beside him. 'I don't usually expect to need a picnic blanket in December, so this is the best I could find at a moment's notice.'

He produced Thea's champagne and two glasses from his bag.

'I thought we'd just have a quick glass of this to celebrate Christmas. It seems the perfect spot for it, don't you think?' He opened the bottle and poured the wine into the glasses, handing her one.

'It does,' she agreed, staring out to sea. The waves were hurtling in, coming up to high tide and washing away the edges of the snow.

'A toast to the Woody-god.'

'Here's to Woody,' she said, as they clinked glasses.

Sean chuckled. 'I bet you had no idea that this was how you'd be spending Christmas Eve, did you? I certainly didn't.'

'It definitely wasn't something I'd planned, back earlier in the year, no.'

'Did you have something else you'd expected to do instead?'

Thea thought for a minute. She could tell him. It was another topic that wasn't being mentioned by anyone else and it felt wrong for it to be so completely unacknowledged.

'Actually, yes,' she said. 'If all had gone as it should have done, right now I'd be having a baby.'

ELEVEN

'I saw you earlier,' Jimi whispered to Thea, halfway through supper. 'What were you doing on the beach?'

'You were on the *beach*?' Rosie, overhearing, didn't go in for whispering and the others all turned to look at Thea.

'You went down there in all the snow? Why?' Emily looked anxious. 'Are you all right?'

'She means, were you sulking?' Charlotte put in. 'I heard you two having words earlier.' She pointed her knife at Emily. 'I think your sister was a bit upset.'

Emily glared at Charlotte. 'My sister does *not* sulk. And I don't know what it's got to do with—'

'Emily,' Mike said. 'Don't.'

Charlotte turned her full-beam smile on him, reached across and squeezed his hand. 'Thanks, but I can fight my corner.'

'We don't want fights, though, do we? In or out of corners,' he replied.

'Oh God, this is like when we were *ten*,' Emily huffed. She shoved a slab of the creamy Anna potatoes to the side of her plate and clanked her knife and fork together.

'It is, isn't it?' Anna said, looking faraway and smiling. 'Doesn't it take you back? All of us together for a lovely family Christmas and—'

'Squabbling, being told off,' Jimi said. 'Whatever must our guests think?'

'Pretty damn normal, I'd say. My mum's always telling me off, still, at my age,' Alec said. 'She says I shouldn't have married Suki, that I shouldn't have got divorced, that I shouldn't have given her the house . . . you name it, she can have a go about it. Not that you are, Anna.'

'No, she wasn't. Quite the opposite actually,' Mike said, sounding frosty. Thea watched as Alec and Charlotte exchanged glances.

'It'll just be Emily then, been stirring things,' Jimi said.

'I was building a snow cat.' Thea thought probably the safest tack was to answer Jimi's original question.

'A snowcat? Like a thing you ride on, on mountains and stuff?' Elmo asked, sounding excited. 'Is it, like, a kit?'

'No, sorry, El. It was an actual cat, made of snow. Sean's cat. Snowman style. I hope it's still there in the morning. I don't know how high up the beach the tide will go.'

'So you were with Sean?' Jimi asked. 'Uh-oh, holiday

romance alert, folks.' He drew a heart in the air with his fingers.

'Hardly,' Thea told him, laughing. 'You have no idea how many miles out you are on that one.'

The kitchen door opened and a sleepy-looking Milly came in. She stood looking at them all, rubbing her eyes, clutching her toy owl.

'Mummy? Alfie can't get to sleep. He feels sick.'

'I'll go,' Sam said to Emily, pushing his chair back. 'You stay here and carry on eating.'

'No, I've finished. Let me. You won't notice if it's something serious.'

Sam frowned. 'Of course I will. What do you take me for?'

'He said he ate the sugar mouse off the tree and the sugar mouse is biting him from *in here*,' Milly went on, patting her stomach. She brightened up, watching Anna taking plates to the sink and opening the oven. 'I can smell pudding. Can I have some?'

'It's sticky-toffee pudding, darling,' Charlotte told her. 'Yum!'

'*Shut up!*' Emily hissed at her. 'Do you think I want both of them throwing up?'

'Sugar mice? What sugar mice?' Rosie asked. 'I didn't see any. I wish I'd known – I love them. They're the most disgusting things ever, and divine as well. One of those things you can't resist but then feel ashamed for eating. Or maybe that's just me.'

'There weren't any,' Charlotte told her. 'But I happened to have brought a bag of them with me and I put them on the tree. Maybe I should have put them a bit higher.'

'I might have known it would be your fault. If he's sick all night, you can come and do the mopping up,' Emily said to Charlotte and she took hold of Milly's hand and stormed out, shutting the door with a good hard bang behind her.

'Well, that's me told,' Charlotte said cheerily. 'Is she always like that? All I've seen so far is the miserable cow side. I hope there's another one.'

'She worries a lot,' Jimi told her. 'She should take up Sudoku. I find it calms the brain.'

'You don't do it to calm your brain,' Rosie said to him. 'You do it to opt out of basic polite general communication.' She turned to the rest of them. 'Try asking him anything when he's absorbed in a bloody puzzle. It's like he's in a coma. Maybe it would help Emily, after all.'

'Jesus, what's *she* got to worry about?' Charlotte burst out. 'She should try being a self-employed singer living in a two-roomed flat at my age with a wine habit to support, an overdraft the size of Portsmouth, a son who prefers living in Australia – oh, and a very much part-time lover who's still living with his wife.' She stood up. 'No pud for me, thanks. But you all carry on. I'll be back to do my bit with the washing-up, but right now I'm going outside for a fag. I may be gone some time.' She headed for the door then looked back at Alec. 'You coming for one, matey?'

Alec looked a bit shifty then asked Anna, 'You don't mind, do you?'

She shook her head. 'No, of course not. You don't need my permission, Alec.' He shuffled out of his chair and went into the hallway, trailing behind Charlotte. There was silence at the table for a few moments.

'Going well then, so far,' Mike said to Anna.

'Yep. Couldn't be better,' she replied.

This was all she needed. Emily sat on the bed beside Alfie and rested her hand lightly on his forehead. His skin felt warm and dry, but then it was a bit stuffy in the room so that could be the reason, or at least part of it. She hadn't wanted the window open in case of chill draughts and the possibility of the breeze blowing snow onto the children's beds. The combination of snow and children sleeping at night alarmed her. She could barely admit even to herself that this was because it reminded her too much of the most gruesome fairy tales. She knew it was ridiculous, because the worst that could happen was that if snow did blow in, it would only result in a soggy duvet, but she couldn't help thinking of the Babes in the Wood: lost, cold and frightened and being covered with leaves. And then there was the Little Match Girl – no shoes, dying on a snowy pavement for want of a few pennies for food and some shelter. Even now, as a logical grown-up, the thought of it made her want to cry. Cold and snow were about struggle, about not surviving. It was all too unbearable and made her heart hurt.

'Mummy, is it Christmas yet?' Alfie half-opened his eyes.

'Not yet, darling. How do you feel?'

'My tummy hurts.' Alfie rubbed at his stomach. 'The mouse is eating me and going chew, chew.'

'No, it isn't,' Milly said from the other bed. 'You've already eaten it, so it's *dead*. It can't come alive again, that would be stupid.'

'Not stupid,' Alfie protested, starting to sit up.

'Lie down again, Alfie, let me look at you.' Emily lifted up his Superman pyjama top. No rash. That was a relief. Through a gap in the curtains she could see it was snowing heavily again and into her imagination rushed the scenario of a rash that could be meningitis, an ambulance that couldn't negotiate the snowy lanes. It could all happen so fast. Children could— No, she wasn't going to do this. She must deal with the here and now, and stop *projecting*.

'I don't think I feel sick any more,' Alfie said. 'Need a wee.'

Emily picked up her son and took him to the bathroom. The moment he was beside the loo, he was thoroughly sick into it. Holding her breath, she looked down to see if there was anything alarming among the hideous pink and white mush. Not just one sugar mouse then.

'You didn't eat any berries, did you, Alf?' she asked, having a sudden horrific thought. That sodding mistletoe, maybe it had shed a few of its berries on the floor. Mistletoe was poisonous, wasn't it?

'He only had the mice.' Milly came into the bath-room. 'And the white chocolate money. All of them. I don't like white chocolate.'

'Better now,' Alfie said, looking rather pleased with himself. 'The mouse has gone. Did Santa come yet? We had a sleep.'

'One sleep has to be a whole night,' Emily told him. 'In the morning there'll be presents. Milly, I've put a clock by your bed. Will you see if you can both stay in bed till the little hand is on the seven? Please?' It was a hopeless request and she knew it. They'd be dragging their stockings along to Emily and Sam's room long before the night was over. She'd go to bed right now, herself, just to get as much rest as she could, but there were the stockings to fill and to sneak into the children's room, and at this rate it would be midnight before they were deeply enough asleep. It was no good leaving it to Sam. Even though she'd got presents wrapped and in separate, labelled bags ready to go into the stockings, he was quite likely to get a bit random with the filling and forget whose were whose. He wouldn't think it mattered, but it did – she'd gone to a lot of trouble with them.

'How's the patient?' Sam's face appeared round the bathroom door.

'He vommed all the mice. I didn't,' Milly boasted. 'I had just as many but I'm not ill.'

'You got lucky then,' Sam told her, 'because it's not a good idea to sneak off and stuff your faces with things you haven't been told you can have. It could have made you very ill, you know.'

Emily smiled at him. 'Daddy's right. You mustn't do it again, you promise?'

'I promise,' Alfie said.

'Milly?'

'I s'pose.'

'No, you don't suppose, Milly, you *promise*, OK? And you stick to it. It is a rule,' Sam insisted.

'I promise.'

Sam took Milly back to bed while Emily washed Alfie's face and got him to rinse his mouth and brush his teeth. She fervently prayed that this was a one-off and that he wouldn't spend the night being sick every half-hour. She'd put the child-alarm on and hoped all she'd hear from it would be soft, even breathing. Tomorrow promised to be a long, long day.

At last the children were tucked up and on their way back to sleep and Emily and Sam left the room, softly closing the door behind them.

'Thanks, Sam, for the back-up,' Emily whispered as

they went down the stairs and waited in the hallway for a moment before rejoining the others.

'Just being the hands-on dad,' he said, putting his arms round her. 'Nice mistletoe, isn't it?' he went on, glancing up and nuzzling the side of her face.

'It is,' she said, her mouth getting closer to his. 'Very impressive.'

'Hey, you two, stop snogging and get in here!' Jimi called from the sitting-room doorway. 'Trivial Pursuit is under way. That Alec is winning and he's ganged up with Charlotte who is arguing about the answers. Mum said she wishes we'd gone for Pictionary.'

'Do we have to?' Sam asked. 'We fancied an early night.'

'Oo er, get you. And you with early-rising kids. Such stamina. But hang on. Come over here for a sec. I want to know something.' They followed Jimi into the second sitting room and he closed the door.

'What's up?' Sam asked. 'Are you worried about Santa burning his boots in the chimney?'

'No – I just want to know about the sleeping arrangements. Where's Mum sleeping?'

'In her room,' Emily informed him.

'So where's that Alec bloke sleeping?'

'In the spare room.'

'So that leaves Charlotte – where, exactly?'

'In Dad's room.'

'Really? So he is sleeping . . . ?'

'In Mum's room.'

'Oh.' Jimi looked confused. 'So our parents have two new – what? Lovers? Partners? Boyfriend/girlfriend? Though that sounds all teenage.'

'How about "gatecrashers"?' Sam suggested with a grin. 'Certainly in Charlotte's case.'

'But either way, the new whatevers have to put up with our parents sharing a bed! Where does that leave the divorce?'

'Same as before, I expect. It's only about beds and being polite to us all. It wouldn't really be very good manners, would it, to shack up with a new body in front of the rest of us,' Sam said.

'Embarrassing, too.' Emily shuddered. 'When it comes to my parents, I really don't want to know.'

'They're not quite ready to take on the full-Scandi mode yet then, any more than we are. But hey, I suppose it's none of our business really,' Jimi concluded. 'Anyway, to the Triv game in hand. Come on.' He opened the door and waited for the other two.

'I really think we could just duck out of that and go and see about being Santa,' Sam demurred, pulling Emily after him towards the door.

'Not a chance. It's on the schedule for tonight and we're not allowed to argue with that. What is writ is writ,' Jimi declared. 'And besides, mate, it's your go.'

*

Three bottles of wine down, two cigarette breaks for Charlotte and Alec and two tiptoed trips up the stairs by Sam to check on the children and the final game was almost over, at long last. Thea really wanted to go up to her room and diddle about mindlessly on Facebook in peace and quiet. The game had gone on too long and they were a rowdy lot. Rosie was rubbing her temples and had gone to her room in search of painkillers and managed to 'forget' to come back. Thea didn't blame her; what was it about quizzes and board games that brought out such an argumentative side to people? The answers were on the other side of the cards – so what was the point of challenging and insisting you were right? It was fine by her that the answer to *What is the world's most common non-contagious disease* was *tooth decay* but Charlotte and (amazingly) Anna wouldn't accept it because they questioned whether decay was actually a disease.

'Would you have accepted it if they'd written "dental caries"?' Jimi asked.

'No. Tooth decay isn't a disease,' Charlotte argued. 'It's carelessness.'

'You could say the same about syphilis,' Sam said.

Mike laughed. 'But contagious, though, that one. Definitely.'

Anna gave him a sharp look.

They were down to the final question. If Charlotte got it right, she'd win. She looked very gleeful and eager at the prospect. Thea silently wished her an easy question so they could all stop playing. Jimi read it out. '*Which bridge do you cross to get to Kew Gardens?*'

Charlotte hesitated. 'Well, it depends where you're coming from. I mean, if you're coming from Surrey it would be Richmond Bridge, but—'

Jimi turned the card over. 'Nope. Kew Bridge.'

'Richmond wasn't my final answer,' Charlotte reproved him. 'You were too quick off the mark there. I was only talking it through. Of course I know it's Kew Bridge! But they didn't even ask which river. Or which road you might be on. If you're on the A316 you'd go over Chiswick Bridge and turn right.'

'Sorry, I had to accept your first answer.'

'Back me up here, Mike!' Charlotte demanded, getting up and pouring herself another half-glass of red.

Mike shrugged. 'Sorry – can't challenge the question-master.'

Charlotte stomped round the room. She kicked a sofa and Thea heard her do a kind of low, furious growl, like a cat issuing a final warning to a teasing child.

'OK, Mum, your go,' Jimi went on, ignoring the dramatics, and picking out the next card. '*What did Walter Raleigh's wife carry in her bag for twenty-nine years after his execution?*'

'Jesus, I don't know. Hang on, let me think.' Anna closed her eyes in concentration.

'You said Jesus,' Charlotte challenged, pointing at her

and waving her glass at a near-spill angle. 'Jimi has to take that as the answer.'

'Don't be ridiculous, Chazz, you can't carry Jesus in a bag,' Mike said, laughing at her.

'Don't you dare sneer at me, Mike. Of course you could carry *a* Jesus. A model of one. Like a good-luck thing. A crucifix would be perfectly reasonable.'

'His head?' Anna guessed.

'A Jesus in a bag is more likely than a head in one,' Alec said. 'Even if head is right.'

'It is right,' Jimi said. 'Manky and disgusting it would be, but it's the right answer. Mum's won the game and we can all go and sleep and wait for Father Christmas to come. Phew.' He started putting the game away in its box while Charlotte still grumbled from the sofa about bias and unfairness and how it was good manners to let guests win. Emily's eyebrows went up at that but she didn't actually point out that Charlotte wasn't the usual definition of a 'guest'. Thea was glad she'd managed a bit of restraint there. For all Charlotte's breezy bravado, her position in the household could hardly be a comfortable one, and besides, she liked her.

In spite of her tiredness, and probably too much wine over the evening, Thea lingered after the others had said their goodnights and left the room. Alec and Charlotte went back to the porch for a final cigarette, Jimi had gone for one by the back door on his own, and she sat on the rug by the remains of the fire along with the carrot for the reindeer and Santa's mince pie. She checked her phone for messages. There were a few Happy Christmases from friends back home, but nothing from Rich, which in true contrary style, she quite minded about even though she didn't want to hear from him. Did he, she wondered, have any memory of the significance of tomorrow's date other than it being Christmas Day? Would he have *any* tiny twinge of 'what-if' about it? She clicked on his contact details and her fingers hovered over the phone's keyboard.

If she sent him a Merry Christmas message now and he then sent one back to her in the morning, she'd never know if he'd simply been responding to hers or if he would have sent one anyway. Also, it looked needy. Regretful. Lonely. She no longer was any of those things, not when it came to him, not now. She switched off the phone and got up. She batted down the embers of the fire with a poker and put the guard across. Then she went to switch off the Christmas-tree lights, waiting first to take in the sight of the heap of wrapped presents beneath it, at the back the big bulk of the wrapped bikes that would so delight the little ones, though possibly not as much as if there wasn't nearly a foot of snow in the garden and no real chance of immediately playing outside on them. She took a quick photo with her phone, switched off the lights, then the room lights and went to the kitchen to get a cup of tea to take up with her.

She wasn't quite the last up. As she went across the hall-way she could hear low laughter from the two smokers outside and the door was open a couple of inches.

Thea munched Santa's mince pie while she made herself a mug of tea. She thought briefly of Sean over in the stable block. In the morning she'd go down and watch him surfing – she was looking forward to that, and to being in the cold, fresh air with plenty of room to breathe. The house was hot and the atmosphere between them all was almost quivering with the tension of everyone trying *not* to be tense. Probably one day they'd all be able to get together and say, 'Do you remember that mad Cornish Christmas?' and laugh about it, but for now it simply had to be got through as good-naturedly as possible.

She switched off the kitchen light and was about to go back across the hallway to the staircase when she realized there were voices whispering together just ahead of her. Charlotte giggled and Alec said, 'Shh!' Thea saw Charlotte close and lock the front door and point upwards to the ceiling.

They were under the mistletoe, though to be fair, given the size of the clump, it was hard to be in the hall and not be under it.

'G'night. Sleep tight,' Alec whispered loudly to Charlotte, who giggled again.

'Tight's the word. Though not like that, not me.' And the two of them collapsed against each other in a fit of suppressed laughter. Thea crept backwards out of the hall as they went silent, not wanting to see them twined together beneath the huge bough, kissing in a far more than politely-because-it's-Christmas way. Oh terrific, she thought as she tiptoed to the far side of the house to go up the back staircase. Now there was a potentially wild complication.

So Mike still did that thing with his socks, Anna thought as she pulled the duvet up to her chin. The socks were in the far corner of the room, rolled together into a ball. It had mildly irritated her for years, that, the way he peeled them off, coupled them together and then hurled them like a county cricket-level bowler across the room instead of simply putting them in the laundry basket in the bathroom. To be fair, there wasn't a laundry basket here for them to go in, but still. Also to be fair, she now found it quite sweet that he still had this same little quirk. She'd bet serious money, though, that he didn't do the sock thing when he was bedding Charlotte. The thought gave her a little painful knot of grumpiness inside, though it might have been Maria's sticky-toffee pudding which had been far too more-ish than was good for her.

The bathroom door opened and Mike came out, glistening and pink from the shower and stark naked. She avoided looking at his body in case he thought she was missing him in *that* way.

'Lights out, or are you reading?' he asked, climbing into bed on the far side of her. There seemed an acre of cool white sheet between them as each of them lay on their separate islands of bed.

This wasn't a situation either of them would have chosen, after all, Anna thought. It was a case of needs must. The idea of sleeping with Alec when all her family were around her was a completely dreadful one. They'd never even done a whole night together and she didn't really want to. It would be too domestic. Far too coupley. They hadn't got to that stage yet and she wasn't in any hurry. In fact, she didn't think she'd want it at all. What was that awful term? 'Friend with benefits'? It was a pretty unattractive phrase but it summed things up for her. It was about the most she would go for. What, after all, was the point of divorcing her sweet husband with his quite mild (if slightly irksome) sock-throwing habits just to take up with someone who might have far worse ones? Alec might be a toenail picker who went click-click at it when he thought you weren't taking notice. You had no idea till after the early polite days were over and old unthinking ways kicked in. Ugh. Sometimes there really was a case for the devil you knew. Or no devil at all.

'Lights out, I think. I expect we'll be woken by the children in a couple of hours. I doubt they'll open their stockings in silence.'

'You're right. Ours never did. Do you remember them

rushing in all shiny-eyed, to tell us Santa had been? You have to pretend you have no idea.'

Mike switched his light off, turned his pillow over – something else he'd always done, as if it had already become hot before he'd even put his head on it – and lay down. He sighed.

'Great beds, these,' he said.

'Very nice,' she replied. Beneath the duvet she quickly pulled her silky nightdress down over her thighs. She felt a bit awkward, as if she were sharing her bed with someone not that familiar to her. Ridiculous. But she didn't want to risk skin-to-skin contact with him, not now she was also sharing the premises with that Charlotte woman.

'Yours is an odd bugger,' Mike then declared.

'My what?' she answered him, knowing quite well what he meant but wanting time before she answered. A whitish light shone through the curtains. A reflection of snow, she realized. It had made the air a misty shade of grey-blue instead of being proper night-dark. She liked the way it made the room not quite dark but not annoyingly so, the way a too-bright streetlamp further up a road could, back home.

'Your bloke. Your Alec.'

'He's not really "my" anything,' she said, then because it felt unfairly dismissive of her friend, she added, 'And he's not at all odd.'

'He's terrified of us all. Apart from Thea and you.'

'Well, of course he is! Who wouldn't be? It's a bit overwhelming, joining a big party of related people. Have some sympathy.'

'Why? It was his choice to come. I wonder what the hell he expected? To be having Christmas jollies in your bed?'

'Certainly not. He knew you were here.'

'But he also knows we're divorcing.'

'Oh, for heaven's sake, are you jealous, Mike? You sound it.'

'Jealous? No! Are you?'

Anna laughed. 'Of Charlotte the harlot? Hardly! She's a piece of work though, isn't she? What on earth were you thinking? Talk about obvious.'

'Obvious what?'

'Obvious as in not a shrinking violet. Brash, loud, boozy.'

'OK, OK, I get the drift. She's a laugh, Charlotte. And you've got to admit, she's handy in the kitchen.'

'She's not lazy, no. And I do appreciate that.'

'Well, there you are then, that's a plus: she's very willing.'

'I bet she is.' Anna wished she hadn't said that. It sounded mean and snitty, and also possessive towards Mike. Not that she was, of course. Far from it.

'Not worthy of you, that comment. Especially given the circs.'

'So are we going to sleep or are we going to lie here, slagging off each other's squeezes?'

Mike chuckled. 'Oh, don't spoil the moment. Let's carry on slagging.'

'It's tempting. There's plenty of scope with yours. You'd think a singer would cut out the fags.'

'It gives her voice a husky edge. Yours is a smoker too. You can't beat up on Charlotte for that.'

'She's a bad influence. I've never seen Alec smoke more than one in an evening before.'

'Aha, he's weak-minded then. I'll add that to his downside list.' Mike rubbed his hands together, relishing his argument.

'Are we getting a bit silly here? These are people we choose to spend time with. Shall we cut them some slack?'

'Hell, no. This is war. But I promise I'll behave in public, as it were, if you will.'

'I'll be as nice as pie to yours then. In the spirit of Christmas cheer.'

'Thank you. And so will I. We should shake on that.' He held out his hand and she shook it, solemnly.

'This is so silly,' she said, smiling at him.

'I know.' He turned and leaned on one arm, looking at her face.

'What is it?' she asked.

'Christmas kiss?'

'OK.' She moved across, and he held her close.

'I'm feeling rather pleased to see you,' he said.

'I can tell,' she murmured, feeling rather pleased herself about the fact. She wriggled closer to him. So much for the not-touching thing. This was good, warm and tender and rather delightful.

'I didn't expect this,' Mike said rather breathlessly. 'And before you ask, I didn't plan it either.'

'It's OK, we won't blame ourselves for anything that happens now,' Anna said as she kissed him. 'It's that massive mistletoe Thea brought in – it has a long-range effect.'

TWELVE

The pounding of small footsteps and some excited squealing in the corridor outside her room woke Thea at 6.30 a.m. And while she'd admit that Milly and Alfie had done well to sleep as late as that, she pulled the duvet over her ears and closed her eyes again, in hope of another hour's peace.

'Thea! Thea! Father Christmas came and we got stockings with lots of things!' Alfie ran into her bedroom and bounced onto the bed, thumping his stocking full of now-unwrapped presents onto her stomach.

'Oof!' she protested, moving over to make room for her nephew. Milly followed and the two of them sat beside her, tipping out their loot onto the duvet.

'We get our other presents after breakfast,' Milly said excitedly, opening a pot of bubble mixture and spilling some on her pyjamas. 'So can we have breakfast now?'

Thea reached for some tissues and mopped up the spilled gooey liquid. Milly dipped the wand into the pot and blew a string of bubbles across the bed.

'I've got colouring pens. Look!' Alfie was taking the lid off a fat orange marker and Thea realized she'd have to wake up properly now to guard the room from possible indelible damage.

'Do Mummy and Daddy know you're in here? Have you shown them what Santa brought yet?' she asked.

'Mummy said we should come and show you first,' Alfie said.

Milly hit his arm. 'Ouch!' he wailed.

'We're not supposed to say that,' she said crossly. 'Mummy said she wanted a bit more me-time but that you'd like to see our presents, only not to say she sent us.'

Thea smiled. 'I won't tell her you said it. I expect she's just needing a bit more sleep because it's going to be a busy day. But even if I get you some breakfast, I can't let you open your other presents, not till everyone else is there. You know that really, don't you?'

'Yes. S'pose,' Milly conceded, looking gloomy, then she cheered up and said with glee, 'Alfie sicked up the sugar mice. It was *gusting*.'

'Yes, I heard about that. I also heard you'd been a greedy pair of rabbits and eaten far too much.'

'I've got more chocolate money,' Alfie said, delving

into his stocking and pulling out a gold-mesh sack. 'I'll have them for breakfast. Can I, Thea?'

'Sorry, sweetie, I think those had better wait for later. And chocolate and white duvet covers don't really go, do they? Maybe we'll all have some down on the beach later when we go to watch Sean surfing.'

'Is Sean the man? The one with the cat?' Milly asked. 'You went out with him for the mistletoe. Is he your boyfriend?'

Thea laughed. 'He is the mistletoe man. This is his house and he's not my boyfriend.'

'I wish he was your boyfriend, because then you could marry him and have some babies and then we'd have more cousins than just Elmo.' Milly blew another stream of bubbles which popped with little bursts of mist on the bed.

'I want more cousins too,' Alfie demanded, followed by, 'What are cousins?'

'They're Elmo and they're what Thea's babies would be because she's Mummy's sister. They'd be our cousins,' the little girl declared. 'And we'd love them.'

Thea felt choked up suddenly and reached out to pull the children to her for a big hug. 'And they'd love you too,' she told them, as soon as she could trust herself to get the words out.

'So this is where you are.' Sam looked in through the open door and grinned at them all. 'Happy Christmas, Thea! Sorry about the invasion. Em was feeling a bit headachey. She's better now she's had a soak in the bath.'

'These two have been showing me what was in their stockings,' she told Sam.

'I hope they're behaving.'

'They are. But they want their breakfast.'

'Come on then, you two, let's go and see what's in the kitchen. I think there's some pigs in blankets for a treat.'

'Ugh! Pigs!' Milly wrinkled her nose up.

'And angels on horseback too. After you've shown Mummy what you've got, just quickly.'

Alfie laughed. 'Horses and pigs! Like a huge dinosaur's breakfast!'

Sam refilled the stockings and took the children back to his room. Thea curled up under the duvet again and thought about the baby she hadn't got. What would it have been like? She indulged herself with a moment's imagining, thinking of these two bickering over who got a go at pushing the pram in the park. She pictured a picnic blanket on a sunny lawn, her baby in a sunhat and Milly helping him or her with a shape sorter. She'd pretty much avoided letting these pictures into her head over the past six months, but today, of all days, she thought she could allow herself a few last if-only moments. It didn't make her horribly sad, not like in those first few weeks, but it did make her send up one big Christmas wish that, just because it hadn't worked out last time, then please – one day – could all these imaginings actually come true.

It all looked very lovely. Anna, lighting the fire, looked at the many gaudily wrapped presents arranged beneath Emily's glittery tree and couldn't help wondering what next Christmas would be like, once she and Mike had moved on to separate premises. It was all very well being so cheerfully civilized about it all, but they weren't likely to have a regular family Christmas like this in future. Other new partners, if any, weren't likely to put up with it and they'd have family ties of their own to be catered for. Charlotte and Alec weren't finding it that easy being here, though Charlotte was brazening it out with the help of wine, and these two were still only in the category of being occasional dates rather than full-scale partners.

The fire started to crackle and she added more wood and put the guard across it, then went to the window. Dawn came later down in Cornwall than it did in London, and the last pearly remains of night grey were still in the air even though it was past nine. Thick snow sat frozen-edged on the trees and the ground, showing no signs of melting any time soon. Here and there, the spikes of daffodils poked above the white, and footprints from the night's marauding wildlife criss-crossed the garden. Anna identified a cat's paw-prints and some bigger ones that were probably a fox, and beneath the window on the terrace were twiggy little marks from birds' feet. The bird table had a couple of furious starlings squabbling over yesterday's toast crumbs and bacon rinds, and she reminded herself she must put out more for them. It must be hard, foraging for survival in this weather. The birds of Cornwall must be thoroughly confused by all this snow.

'Happy CHRISTMAAAS!' Footsteps thumped down the stairs along with the bright, brash sound of Charlotte. 'Oooh, a victim!' she shrieked and Anna opened the door just in time to see her ambush Mike, who was crossing the hallway. Charlotte planted a fat, wet kiss on him beneath the mistletoe and flung her arms round his neck, hugging him close and wriggling against him.

Mike grimaced at Anna over Charlotte's shoulder. He was gently patting her as if she were a child to be indulged or comforted, and Anna escaped into the kitchen to avoid seeing whether Charlotte inveigled him into some full-scale snogging. Some things you really didn't want to witness. Especially not when you'd been doing much the same only hours before. It was probably wiser just to go and have breakfast: she was sure the slight gnawing feeling inside must be hunger. Of course it was – the scent of bacon and sausages was all that was stirring her insides. It couldn't possibly be the thought of having to face Alec.

If Anna were a young twenty-something or in her

early thirties like Thea, she'd probably put what happened the night before down to 'a mistake', but she'd been a long time grown up, and she and Mike had both known exactly what they were doing. She still felt a tingle of excitement thinking about last night. It had been like newly discovering both a best friend and a lover, and it had felt a lot like when she'd first met him nearly forty years previously. As she opened the fridge for milk for her tea, she wondered how Mike felt about it. The thought that he might not feel the same was a possibility that she didn't want to consider. Not today, anyway. Not when there was still so much of Christmas to get through.

The turkey went into the oven while everyone was still helping themselves to breakfast around it. Thea and Emily closed the door on the huge bird and breathed big sighs of relief.

'It's massive,' Thea said. 'Poor thing, don't you always feel sorry for them? They get stuffed at both ends and gussied up and blanketed in bacon and surrounded by dinky sausages and then in the end we just *eat* them as if they're just big old everyday chickens.'

'They are, though, really, aren't they? What did you want for it, a state funeral?'

Emily's tone was a bit sharp. Thea stepped back and went to clean the worktop, scooping stuffing crumbs and bits of onion into the bin. She wasn't going to snap back at her, not today.

'Sorry, Tee. Didn't mean to be horrible. I feel a bit yuck this morning, that's all.'

'Headache? Shall I get you something for it?' Thea asked.

'Oh no, it'll go off. I don't want to take anything.'

'Come down to the beach and watch the surfers later. The air will clear your brain,' Thea suggested.

'I will. The children want to go down the hillside on their sledges. I'll go and get them dressed, then they can open their main presents. It's going to be chaos in that room, all the unwrapping.'

'It's OK, it's only paper, easily cleared. Em, are you all right? You haven't really looked relaxed since we got here.'

To Thea's surprise, Emily's eyes filled with tears. 'I'm OK. It's just' – she waved her arm vaguely – 'all this. Mum and Dad. These random people they've brought in. I mean, why? Were we never enough? What bloody more do they want?'

Thea shrugged. 'They want the same as the rest of us, I expect. To be happy, to be loved, to get by.' She'd quite like some of that too, she thought. *Here's hoping for the new year.*

'But that's what I mean. We love them – why do they want to hook up with new people? Is this what happens? You think everything's going really well and you love your partner and your children, and then all of a sudden you get to a certain age and you think, You know what? There's more to life than *this*. Will it happen to me and Sam like it did with— Sorry. Forget I even started this. I'm so stupid.'

'With me and Rich, you mean. Thinking about it, I know we were supposed to be engaged and everything, but really, we never got even halfway to what you've all got,' Thea said. 'We wanted different things. I wanted a family and he wanted' – she felt her face give way to unexpected laughter – 'poodles.'

'There's a lot to be said for a dog,' Emily agreed, laughing along with Thea, 'but not *that* much.'

Milly and Alfie came into the kitchen, dressed and washed. 'Presents now!' they demanded.

'Not as much to be said for a dog as for these two. You are so lucky, Emily. Please don't waste your time waiting for it all to go wrong.'

Emily came up and gave her a quick hug. 'You know, you can be quite wise at times,' she said. 'It's just one more annoying thing about you: you got the looks *and* the brains.'

'I never know when you're joking,' Thea said gently. 'So you got the inscrutability gene.'

'I wasn't joking, not really.' Emily laughed again. 'And you can be quite annoying at times.'

'It's never too early for champagne, is it? Especially not on Christmas Day.' Charlotte wasn't so much asking

Mike as simply stating a fact as she opened the fridge and took out a bottle. To be fair, he thought, she had brought a couple of bottles with her, but given her consumption rate there was a danger they'd be all out of wine by the time dinner was served. Luckily she didn't know about the dozen bottles of Prosecco he'd still got stashed in the Sierra. There hadn't been any point in bringing them in. The car was serving perfectly well as a fridge – that's if he could get to it under the new snow that had fallen in the night. In fact, it wasn't easy to tell which of the cars was even his.

Charlotte was looking a bit haggard this morning, he thought, though she'd dressed up in a velvety dress and plenty of defiantly glittery jewellery. Her make-up seemed to have been put on without the use of a mirror, and one eye had a lot of dark blue eyeshadow and the other only half as much. He felt a bit guilty. Maybe she hadn't taken to being a house-guest with quite the casual breeziness that she'd shown. But the two of them weren't properly what his children's generation would call 'an item'. It was far looser an arrangement than that. Or so he'd thought. She'd never made any demands on his time. They'd met at a pub gig where she'd been doing a couple of numbers with a blues band and he'd been (until she'd turned up here) under the impression that she was a completely free spirit. Now he wondered if she really did want more.

Even so, he thought as he fetched her a glass from the

cupboard, it was a bit of a cheek on her part to come here claiming that something more under the noses of his whole family, especially his not-yet-ex-wife. Talking of which, last night had been a jolt. Over a year of sleeping apart. And a good year before that of a fading-out and perfunctory sex life and now, suddenly, *oomph*. What to do? How to be?

Charlotte slumped into a chair and fanned her face with her hand. She was looking a bit over-heated. It should probably be a glass of water he was handing her, not opening the champagne. He didn't want to think what her blood pressure must be like.

In the background Mike could hear the squeals of Alfie and Milly opening their presents. Any minute now they'd be riding their bikes into the kitchen.

'Are you all right, Char?' he asked as he handed her a glass of the bubbly stuff.

She took it and had a sniff at it. 'Ah, bliss. That biscuity scent. They should sell it on the perfume counter.' Then, 'Yes, I'm fine.' She gave him a questioning look. 'How about you?'

'Me? Oh, fine, yes. I hope you're not having too terrible a time, that's all. Sorry about, you know.' He looked up at the ceiling.

'Oh, don't even think about it, sweetie. I may be an old slapper but even I don't expect to shag you right under the gaze of your entire family.' She gave him a seductive smile and said, 'I can wait. Or not. Whatever will be and so on. I see my job here as cheering up that Alec. Poor chap is pining for your wife like a lost puppy. What on earth is he doing here?'

'An accidental invitation. Anna crossed some wires for him. Didn't mean to.'

'I think he loves her,' Charlotte said.

'I don't blame him.' The words slipped out before Mike could stop them.

Charlotte looked at him and took a large gulp of her drink. 'I knew it,' she said. 'You two will never be over each other.'

'Probably not, not completely. Sorry.'

'Don't be. We've had fun. We can still have fun.'

He took her hand. 'Of course we can.' But he knew that the fun he meant was to do with music, and the fun she had in mind wasn't.

'We won't see him all day now,' Jimi said to Thea as Elmo got his head down over his new iPad and started tapping away at it. 'Awesome,' had been his response on opening all his presents, just as a huge squeal had been the reactions of Milly and Alfie when opening theirs. The rug had vanished beneath a sea of wrapping paper and dollies and cars and dressing-up clothes and Lego and packaging and Milly rode her new scarlet bike across the lot, howled at by Alfie.

'Can I go out?' she yelled from the hallway.

'What do I do?' Emily asked Thea. 'I can hardly give

her a bike and then say, "No, you can't ride it," can I? But look at it. It's like an ice rink out there.'

Thin snow was falling again. It wasn't as pretty as the fat flakes of the day before but it was quickly covering up any footprints that were still visible.

'You could walk out there with her, show her how slippery it is and suggest she waits till the snow's gone?' Thea suggested.

'Good plan. It beats saying yes and then having her fall off on the snow and break her arm.' Emily took hold of her own forearm and rubbed it, as if putting a no-breaks spell on all bones on behalf of her children.

Emily opened the door and she and Thea and Milly put their boots on and went outside. 'I'm bringing my bike,' Milly insisted, pulling it through to the porch.

'It'll get all snowy,' Thea told her.

'I don't care, I want to ride it.'

'Just walk about a bit first,' Emily said, as Milly wheeled the bike out to the garden. Thea's phone rang suddenly and Emily, distracted, could only watch as Milly climbed on to her bike and sped away from her, towards the side of the house where the cars were parked.

'Milly! *Stop!*' Emily yelled.

'I'll be back in a minute,' Thea said, fishing her phone out of her pocket and turning back towards the house. There was Rich's name on the screen and she was pressing the green answer button when there was a crash and a scream from around the corner of the house.

'Is she all right?' Thea shouted, abandoning the call and quickly slithering round towards the stable block. Milly was lying against the side of Mike's Sierra, tangled up in her new bike. She prayed the child wasn't damaged and the same for the bike – how awful for the poor girl would it be for the first ride to make it a buckled write-off?

'Oh God, I don't know. Milly? Does anything hurt?' Emily was crouched over her child.

'What's happening?' Sean came out from the Stables, pulling on his sheepskin jacket. 'Hello! Happy Christmas, all of you. I see you've celebrated by having a bit of an accident. Are you OK, little one?'

'Owww!' Milly wailed as Emily started to move the bike from her.

'Hang on a sec,' Thea said. 'Let's just check a couple of things first.'

'You're a first-aider?' Sean asked.

'Yes – goes with the teaching job. Milly, did you hit your head?'

'Nooo! I'm getting cold!' she wailed. 'And my knee hurts.' She wriggled about, trying to get up.

'Limbs all seem to work,' Sean said. 'That's a good sign.' He and Thea pulled the bike off Milly and she bounced up like a lithe kitten and prodded at her knee.

Thea wheeled the bike in a circle and nothing seemed to be wrong with it.

'Do you want to come in for a plaster and a bandage or anything?' Sean asked.

'Oh – that's kind, but no thanks,' Emily said. 'I'll just get her inside and into dry clothes and see what she's done to her knee.'

'But I want another go,' Milly said crossly. 'Not going in yet.'

'I think you are, darling, just for a while. The snow will go soon and then it'll be safe to ride your new bike. Come and play with your other toys now. Shall we make a bracelet with your Rainbow Loom?'

On that thought, Milly cheered up and went back to the house with Emily.

'Can I tempt you to coffee and one of your own mince pies?' Sean asked. 'I've managed not to eat them all so far.'

Thea thought of the call she hadn't taken. Should she call Rich back? It would be madly unfriendly to let him think she'd deliberately cut him off so abruptly. What could be so bad about wishing each other a Happy Christmas? All the same, Sean was here looking bright and friendly and far more deserving of a positive response than Rich was. Rich could wait.

'Yes, please, that would be good. I could do with a few minutes' peace – it's all go in there.'

'I bet it is,' Sean said, laughing as they went into the house. 'I remember it well. I'm one of five children and there are several nieces and nephews. Last Christmas was at my sister's in Scotland, and by lunchtime there wasn't an inch of floor that wasn't covered in toys and wrapping.' He filled the kettle and took the box of mince pies out of the cupboard and turned down the music that was belting out from the computer – the Phil Spector Christmas album, with the Ronettes singing 'Walking in a Winter Wonderland'.

'Don't you miss that family stuff, this year?'

'Not really. It was fun at the time but I like being here too. It's something different. I like the something-differents in life. Though I can't pretend I wouldn't give a lot for one of those Australian surfer barbecues with a few tinnies with mates in the blazing sun right now. But then if I was there and knew there was a once-in-a-lifetime white Christmas over here, I'd be gutted.'

'Well, you'll have the surfing later, so that's that bit covered.'

His wetsuit was hanging over the back of the sofa and one of the boards was down from where it had hung on the wall and was propped up near the door.

'You'll freeze out there,' she commented. 'Is Paul coming to the beach to watch?'

'Paul? No – he'll be swanning about at his folks' place in the velvet monogrammed slippers his mum will have bought him. He 'fessed up a couple of months back, when he was telling me which rugs we needed, that he's always fancied a pair so I let on to his mother. He only needs a quilted smoking jacket to complete the look, the big fairy.' He laughed. 'And yes, I'm allowed to call him that. He calls me worse.'

Thea was amused. 'Some couples do go in for insulting nicknames, don't they?'

'I expect so,' he said, looking vague. 'It's been a while since I called anyone anything fond. Apart from you, Elf.' He smiled at her, looking strangely bashful. Before she could reply to that, he asked, 'Do you want a slug of medicinal Christmas brandy in this?' He indicated the coffee.

'No, thanks. There's a lot of day to get through. I'll wait till later.'

'Me too. So sensible, aren't we?' They went and sat by the fire where Woody was lying with his tummy turned to absorb the heat. His little face seemed to be smiling and his body twitched in his sleep.

'Dreaming,' Sean said quietly. 'Who wouldn't want the life of a pampered cat? He must have been a human who had a very saintly life. To be reincarnated as some-one's loved cat has to be a reward, doesn't it?'

'It does. It makes being a dog seem like really hard work, by comparison. They always look as if they're trying so hard to please their people.' She was thinking of Benji, that great mass of curly orange fur who'd stand in front of Rich panting to be taken out, bringing his ball and his lead and waiting with his black tongue hanging out and trembling with eagerness. He'd been a sweet dog and she suddenly missed his big soft presence. She didn't, she realized, miss Rich any more. Not at all.

'Hmm – not sure. I never think those tiny handbag dogs look as if they want to please anyone but themselves. Nor do they ever look particularly pleased by anything, the same way cats do.'

'True. Coming back as one of those must be a disappointment. It says, "Sorry, nice try but not quite good enough".'

There was a small silence. Sean was looking at Thea. 'You're very silly, you know, Elf.'

'Am I?' She felt slightly hurt.

'Yes. In a good way. You're almost as silly as I am. I love it. There aren't many like you out there. You're a rarity.' He clinked his mug against hers. 'A very Merry Christmas to you.'

He hadn't kissed her this time, she thought as she left the Stables. Not a Christmas peck or a hug or anything. Thea rather wished he had – she'd have been ready for it, not awkwardly caught by surprise. Sean was so warm and – she had to admit – rather beautiful. OK, so he wasn't on the available list but she liked the easy way he'd gone for some minor physical contact with her in the last few days. It felt good to be hugged, to be stroked a bit. She hoped he hadn't thought she'd been wondering if he fancied her and was now withdrawing to a safe distance to make sure she got the message. It was fine – it didn't need spelling out. Or maybe it was what she'd so stupidly blurted out about this being the day she should have been having a baby. He hadn't asked her about that – he had just let it go and now she wondered if it had embarrassed him or whether he'd thought it was just too much information. After all, what a thing to come out with to someone you'd only met a few days before! It probably wasn't a great idea to give them instant pictures in their head of you going through childbirth. They'd want to press 'delete' on that, immediately.

She was about to go into the house through the side door and up the back staircase to her room, but instead she took the phone out of her pocket and looked to see if Rich had left a message. There was a voicemail. She didn't feel like being on the premises with all the others while she listened to it; even her own room wasn't safe from invasion by a family member wondering where she was, the children showing her a toy or Emily wanting to borrow some eyeshadow, so she wandered down the driveway and into the shrubbery.

Happy Christmas, Thea. Just wanted to talk to you, see how you are on this day of all of them. Call me, if you get a chance. Lots of love to you.

Well, that was a surprise, she thought, leaning against a tree. So he'd remembered. She'd thought he'd obliterated all awareness that there'd been the beginnings of their baby from his mind for ever. She'd call him back. Maybe at last he realized it could have meant more to him than the inconvenience that he'd thought it at the time.

'Rich? Hi, it's me.'

'Thea. How are you?'

'I'm very well, thanks.' The 'very' mattered. She didn't want him to have the slightest doubt that she was OK without him. 'I'm down in Cornwall with the family.'

'*Cornwall?*' He made it sound as if she was halfway to Mars. 'Well, that's nice. Do send them my kind regards.' He sounded so formal. She remembered how he'd always seemed years older than he was, with the vocabulary of his parents' generation as if he'd never really mixed with his own age group.

'I just wondered, Thea – I wanted you to have something. But obviously I have to ask you first.'

For one awful moment she wondered if he was about to tell her he'd changed his mind and would she marry him after all. She could imagine him down the phone, turning that diamond ring over and over in his hand as he had done the first time. It would be a no. A polite and gentle no, but a definite one.

'I wanted to ask you . . . would you like a puppy? Benji's sired a litter.'

'Oh, how sweet! Give him a pat from me, won't you? I do miss him sometimes.'

'You could have your own Benji then.'

Did she want a puppy? Not really – she was out working most of the day. What on earth would she do with it? Take it with her? The class would love that. The school, less so.

'That's very kind of you, Rich, but I really can't have a dog. It wouldn't be fair on it.'

'Are you sure? Liz says we can let you have it for half the going price. Great pedigree, obviously.'

Price? So it wasn't even a gift? If ever there was a moment to have your breath taken away, this was it.

'You want to *sell* me a puppy?' she managed to say.

'Well, yes. So you don't want one then? Shame. It would have been nice for you to have something to remember us by.'

'Yes, it would,' she said, feeling very down, suddenly.

'Well, never mind. I'm sure I'll find him a good home. And it's good to talk to you again, on this special day.'

'It is special, isn't it?' she murmured into the phone. Well, at least he acknowledged that much; it was something.

'Yes. Christmas Day – always the year's highlight. Anyway, I won't keep you. Liz says hello.'

And he was gone, just as she realized he had completely forgotten the day's other significance.

Thea rolled a good solid snowball and hurled it at a

tree trunk. 'Fucking *tosser!*' she shouted as loudly as she could, hoping the essence of the message made it all the way up the country to Cheshire.

THIRTEEN

There wasn't much more preparation that needed to be done, foodwise. Charlotte had dealt with the sprouts the day before and had now impressed Anna by attacking the potatoes like a demon and peeling a mountain of them, a glass of wine already by her side. They were waiting in the biggest saucepan, which Charlotte had referred to as a cauldron, doing a bit of witchy cackling as she peeled. Maria's red cabbage with apples was ready in its casserole dish to be heated up, and Anna had made sorrel and parsnip sauce to put in the little puff-pastry vol-au-vent cases she'd already made the previous afternoon. All this would wait to be cooked till the turkey came out of the oven later and was resting. Alec contributed a jar of spiced cranberries that his mother had made before she left for her cruise, and Elmo and Rosie had chopped a lot of holly and ivy from the driveway and were going to use it to decorate the table once the melted snow had dried from it.

'Maybe we should add bits of that mistletoe as well,' Jimi suggested. 'It's not as if there isn't enough of the stuff.'

But Anna wasn't keen. 'I think we should leave it where it is,' she said. 'I don't trust it. I have a feeling it's too powerful to sit tidily on a table and not get up to any mischief.'

'Along the lines of "bad vibes, man"?' Alec said, teasing her, but Thea noticed him giving Charlotte a bit of a look. The mistletoe had worked some kind of spell for them, she recalled from late the night before. That had been some clinch she'd accidentally witnessed – Christmas spirit by the truckload. Charlotte's face gave nothing away but she wriggled her hips a bit as she stirred the bread sauce.

'Something like that, yes,' Anna admitted with a grin. 'I'm not superstitious but I can't help thinking it shouldn't be mucked about with. It's safer to leave it where it is.'

'We could take it down and put it outside,' Rosie said. 'Or would it not like that either?'

'I really don't think it would,' Anna said. 'In fact, I don't think we should even talk about it. It might hear.'

'Have you been at the fizz, Mum?' Emily asked, with no hint of a smile. 'It's only a bit of a plant, you know.'

'No, of course I haven't! Though I intend to as soon

as I've had a walk to the beach and back. Thea, do you know what time the surfers are going out?'

'Pretty soon, I think. We should probably make a start. I want to watch Sean. He's world-class, ex-pro, and apart from on films, I've only ever seen people on boards do a couple of metres and then fall off.'

It was good timing, in terms of the planned mid-afternoon lunch. The turkey was cooking away in the Aga and when Anna opened the oven door to baste it, it filled the house with the gorgeous scent of Christmas and there was now time to go out and work up an appetite on the beach. Charlotte and Alec went outside to the back terrace to have a cigarette and then came back in and asked if anyone minded if they didn't go with them.

'Of course we don't mind. It's not compulsory,' Anna told Alec. 'It's fine – you can do whatever you like.'

'Isn't it compulsory, though? What about that big list of who's doing what and when?' Charlotte looked at Thea.

Just as Thea was wondering with mild suspicion what the two of them had in mind for when everyone else was out of the house, Alec surprised her.

'We thought we might go to the service down at the church,' he said. 'Do you want to come too, Anna? And what about you, Mike? I heard you both missed out on the carols yesterday and Charlotte fancies a sing.'

'No, actually, I won't, thanks,' Anna told him guiltily. 'I just want to get out and feel the salty air on my face. If I sit around in a hot church with masses of others I'll only wish I was having a fast, cold walk. I'd start fidgeting.' She went with him into the sitting room. 'You don't mind, do you, Alec? I feel as if I'm neglecting you. It's just there are so many of us, you know . . . and it's not the easiest of situations, is it?'

They were alone in the room and he put his arms round her, which didn't feel as comfortable as it used to, not after the night before and Mike. Alec no longer seemed to 'fit'.

'It's not a problem,' he said immediately. 'I'm not a child, you know; I don't need mummying.'

She pulled away, a bit miffed at the reminder, intentional or otherwise, that she was so much older than he was. Freeing herself from his grip, she went to put a couple more logs on the fire.

'Here, let me,' he said, taking the logs and placing them in a way that she wouldn't have chosen. They wouldn't burn like that – they needed to be crossways and have better contact with the hot base. That annoyed her too. She really must try to be less prickly.

'You coming to the beach, Mum?' Emily appeared with her children, all wrapped up in their coats and each of them wearing new matching hats and scarves, a present from Rosie. How sweet they looked, Anna thought.

'Right with you,' she replied. 'I'll just get my coat and boots on. I'll see you later, Alec. Enjoy the service.'

'We will.' He nodded. 'We'd better get going too – it starts at eleven thirty. I'll go and find Charlotte.'

He moved towards her and Anna realized how much she really didn't want him to kiss her, especially as the children were still in the room . . . but not only because of that. But he simply squeezed her arm and walked on past her. Oh, the relief, she thought as she sneaked back to prod the logs into a better position and put the guard safely in place, but there was a tinge of sadness too. She'd very much enjoyed their minor romance but now it really would have to end. She just didn't feel like 'that' about him. If there was a way to stay friends then she did hope they'd find it, but otherwise – well, she doubted there'd be a broken heart on either side but it would be a shame not to be able to meet again back home.

Still, for now it was time for a proper Christmas family walk. The thought very much cheered her.

The snow had stopped and the sky was blue and bright, but it was still too cold for thawing. Thea wrapped her scarf across her mouth and wished she still had long hair, which had always kept her neck from being chilled in the depths of winter. She pulled her furry ear-flapped hat down tight for maximum warmth and descended the path as fast as the holding of Milly's hand would allow.

'Want to go on the sledge!' Milly protested, trying to pull away from Thea. Sam was ahead, carrying the sledges of the small children. Elmo had been persuaded away from the sofa and his iPad and was on his sledge, bumping and bouncing and whooping his way down the hillside in a terrifying manner, incurring the envy of Milly.

'It's too steep here, darling. When we get to the bit near the bottom you can have a go on it.'

Milly stamped and pouted. 'Want to do it now! I want to go on the steep bit then it'll go really fast, like Elmo.'

'But it's all rocky under the snow. You could hurt yourself. And anyway, we're nearly there now.'

'Elmo could be hurt too, so why can he do it?'

'Because he's much older than you and his mummy and daddy haven't said no.'

'It's not *fair*.' Milly dragged the word out for several seconds. For a moment, Thea was tempted simply to tell her that no, it wasn't. Life often sodding well wasn't. But it was also not fair to inflict the mildly resentful mood that was left over from the conversation with Rich on a child of seven.

There were more than a dozen surfers on the beach. A few others were already in the water, lying on boards and slowly paddling out to sea. In wetsuits and neoprene hoods, they made Thea think of seals that had been dieting as they bobbed about in the waves. The air was still and calm, but the winds and storms of the pre-Christmas weeks had left the waves big and rolling.

'Hmm – he's pretty buff, isn't he?' Thea was surprised by Emily's statement and looked across the beach to the object of her sister's unusual admiration. It was Sean. He was pulling his wetsuit up over a tight Lycra rash vest. He saw Thea and waved, and came over to her and Emily, still squeezing his arm into a sleeve.

'Should be a good one today,' he said. 'Hope I don't disgrace myself out there in front of you.'

Emily smiled at him. 'Oh, I'm sure you'll be highly impressive.'

'Are you?' He looked a bit puzzled. Thea could feel her face getting warm. What on earth was Emily doing, putting on a voice that was almost a purr? Was she flirting?

'How's the patient?' Sean rallied a bit and asked Emily. 'She doesn't look like she's still suffering from the fall.' Sam was putting Milly on the sledge and the little girl was squealing with anticipation, even though she hadn't yet moved an inch on the snow.

'Oh no, she's fine. Just a couple of bruises to her knee. Thanks so much for coming out to help.'

Thea would swear Emily was fluttering her eyelashes. She hadn't even realized women actually did that and she'd never have thought her sister would be the type who even gave it a go. She could feel herself getting cross, and jealous that Sean was smiling back at Emily the way she liked him smiling at *her*. Childish and silly, she thought, deciding this too was entirely Rich's fault. Trying to sell her a puppy and actually forgetting their baby totally. Jeez.

'It was nothing. You and Thea had it covered anyway. Look, I'd better go and get on with it.' He then said to Thea, 'Could I ask you a quick favour?'

'Of course.' She hoped it wasn't a request to leap into the freezing waves with him, though maybe it would jolt her glooms away.

'Part of the leash on my zip has come adrift.' He turned to reveal that the back of the wetsuit hadn't yet been fastened. 'Would you mind . . . ?'

'Oh – yes, sure.' She grasped the broken neoprene tag and pulled up the zip. It felt like a very intimate thing to be doing and she also had a slightly shocking urge to put her hands on his broad back and simply stroke it, even to lay her head against it. Then the moment was over. He'd have thought her completely mad and possibly it would have counted as sexual harassment. Not that she was thinking sexual, just warm affection. It was a good feeling, way better than the one where she was pointlessly cross with Rich, and one she'd be reluctant to leave behind when she went back home.

Thea and Emily watched as Sean picked up his board and jogged down to the water's edge where surfers –

mostly male but a few girls as well – were assembling.

'Funny how they all do that, isn't it?' Thea commented, seeing a few others running for the sea. 'None of them just *walk* down there.'

'Like athletes running up and down on the spot before a race, I suppose,' Emily agreed, looking round for the children. Sam was now hauling them both up the snowy slope on their sledges. 'All this activity,' she murmured. 'I suppose we should do brisk walking across the bay and back, to get the appetite going for lunch.'

She didn't seem terribly inclined to move, though, and Thea was glad. She really did want to watch Sean, who was now with a couple of his mates, standing on the edge of the shore doing some warm-up stretches. Then, suddenly, he turned and waved at her and, board in hand and its curly leash attached to his ankle, he dashed into the waves and threw himself onto it.

'Rather them than me.' Rosie approached. 'How mad do you have to be to go into the freezing sea on Christmas Day?'

'It's probably not that much colder than it is out here,' Thea said, 'though I'm with you – I wouldn't want to put that theory to a practical test. It wouldn't be so much the getting in there as the coming out.'

Soon she was no longer sure which of the surfers was Sean. They were weaving about like a pod of porpoises, heading out for where the breakers started. Some caught waves and took to their boards for a while before tumbling into the water again. Several were on body-boards and whooshed onto the shore. But then, just as she and Emily were about to start their walk across the beach, one of the surfers was up on his board and riding the wave as if the sea – and not the land – was his element. Sean.

'Wow,' Emily said. 'Would you look at that . . .'

'I am, I am.' Thea watched in admiration as Sean wove about, alternately leaning into the breaker and leaping with the board over the foam. It was an astounding display. At last he reached the shore, stepped off the board as easily as if walking off a pavement edge, waved to her again and grinned. She waved back and he turned away to the sea, swimming back out to catch more waves.

She and Emily set off across the sand towards the far side where a group of teens, Elmo among them, were having a noisy snowball battle. Thea started to laugh.

'What's so funny?' Emily asked, giving her a suspicious look.

'Nothing really,' Thea told her, fighting back a fit of giggles. 'I just had a sudden thought, imagining Rich in the sea doing something like that. I can't picture it, him getting so loose and agile and – you know, *into* it. What Sean was doing was almost like dancing or something out there. Rich would have hated it.'

'He hated a lot of things. Mum thought he didn't like us, even.'

'He liked *you* because you have a proper job. And me too, I suppose,' Thea told her. 'But the rest of us' – she laughed again – *'way* too arty-farty for him. He kind of understood that Dad made a great living from the commercial end of art, but he'd never have loosened up . . .' She stopped. 'If, you know, in the future, if we'd had a child . . .'

'Yes, but—'

'Please don't say "yes, but you didn't", Em. I know that all too well.'

'I wasn't going to.' Emily took a deep breath. 'I don't want to sound after-the-eventish, but I was going to say that even if the baby had worked out, in the end I think sooner or later you'd have finished it with him. You were too different.'

'He was fun once, you know.'

'It takes more than fun.'

'I know. Well, I do now. No, you're right, I expect. What I meant was, suppose a child of ours had had a massive talent for, say, drama? Or tennis? I don't think for a minute he'd have let it go any further than a part-time hobby. He wouldn't have thought it *sensible*. It would have been something they'd be expected to grow out of before taking up being a lawyer and then golf or tennis or something that would be socially useful.' She looked back at the sea where Sean was weaving in and out of the other surfers. 'To get to be that good at something, you have to have the kind of parents who let you *fly*. I'd have wanted that. Rich simply – wouldn't.'

'Unless it was dog shows and poodle breeding,' Emily reminded her, starting to giggle.

'Oh yes. Very important and sensible, that.'

'What do you think so far? Do you reckon everyone's having an OK time?' Mike asked Anna as they sat on a rock and watched Elmo with a handful of snow chasing a pony-tailed girl – the daughter (Daisy, was it?) of Maria. She was laughing helplessly, and when Elmo caught up with her and stuffed snow down into her hood then pulled it up over her head, she shrieked but didn't seem to mind.

'I think they're having both a better and worse time than they expected,' Anna finally replied.

'Which side of that is your version?' he asked.

'Better time,' she said, smiling at him. 'Not quite what I had in mind, the way it's turned out.'

'Nor for me. Do you feel bad about Alec?'

'Yes and no. Probably about the same as you feel about Charlotte, I'm guessing.'

'She's up to something but I can't tell what,' he said suddenly.

'She should be up to a massive hangover, the amount she puts away. Still, an hour singing in the church will clear a few of the cobwebs.'

Mike looked thoughtful. 'Hmm, possibly.' He glanced up at the sky. 'More clouds coming in. The weather forecast said more snow is on its way. Unbelievable, isn't it?'

Anna shivered. 'It's so cold when the sun's gone. Shall we go back? I think it's time to check the turkey and start getting properly organized. And not wanting to sound like your girlfriend . . .'

'Ex,' he interrupted. 'Not that she really was very girlfriend-ish in the first place.'

'Well, whatever she is, was or isn't, I'm not wanting to sound like her but I could do with a drink.'

Thea hung around for a bit after the others had gone, hoping she didn't look like a star-struck idiot or something, but she was fascinated by Sean's surfing. After a few more rides, Sean came out of the water and up the beach to where she was perched on a rock. She'd cleared it of snow, but the residual dampness was seeping through her jeans and she was starting to get a bit numb with cold. The snow cat they'd made the night before was still intact, though Milly and Alfie had made a couple of dents in it and it seemed to have a new spine of pebbles along its back.

'I think Elmo would say "awesome",' Thea said as Sean approached. 'That was brilliant.'

'Thank you,' he said, dripping seawater all over her boots. 'I was showing off a bit because I knew you were there. I probably shouldn't admit that.'

'I don't see why not. A performer needs an audience.

It's what drives the show.' She thought of the children in her school class, her occasional despair that a class assembly or a show they were doing would never get beyond the hopeless-rehearsal stage. And yet, give them a hall full of eager, proud parents, and they all upped their game. She'd be back to work in under two weeks, she realized, far away from here. Normal life seemed, right at this moment, like another world and another lifetime.

'True. We all do our best moves in competitions with the biggest load of spectators. And with surfing there's the huge buzz from seeing the photographers gear up on the beach to take the shots because you know then that they rate you. It's when they don't bother and take the chance to fiddle about with their lenses or go for a beer that you get a bit down and your standard flops.'

He ran his fingers through his wet hair. It was going into long twirly curls. He must be freezing, she thought.

'Right – I'd better leave you to get dry and warm up again,' she said. 'When are you off to Paul's, and' – she looked up towards the snowy hilltop – 'how will you get there? Is the road clear?'

He laughed. 'Not clear at all. Even the Landy wouldn't make it back up the hill to here on the way back.'

'So it's walking distance then?'

'Not quite. But it is skiing distance. I've got some

cross-country ones that I've just hauled out from the back of the barn. I never thought I'd get to use them in the UK, that's for sure.'

'No, not a lot of call for skiing in Cornwall, I guess. Anyway,' Thea said awkwardly, feeling she was holding him up but reluctant to lose his company, 'I hope you have a good day. I guess you won't be back tonight.'

He looked surprised. 'Unless my head-torch breaks, in which case I'd be a loony to ski in the dark, I'm planning to get back later. I don't want to leave my clients – that's you lot – overnight, not in this weather, so I should be back. Late, though. See you tomorrow?'

'OK. Yes. On our list – the famous list – is a barbecue lunch on the beach, just simple things like sausages in buns, that kinda thing. You could join us if you're not busy. Just a thought.' She felt suddenly shy about the suggestion. He surely had plans of his own and now she wished she hadn't asked because she didn't want to hear him say no.

'I'd like to. Thanks. And' – he gave her a grin – 'could I ask you something in return?'

'Of course,' she said. 'Go ahead.'

'Will you unzip me, please?' he said, turning and pointing to the neck of his wetsuit. He looked at her over his shoulder. 'And that's not something I ask just any girl.'

'No,' she said, returning the grin. 'I can imagine it isn't.'

She left Sean chatting to his mates on the beach and walked quickly back up the hill and into the house through the back door. As she started up the staircase she heard the sounds of low giggles and whispers, and as she reached the first floor the connecting door to the staircase opened and Charlotte and Alec then started coming down towards her, dressed for the cold outdoors.

'Oh hi. How was the church?' Thea asked.

'Oh, you know, sort of carolly?' Charlotte said, clearly trying not to laugh.

'Lots of people there?'

'Mmm. One or two,' Alec said. Charlotte giggled.

'We're just nipping out to look at the view,' Alec continued. 'Won't be long.' And the two of them passed her on the stairs and went out through the back door, heading for their usual ciggy spot on the back terrace overlooking the bay.

They'd looked pretty shifty, Thea thought. It was nothing to do with her what they got up to, but she was overcome by a nosiness that she wasn't very proud of feeling but was going to give in to, all the same. Instead of going to her room she veered off along the landing and ran quickly down the front staircase. She looked up at the mistletoe, wondering if her mother was right and that it had powers. You certainly couldn't miss its presence, and it was witness to all the comings and goings both inside the house and of those on their way out of it.

As silently as she could, she opened the front door and went outside into the snow. There were plenty of footprints close to the house from earlier when she and Emily and Milly had been out with the bike. But the only ones further down the driveway were her own from when she'd taken Rich's call only a couple of hours earlier.

So, as there wasn't another way out to the road from the house, it looked like they hadn't gone to the church after all. Thea went back inside, took off her boots in the porch and ran up to her room to change into something drier and more party-ish than the damp-edged jeans and big comfy jumper she'd worn to the beach. It looked like Charlotte and Alec had changed their minds about singing carols. She imagined they'd probably opted for a bit of peace, just some time to slob about on the sofas, possibly with a sneaky drink and some of the smoked salmon from the fridge and without being surrounded by a large and overwhelming family that wasn't their own. Good for them. But why on earth had they not thought they could say so?

After so much time on the freezing beach, Thea was feeling as if her bones were chilled right through, so she went upstairs and had another quick, hot shower, fluffed up her hair and put on her purple Zara dress. It was shorter than she remembered and she thought for a second it was a bit of a waste not to have someone who would admire her legs in it, her black tights with a silver thread running through and some clunky silver jewellery and plenty of make-up.

Down in the kitchen, Anna had made up a big plate of smoked salmon with brown bread and lemon as lunch was going to be later than planned. She was carrying it through to the sitting room, behind Thea who held a bottle of champagne and glasses, when there was a knock on the front door. Thea handed the bottle and glasses to Elmo to take in to the others and she opened the door.

Sean came in, looking slightly shy. 'Sorry to interrupt you all,' he said, 'but could I ask a favour, Thea?'

'Is it to do with zips again?' she asked and then immediately blushed, horrified at how that must sound. Anna, still behind her, looked at her with eyebrows raised and a broad smile.

'Gosh, tell us more,' she said. 'Or maybe it's best not to.'

'Mum, *please*,' Thea murmured. 'Sean, come in. Would you like a drink?'

'No, thanks, better not. I'm about to get under way and I don't want to be drunk in charge of skis.'

Anna and Elmo had gone into the sitting room, leaving Sean and Thea alone. 'And no, it's not zips this time,' he said, chuckling at her.

'Sorry, you must think I'm mad.'

'Oh, *I* don't, Elf, I don't . . . but your family might,' he said cheerfully, 'but I expect they're used to you.'

He stood back then, looking as if he'd only just noticed her. 'You scrub up bloody well, you know. Great dress. And you've' – he looked down – 'got some actual legs. I wouldn't have known – I've only seen them hidden away. I was assuming you weren't the dress type.'

'I have my moments.'

'You do, don't you?' He carried on staring, as if he'd forgotten what he came over for. 'Sorry, you just look so – well, you know – gorgeous.' He looked awkward as soon as he'd said it.

'Thank you. So do you.' The draught from the outside breeze set the mistletoe swinging gently and it crossed Thea's mind that it was as if it were reminding them – as they stood beneath it – what it was there for.

'It's Woody,' Sean said, then put his hands over his face and laughed. 'Oh God, that sounds so wrong! I mean the cat. Shall I go outside, knock on the door and start again so we can both cut the double entendres?'

'Too late now!' she said, giggling. 'But I take it you mean your cat?'

'The cat. Yes, the cat. It's just in case I don't make it back tonight. I'm intending to come home but if there's a blizzard I'm not leaving Paul's place to end up dying in a ditch, so if I give you the key to the Stables, would you mind feeding Woody in the morning if I'm not there?'

'Of course I will; I'll be glad to.'

'Thanks. His food is in the cupboard over the sink,

and he likes to drink from the downstairs loo, so maybe you could flush it so it's all fresh for him?'

'Wow, that's a new one – there must be things I didn't know about cats.'

'He is a bit mad. He'll drink from the loo and also water from the shower. Never out of his bowl, though there's always some in it.'

'Right. Loo flushed, food. Got it.'

'Thanks, Thea.' He handed her the key. 'Happy Christmas again, Elf. Hope the meal goes well.'

'Thank you, surf dude. And you have a good time too.'

Sean didn't seem in a hurry to go and Thea wasn't in any hurry to let him so she felt very happy when he smiled, pointed up at the mistletoe and murmured, 'It would be rude not to, wouldn't it?' He pulled her gently towards him and kissed her. This time it wasn't awkward and mis-aimed but was soft and tender and exciting enough for her not to want it to stop, but of course it did, all too soon. She knew it was just a friendly gesture, just a thank-you about the cat. Just plain lovely, though, and it felt fabulous to have her heart thrilled, racing like that after far too long.

'I'll see you tomorrow, Elfie,' he said, opening the front door. The snow was falling again. He looked at it and frowned. 'With luck . . .'

FOURTEEN

It was all going out of control and Emily was feeling twitchy and tense. Anger at nothing in particular was building up and she felt as if she were a terrible person because she knew perfectly well you were supposed to enjoy Christmas Day. You were especially supposed to enjoy it when you had a family of whom you were deeply fond, a loving (if a bit casual in general attitude) husband, brilliant children who were healthy and bright and for whom you could provide a warm home and love and good food and enough toys to brighten their lives, but not so many that they'd be spoiled and sullen. You shouldn't feel like she did – that you want to slide out of the house and run away, alone.

Emily lay on the bed and tried calm logic on herself, breathing slowly and deeply and joining her forefingers and thumbs together as a gesture of spiritual connection. She only, she surmised, wanted to get out of the house and race off for miles in the car because at the moment, given the snow that refused to thaw or even to stop falling in entire clouds-worth quantities, she absolutely couldn't. It was the locked-in feeling that was getting to her. That was all. And maybe it was perfectly reasonable to feel like this. Perhaps everyone in the house was feeling something similar. Perhaps they were only just keeping a lid on this sense of being isolated and imprisoned, and it was rattling away beneath their surfaces just as it was in her.

She sat up and arranged her legs into a lotus position, thinking that some yoga might help, but her thighs ached. To stay supple you had to do this every day and she hadn't done any since they got here. That was something else that chewed at her mind, the sense that if she didn't keep all the plates of her own life and those of the children madly spinning, then the whole lot would crash down. She unfolded her legs and stretched them out in front of her, leaning slowly forward and placing her hands across the top of her feet. That thigh pull again. And she couldn't put her nose to her knee either, whereas she could this time last week, she was sure. It would come back, but it would take work. You couldn't take a single thing for granted, not even that. Nothing stayed the same, especially the children. Just as you think you've got the hang of your child, just as you are used to how they are, they change and are on to their inevitable next stage, and they're gradually moving away from you all the time, and will eventually fly from the nest like a winter robin. What parent of young children could bear that thought? She tried not to think of the Abba song, 'Slipping Through My Fingers', which always made her cry – but this never stopped her playing it when she felt like poking at a melancholy mood till it really hurt.

She could almost laugh at the irony – that she felt frustrated about the speed at which Alfie and Milly were growing up, but that she had this chance to do it all over again and was thoroughly frightened by the idea.

She got off the bed and went into the bathroom where the pregnancy test kit was hidden at the bottom of her sponge bag. A pee on a stick, that's all it took to find out whether you were about to make a whole new person, maybe a major cultural figure: an artist who'd change all creative perspectives or a giant of political importance. Or a serial killer or a shoplifter or someone emotionally fragile who couldn't get a grip on life. All these possibilities were inside her right now and she was fearful already for who her baby would become. She'd settle for ordinary. Healthy and ordinary would be a blessed bonus because having another baby was pushing the Luck Fairy very hard. Or maybe she wouldn't settle at all. When you'd already got everything you'd hoped for in your children, wasn't it a huge risk to go through it all again? What about Sam? Suppose it was the one extra thing too far for him?

The lines would appear on the little white wand; Emily didn't really need to do the test because her body was already telling her what it was up to, but it was part of the process. Once the evidence was there in its own little plastic form of writing, then she could decide what to do. One thing she wouldn't do, on this day of all of them, was say anything about it to Thea.

The table looked wonderful, thanks to the efforts of Elmo and Rosie. The long white cloth was decorated all down the centre with holly and ivy. There were scarlet and gold crackers and gold paper napkins that the small children had folded into star shapes under the patient and expert guidance of Thea. Rosie had finished it all off by scattering silver paper stars over the whole lot. Mike couldn't help wondering if a bit less foliage would have been a good idea if they were to have somewhere to put all the dishes of vegetables.

'Will you take some photos,' Anna asked him as she drained the carrots, 'before we all sit down and clutter it up? I thought I might make some sort of collage thing out of the pics of this Christmas.'

'Are you sure?' he murmured, coming up close, out of range of Charlotte, who was uncorking another bottle of red. 'Will it be one you really want to remember?'

She poured the carrots into a serving dish, applied butter, tarragon and pepper to them and turned to look at him. 'Well, I was thinking I might. Would I do better to forget all about it?' She gave him a questioning look.

Mike felt flustered. 'No. I mean, we are talking about Christmas here, aren't we? Are we?'

'I don't know. Are we?'

'What are you two whispering about?' Charlotte came and linked her arm through Mike's. Although he wished she hadn't, this wasn't a moment to wriggle away from her – that would be unkind and uncalled for. Besides, he was very fond of her brash personality and he admired the way she'd got stuck in and pulled her considerable weight, domestically speaking. She was a trouper, he'd give her that. All the same, he did wish she hadn't made this 'claiming' gesture right now, and right in front of Anna.

'We were just discussing whether the carrots need nutmeg,' Anna lied, but it was only a white one. 'I say they don't, because nutmeg is a hallucinogenic and the children are wired enough today as it is, without scrambling their brains even further.'

'You old hippies.' Charlotte laughed. 'You know some crazy stuff. I bet you once smoked banana skins and tried to get stoned on morning glory seeds. I read about that somewhere, some history thing about the end of the nineteen sixties.'

'I didn't know that about morning glory,' Anna admitted, deciding she'd ignore the idea that her teenage years now counted as 'history'. 'And I grow them every summer too. I must remember to give it a go next year.'

'Are you serious?' Alec asked. 'Isn't it dangerous?'

'Probably,' Anna said vaguely. 'Or not. If it really worked, they'd have taken them off sale long ago, life being all about health and bloody safety these days.'

'Here, let me take that and put it on the table,' Charlotte offered, taking the carrot dish from the work-top. 'And are you all traditional and the senior man carves the turkey, or do you do it, Anna? Whoever does it, don't give me any, will you. I don't eat meat.'

'You're a vegetarian?' Anna glared at Mike. 'Why didn't you say?'

He shrugged. 'Why me? I didn't know. I've never seen her eat.'

'Now *that* I find hard to believe,' Anna said, glancing at the ample rear end of Charlotte as she leaned over the table to put down the carrots.

'And anyway,' Mike went on, 'as I didn't know she was coming till yesterday there wasn't much I could do about it.'

'I am *in the room*, you know,' Charlotte said.

'I'd have made you something special this morning if I'd known,' Anna told her, feeling rather grumpy. There seemed something a bit passive-aggressive about Charlotte keeping this little piece of information to her-self when they were about to have a meal where the star of the event was a massive meaty bird – and then coming out with it right at the very last minute. Still, it was too late now, and come to think of it, why would she be expected to do special catering for an uninvited vegetarian? Her own upbringing told her the answer to that: in her head she could hear her mother firmly stating that if someone is staying in your house you do what you can to make them comfortable. Back in those days, though, Anna would have been pretty certain it didn't include dithering about whether or not you should be tucking them up in bed with your husband.

'No need, it's only the turkey I won't eat. There's masses of other stuff – but if there's an extra one of those little vol-au-vent things going, I wouldn't mind putting my name on it.'

'It's yours, no problem. Have as many as you like.'

'OK – everyone got a glass?' Mike said once they were all sitting down and just before they began to eat. 'Can we have a toast to the cooks – to all of them? Emily, shall I pass you some wine?'

'Er, no. I'm OK, thanks. I'm sticking to water for now.'

Thea looked at her. 'You OK?'

'Fine. Bit of a head still, you know.' Emily indicated the children who hadn't stopped moving, shouting and playing all day.

'Cheers to the cooks,' was the toast, and Mike then looked a bit awkward. 'And thanks to ... ahem ... whatever deities any of us might believe in for, well – all this. We might be snowed in but we're a lucky bunch, aren't we?'

Charlotte hiccuped and stifled a giggle. Alec, sitting beside her, gave her a nudge.

It took an amazingly short time to reduce the beautifully decorated table to a wreckage of screwed-up napkins, the carcases of crackers, spilled gravy (Milly), spilled wine (Rosie) and a line of rejected sprouts on the tablecloth (Alfie). All this effort, Thea thought, for what was essentially just a rather big roast dinner and it was a scene of near-devastation in no time. But it was happy devastation; everyone seemed very jolly and positive, which was quite an achievement, given the dynamics of the situation. Even Elmo, for once, hadn't sneaked in his phone to play with under the table, and Jimi hadn't got a pen ready beside his plate and a newpaper open at the puzzles page tucked down the back of his chair, in case of quiet moments where no one would notice what he was doing.

Crackers were pulled, a lot of cheering went on and nobody was too uptight to wear their paper crowns.

'OK, listen, everybody, joke time,' Jimi announced, unfurling a piece of paper from his cracker and reading it. 'Are we ready? Right, here it is. What's brown and sticky?'

'No idea,' Anna said. 'Go on then.'

'A stick. Ta-da!'

Thea, across the table from Charlotte and Alec,

watched as the two of them suddenly burst into the kind of laughter that wasn't going to stop before tears rolled down faces and the point was reached where everyone else was wondering if they'd heard a different joke from the one that had been read out. They leaned against each other, shrieking and silly, out of breath and near-hysterical.

'What have they been smoking out there?' Anna murmured to Mike as everyone else carried on eating and the children played with the tiny coloured pencils from Alfie's cracker and some miniature screwdrivers from Milly's.

'A Christmas spliff, at a guess,' Mike told her. 'I hope Elmo doesn't know. He's at that age.' Elmo looked up, suddenly listening eagerly.

'It was only a bit.' Charlotte had overheard him. She was still wiping her eyes and trying not to break into fresh hilarity. 'Lighten up, you two. It's proper Christmas, not a tinsel tea.'

'What's a tinsel tea?' Elmo asked. 'Is it like, glitter and stuff? Sounds cool.'

'No. Definitely not what you'd call cool. It's an outing for old people. A coach trip to the seaside and a Christmas dinner with crackers and hats,' Jimi told him.

Elmo shrugged. 'Still sounds OK. Apart from the olds.'

'Yes, I'm sure it's great – but in early October? And going for one almost every week?' Charlotte went on,

'I've done singing gigs at them in places like Worthing. Playing carols on the piano in some grim hotel on a rainy seafront, trying to get them to enjoy it while they sit there all glum in paper hats and complaining about the sprouts being under-cooked because they haven't had at least two hours of thorough boiling.'

'Which all goes to show,' Alec said, starting to laugh again, 'that a bit of weed should be handed out on the NHS to everyone over sixty to remind them that life's a laugh.'

Elmo nodded. 'Spliff. Right.' Rosie glared at Charlotte.

'Too right. Who wants to be a miserable geriatric?' Charlotte agreed, banging her glass on the table and slopping wine over the side.

There was a brief silence, broken only by the children squabbling over the last of the potatoes, during which everyone else took in how far that 'over-sixties' crack had been mis-aimed.

'Mike and I, the resident miserable geriatrics here, will bear it in mind then. Thank you so much for that,' Anna said, stony-faced.

'Ah. We didn't mean *you*, darling,' Charlotte said, reaching out a hand across the table to Anna's, which – to add insult to injury – she then patted.

Anna snatched her hand back. 'Don't *darling* me,' she almost snarled.

'Fight, fight, fight,' Elmo started, but was shushed by Jimi.

'Soz,' Elmo said, grinning as Jimi gave him a sly wink.

'It's only that you and Mike seem so much younger. It's easy to forget you're actually as old as you are,' Alec said, trying to back-pedal.

'Would you like me to get you a spade, mate?' Mike asked. 'Then you can dig a bigger hole.'

'If I do, I'll make sure I get right in it and cover it up over me. Sorry, honestly. Maybe we should completely shut up now, Charlotte, in case there's another foot-in-mouth episode.' He looked at her and they both started sniggering again.

'No feet in my mouth, sweetie. I don't eat meat.'

'That's not what you said bef— Oops.' Alec put his hand over his mouth and looked around the table.

'More turkey, anyone?' Mike asked tightly. 'Or are you all leaving room for the pudding?'

It was when Thea saw Sam reach across the table and take Emily's hand, blowing her a kiss at the same time, that she had a massive tweak of loneliness. One way or another, all the adults here had *someone* – and in some cases two people. She'd pulled her cracker with Milly, which was fine – and who doesn't love a child's delight and squeal at the flash and bang – but not with a life-time partner. It was probably the champagne getting to her and giving her a sneaky dose of the morose, but it did bring to mind how she, this time last year, had been half of a couple, on holiday with friends in a French Alpine chalet, confidently expecting to spend a contented lifetime with Rich and not even letting the idea that it could all fall to pieces have a centimetre of space in her head. And today, the date the ·baby that didn't make it had been due to be born, was passing with no one knowing about it, apart from her and Emily, who was looking as if she had something of her own on her mind.

Maudlin thoughts like these were not to be allowed any more time, Thea resolved. And besides, Anna was switching off the kitchen lights, pouring brandy over the pudding and bringing it to the table. Milly and Alfie gasped and squealed at the flames – even the adults went silent for a few moments before the flames died down and the clatter of dishes broke the spell. Jimi had insisted on custard, Emily favoured brandy butter and Anna had bought Cornish clotted cream. They were all pretty damn lucky, Thea considered. What did being fiancé-less matter? Especially one with whom you'd expected to be 'content'. It was hardly a term that anticipated a long partnership of great love and passion, was it? But somebody else some day would be good. Thea decided it would *not* be her New Year resolution to look for somebody new. She would rely, at least for a while, on going out a lot, being sociable, and on luck. And that way, who knew what would creep up and bite her when she was definitely not looking. She only hoped, as she took a first spoonful of her pudding, that it would be someone just as lovely as Sean but an awful lot more available, damn it.

*

They were all afflicted by post-lunch idleness. It was after six by the time the dishes were done and everyone was flopping around in front of the fire, tired and – in Emily's case – a bit tetchy.

'There's more to life than television,' she told the children, who wanted to watch a DVD, taking the lead from Elmo who was again absorbed in something on his iPad.

'It might calm them down a bit,' Sam said, still picking up bits of paper and the endless multi-coloured circles of elastic from Milly's Rainbow Loom that had gone all over the floor. 'Why don't you make another loom band, Mills?' he said as she rolled about on the rug and glared at everyone.

'Don't want to,' she whined. 'Wanna watch something. I'm bored.'

'Bored isn't allowed,' Charlotte said sharply. 'How can you be bored with all these lovely presents you've got?'

'Thank you, Charlotte, but I'll deal with her,' Emily said.

'Sorry – I just can't bear to hear children say they're bored like that,' Charlotte went on. 'It sounds so spoiled.'

'They're not spoiled,' Emily said tersely.

'I didn't say they were; I just said "bored" *sounds* spoiled. I was never allowed to say it when I was little. I was always told to go and read something.'

'We always read to them when they go to bed.' Emily wasn't going to let it go. 'We don't need to be told.'

'Em, I'm sure Charlotte was only trying to be helpful,' Sam said. 'And frankly, she's not wrong about Milly sounding spoiled. I mean, God knows the child's got enough to occupy her. *Too* much.'

'She's full of food and could do with a walk. If we were back home in London and had had lunch at a proper time, we'd be out in the park by now, on the swings,' Emily said. 'Instead, we're stuck behind a snow wall in the dark. We're trapped.'

She went to the window and peered out into the darkness. The snow seemed to rise up at her from the ground, the pale, rounded monster-shapes of trees, the garden furniture and the shrubs all looking as if they weren't just innocent items but all kinds of evil scariness, hiding under thick, freezing blankets. Beyond the end of the garden was the hillside edge, leading down to the sea, another of nature's terrors, sitting there looking beautiful but all the time waiting to murder you. She turned away from the window and closed the curtain firmly over the view, wishing she could stop wasting her time – and she knew perfectly well it was a waste – on such morbid thoughts. Maybe it was because of this tiny, vulnerable seed of a baby growing inside her. The potential for so much to go wrong, including the end of her and Sam. Hell, what *was* he going to say?

'Nobody's trapped,' Anna said gently, trying to calm

down her daughter who was looking way too nervy for someone who was having a highly luxurious and supposedly near-effort-free Christmas. She addressed the room in general. 'We can still go out for some exercise, work off that Christmas dinner feeling. Anyone else up for going out to the garden and making a big, fat snowman who can look out at the sea?'

'Meee!' shouted Alfie. Milly stopped rolling her body around on the rug and started to sit up. She seemed to be giving the matter some deep thought.

'Do I have to?' Elmo said. 'I'm at level six.'

'You know you want to really,' Jimi teased. 'So yes.'

'I'll come,' said Charlotte.

'And me,' joined in Thea. 'Come on, Milly, we can give the snowman one of the paper hats from the crackers. He'll like that.'

'*Okaay.*' Milly allowed herself to be persuaded and Sam sent them off to find boots and coats and gloves.

'Looks like it's all of us then?' Anna said, prodding at Mike with her foot. He was lying back on the purple sofa, going through the TV listings in a four-day-old newspaper. If the children weren't to be allowed to watch television, she thought it would be tactless for him suddenly to switch on yet another viewing of the Christmas edition of *Porridge*.

'I'm there, I'm there,' he said, allowing Charlotte to take his hand and pull him up from the cushions.

It was as Thea crossed the hall on the way to get her

coat that she noticed a piece of the mistletoe was missing. The shadows cast by the huge bunch had changed shape. For a moment she put it down to the heat – the foliage and berries were certain to shrink as they became dehydrated. But the shape the bunch had cast until this evening had been something almost perfectly round; now it was like an orange with a segment or two missing. She went over and put her hand up to it; the mistletoe had been snipped close to its centre and a couple of medium-sized twigs of it had gone. Thea felt almost like stroking it, fondly remembering that crazy escapade with Sean to collect it. Was it only a few days ago? It was probably because they were now unable to drive beyond the hill to the village that made her feel as if they'd been in the house for ever. The thought of leaving it in a couple of days' time was also quite odd: was there still an actual functioning world beyond the snow – or had the whole world stopped?

It felt a bit warmer outside in the garden than it had that morning on the beach, maybe because the breeze had dropped and they were in the shelter of the house. All the same, the snow wasn't in any hurry to melt and Thea was glad of her furry hat and sheepskin boots. The children were racing around now on the lawn, rolling up a big fat ball of snow with Sam, illuminated by the lights on the outside of the house that shone on the terrace area. She stood back for a moment and watched them, loving the contrast between Milly's earlier languid ennui in the warm sitting room and the way she now bounced around in the chill air, completely involved in her task. Thea found this with the children in her class at school: give them a project that involved being out in the fresh air – collecting leaves to identify, learning about birds and their habitats – and they livened up enormously.

'Someone's been chopping chunks off the mistletoe,' she said, when most of the grown-ups were within hearing range, curious as to who would own up, and why.

'Good. That thing is obscenely big,' Emily said. 'It's an inducement to far more than a bit of innocent kissing.' She was staring hard at Charlotte, who was laughing with Sam as they added devil horns to the head of the snowman. They seemed to be play-fighting over who got to do what and Thea watched Emily go tense as Charlotte shoved Sam aside using her hip in a way that made it look as if she was somehow rubbing her bottom against him.

'You think?' Anna said. 'It's only a bit of greenery, Emily. And I wouldn't worry about *her*. After a couple of days you won't have to see her again. And it's not your husband she's been – er, close to.'

'So are you still saying Dad's your husband, Mum?' Emily asked. 'You're not really going to get divorced, are you?'

'Oh, I expect so,' Anna said. 'It was what we decided.'

'You can always change your minds,' Thea said. 'People do, one way or another.'

'Let's leave it, Tee,' Anna said. 'I don't want to think about it right now. Here, give this hat to Milly and tell her to put it on the snowman.'

Thea got hold of the terrace's balustrade to go down the steps to the lawn and suddenly, all was dark. 'Power cut,' Mike said. 'Bloody hell, now what?'

There were several moments of utter stillness as everyone's eyes tried to get used to the lack of light.

'I knew it. I knew something like this would happen. No way out of this sodding place and now no lights.'

Thea stepped closer to Emily, whose voice had suggested she was close to tears.

'It's OK,' she said cheerfully. 'I bet it's all back on in a couple of hours. Don't worry. I'll go in and get a torch – there's one in the room where the wellie boots are. You stay right there.'

The moon was hidden by clouds but the snow's brightness helped light her way. Thea stepped carefully, fearful of dropping down into unseen gulleys and dips, and as soon as she could, she felt her way along the side of the house to the back door. Just as she opened it, something furry brushed across her ankles and she almost squealed. Then there was a soft miaow. Woody. She reached down and picked him up, hoping she wouldn't get her hand scratched again, but he settled against her and purred. It was darker in the house than outside and she didn't want him to plait himself round her feet as she walked and trip her up.

The boot-room door was open just ahead. She concentrated on picturing where exactly she'd seen the torch.

'Boo!'

Thea nearly hit the ceiling with fright. 'Alec! What the hell are you *doing*?'

'Looking for the torch that was in here. I didn't know someone else would be doing the same thing.'

'But you were there when I said I was going to come inside.'

'I wasn't – I didn't go outside. I was having a sneaky look on my iPad at Facebook. On the other hand, now you're here . . .'

'Now I'm here, let's get the torch and then we can find the candles and get some light going in here.'

'Yes, but seeing as it's Christmas . . .' Her sight was getting used to the darkness in the boot room and she saw Alec's eyes gleaming at her, looking eager. He held up in front of him a piece of the mistletoe and leaned in towards her.

'OK then,' she said, grinning at him as she watched him close his eyes in keen anticipation only to flash them open again in shock as he found himself kissing the furry, whiskery nose of Woody.

'Whoa! What the fuck?' Alec stepped back, fast,

recoiling from the cat, and fell against the bench, sending wellington boots tumbling to the floor.

'Cats like Christmas kisses too,' Thea told him. 'Now – where's that torch?'

Milly was crying when Thea returned with the torch and with Alec trailing behind her. Emily was cuddling both her children and a brief pass of the torchlight over her face showed a look of terror and panic.

''S'great. Liking the darkness,' Elmo said, still patting a snow nose onto the big figure they'd all made.

'It's *not* great,' Emily snapped at him. 'This could go on for *weeks*. Isn't there someone we could phone? There must be an emergency number. Can we go into the house now, please? All of us?'

The snowman moment seemed to have passed so they all trooped in, following Thea with the torch, Elmo lobbing a final snowball from the rear and making Emily jump as it landed beside her.

In the sitting room, Thea and Anna lit candles and Mike poured more drinks.

'Takes me back,' he said. 'All those three-day weeks back in seventy-four. Then later on, the miners' strike.'

'I don't remember either of those,' Charlotte said morosely. She curled up on a chair and sighed, sounding close to sleep. 'What now? A sing-song? Shall I give you my "Delilah"?'

'Oh please don't,' Anna muttered.

'Save it till tomorrow at the pub,' Mike suggested. 'I'm

not sure we could cope with it in a domestic setting.'

'I was only offering.'

'We appreciate it,' Jimi said. 'In fact, I wouldn't mind—'

'Yes, you would,' Rosie said. 'And besides, we're enjoying the peace and quiet.'

'Cake. We need cake,' Thea said. 'Also cheese. I fancy cheese. I'll go and get it.'

She took the torch and went into the kitchen but felt conscious of someone behind her. Bloody Alec again. 'Alec, what are you doing?' He made her nervous, creeping about.

'I wanted to apologize. About earlier.'

'And to make sure I'm not going to say anything?' She shone the torch into the larder and found the cake tin, pulling it out and holding it against her front in case he made another move. She did *not* want to snog her mother's . . . friend.

'I suppose so. I didn't mean to.' His voice faded out and he went to the fridge and took out the big Stilton.

'Did you think I was someone else?'

'Um, not really. It was just a bit of fun. I mean, you're – y'know – single and it's Christmas.'

'Fair game then, you thought?' she said. 'But I felt ambushed.'

'I had mistletoe.'

'You've also got my mum, for heaven's sake. Oh, and Charlotte, no?'

'Oh.'

'Exactly.' She went to the drawer and pulled out a knife, enjoying, as she shone the torch briefly into his face, Alec's sudden look of fright.

'It's only to cut the cake, Alec,' she said. 'You don't have to look so scared.'

'Really?'

'I promise.'

FIFTEEN

Well, that was an abrupt end to Christmas, Anna thought as she woke up in the pale grey dawn light of Boxing Day. She'd have thought it quite romantic, herself, given perfect circumstances, finishing the day in the candlelit sitting room after coaxing the kettle to boil on the Aga. Its heat had been almost exhausted by the day's cooking and it hadn't had more than a couple of hours to rally before being cut off by the power failure. 'It won't make any difference to it,' Alec had declared rather bossily. 'I was brought up with an Aga and that's the one great thing – they'll still be warm and working even in a power cut.' He'd taken a lot of convincing that in this case he was wrong and it had made the mood in the kitchen a bit edgy.

'These aren't the days of bunging in coal and praying to it,' Mike had told him. 'This sort needs electricity too, you know. A spark.'

'Oooh, it's a stand-off.' Charlotte had giggled, watching the two men square up to each other on the technical details. 'It's you they're really fighting over, Anna.'

Anna, now rolling over and snuggling close to the warm naked back of Mike, would have had to be a saint not to feel a bit pleased at that comment, however throwaway and possibly untrue it had been. So there'd been half-brewed tea for her and Emily and Thea, and more wine with cake and some of Alec's Stilton for the rest of them, and Sam had read to them from Dylan Thomas's *A Child's Christmas in Wales* until they were all dropping off to sleep and called it a night. There'd been some awkward shuffling around where they all failed to work out the etiquette for kissing goodnight (Charlotte hugged Anna, Anna kissed Jimi and Thea), until Mike grumpily stated that he didn't need a night-night kiss and that next they'd be wanting a chapter or two of *Winnie the Pooh*.

Anna had been the last one to go up to bed, lit by the torch in her phone which was possibly not a good idea as it would use up the battery very fast and there'd be no way of recharging it. As it was, she'd been getting into bed and the text message signal had pinged, showing a *Good night, Happy Christmas* message from Alec. Oh Alec, she thought now as she rolled back to her own side of the bed. What was she going to do about him – and had she given him a terrible Christmas? But you couldn't get it right for everyone in a big party and he'd known all along that it was a risk to come and stay. But she didn't like to think of him that last night, getting into bed alone and sending her that poignant little message. Surely he couldn't have been hoping that she'd join him?

Mike had fallen asleep almost immediately as they'd got into bed. There'd been no suggestion of a repetition of the previous night's activities and Anna had been surprised to find she was mildly disappointed. On the other hand, he wouldn't have noticed if she'd crept out and gone along the corridor to Alec's room – not that she would have done. The thought now filled her with – not revulsion, not at all – but a sense of nothingness in terms of attraction, and she felt a bit guilty about that. Only a couple of weeks ago she'd found him irresistible. But then, just as she was lying there with her eyes wide open, feeling bad about Alec, she remembered how he'd been giggling with Charlotte, the unthinking comments about 'over-sixties', and she pulled herself together and became more resolute. What Alec needed was someone his own age to play with. And in Charlotte, he'd quite possibly found her.

Woody was still on Thea's bed where he'd spent the whole night, stretched out alongside her and breathing evenly and slowly, snoring slightly now and then.

There'd been no sign of life from the Stables late last night, so clearly Sean had stayed overnight at Paul's. She was glad and not glad. Obviously she wouldn't have wanted him to risk a horridly frozen death by skiing home alone in the night across goodness knows how many miles of icy roads, woods and/or fields, especially as even the few streetlights there were through the village would be out of action with the power cut. But at the same time, she realized she was really quite envious of Paul. Truly, she'd be glad to get back to her own home now, because having feelings for a man who was not only already in a relationship but also with someone who happened to be of the opposite sex to her was the behaviour of the most desperate kind of singleton. And she wasn't desperate. The words 'you can't help who you fall for' came to mind but she pushed them out of her brain. You might not be able to help it in theory, but please, she thought, let her have the common sense not to make the object of her desire some gay bloke she barely knew. It was true maiden aunt territory, this, and she was *way* too young to turn into the old-fashioned version of that. If she ever told him about it, Sean would probably find it pretty damn funny, but geography being what it was, she might well never see him again after a couple of days from now.

She stroked Woody's flank and he stretched out his front legs, flexed his claws and gave a long sleepy purr.

It had been a risk, letting him stay with her through the night, but she didn't like to think of him all alone in the Stables with no heating and no Sean. If he'd wanted to go out in the night, she had a little torch on her key-ring to light her way down the stairs, but he'd stayed put.

It was nearly light but she thought about staying in the cosiness of her bed for a bit longer so she wouldn't have to face Alec. It made her feel almost queasy, the idea that he didn't think twice about the mother/daughter scenario. Still, he'd apologized and probably thought she was a prissy little twit. Better, though, than assuming she'd be grateful for the attention.

She turned over and flicked the bedside light on just to see if they'd got the power back. They had. Phew, that was a piece of unexpected luck. It must have been just a local blip rather than a full-scale wire-down, which might have taken days to fix, or even the weeks that Emily had panicked about. For a few minutes, she cuddled back under the duvet and shut her eyes, but she was past sleep. On her organizing list she'd scheduled a barbecue on the beach for everyone at lunchtime today. When she'd drawn up the list she'd had the kind of reasonably balmy (if often wet) midwinter Cornwall weather in mind, nothing like the snow and ice that they'd got, and if the power was going to be unreliable then the pair of disposable barbecues she'd brought with her would be brilliantly useful. Perhaps they should save them in case they were really needed. On the other hand, getting out of the house would be a welcome relief, if only for the hour or so they'd be able to cope with the cold. Or maybe a ramble through the snowy woods would be a better idea. She could show the children the beginnings of the new buds on the trees, just as she would on a school nature walk. Perhaps they'd do that in the afternoon, just her and the children, which would give Emily and Sam some time on their own.

Woody opened his eyes and sat up, yawned and stared at Thea.

'Do you want to go out?' she asked him, half-expecting a verbal answer. He seemed quite a communicative cat. Sean had said that Siamese like to keep a noisy running commentary going. He slowly blinked at her and she did the same back to him then got out of bed and went to see if there was any hot water so she could quickly shower before getting dressed and taking him across to the Stables for his breakfast. Amazingly, the water ran hot – so the power must have come back on reasonably fast – and she opened the new Cowshed shower gel called Knackered Cow. Rosie, who had given it to her for Christmas, had said it seemed appropriate for an overworked teacher but hadn't offered any explanation as to why she'd given Emily the one named Grumpy Cow. Thea lavished it over her body, giving her hair a quick wash as well.

She felt almost elated as she dressed in jeans and her favourite floppy turquoise sweater and realized then how much she'd been dreading Christmas Day. It was so good to have it over and done with! Of course, she knew that the due date for a baby's birth isn't set in stone and hers could well have hung on till many days later, but all the same, she did feel very new-startish now that the date was past and the whole episode could fade into something that had been sad but was over and simply hadn't been meant to happen.

With her hair still wet and roughly flicked into place, Thea put on her boots and a scarf, grabbed Sean's door key and bounced down the back stairs with Woody alongside. He was miaowing now and looking keen to get out.

'Whose is that, d'you reckon?' Jimi was outside the back door, having an early cigarette. He pointed to where the cars were parked. Alongside Mike's Sierra stood a big scarlet tractor with a scoop attachment on the front.

'No idea. Someone who's come to clear the snow from the road?'

'Maybe,' Jimi said. 'Whoever they are, they're not in the house, I don't think. Could be lurking somewhere, though, I suppose.'

'Maybe Charlotte sneaked out in the night and made a new friend,' Thea couldn't resist saying.

'Nothing about that one would surprise me,' he said,

chuckling at the idea. 'She's quite a piece of work, isn't she?'

'She's OK, though, I think.'

'Oh yes, I don't *not* like her. She's got a lot of oomph. Don't see her as our new stepmother, though, do you?'

Thea laughed. 'Stepmother? Do you really think it would have come to that?' It hadn't crossed her mind, the idea that after her parents divorced, they could remarry. Of course, they easily might.

'No, I don't think so. I don't suppose they were splitting up just so they could rush into the same old thing all over again. But who knows?' He stubbed out his cigarette, only half-smoked – his version of cutting back – against the wall and opened the door to go back inside. 'Whoever they end up with, if anyone, I'd put folding money on it not being either of these two house-guests.'

Thea went across to Sean's front door and put the key in the lock, only to have the door opened abruptly from the other side and Paul to greet her with 'Well, good morning! The Elf returns.' Paul was looking strangely glamorous for such an early hour, with his George Clooney-perfect hair and a dark blue velvet jacket over a soft and flannelly-looking pink shirt.

'Oh! Sorry – I just came to feed the cat. I assume Sean is back then.'

'Yes, we're both here. Coffee?'

'Well, I don't want to get in the way . . .'

'No, no – come in,' he insisted, holding the door wider and flashing a lime-green lining to the jacket. 'You're very welcome, and if we argue on the doorstep all the warmth will slide out again.'

Thea went inside and Woody rushed to the kitchen and sat on the floor looking up at the cupboard where Sean had told her the cat food was kept.

'We heard about the power cut so we dashed over here first thing to see if you needed anything, but by the time we got here the power was magically returned to us,' Paul said, filling the kettle. 'Sean felt very bad about leaving you all to it and was all for whirling back here at midnight on his skis like that old Cadbury's Milk Tray advert.' He looked a bit dreamy. 'That was one of my first. I was a mere infant, Assistant Art Director on a supposedly ironic version of that advert.'

'Ah, so that's where your background in design came from?'

'Yes. Though on that day I wasn't really up to speed. I remember being told off for getting the wrong type of rope for the actor to swing on through the window. It was the beginning of learning about how much detail matters.'

The door at the far side of the sitting room opened just then and Sean came in, wearing only a large white towel round his waist and rubbing at his wet hair with another one. Thea's heart rate went up a fair bit and she told herself not to be so ridiculous. All the same, whichever bus he was on, his naked and still tanned torso was a pretty gorgeous sight.

'Oh – hi, Thea!' he said. 'Happy Boxing Day. Er, sorry, just fresh out of the shower. Maybe I should, um . . .'

'I'm sure the lady has seen the odd half-dressed chap before,' Paul said, then turned to her. 'Or have you, m'dear? But maybe you should put something on, Sean, love. You might catch a chill.'

'Shall I feed Woody?' Thea asked as Sean started back towards the bedroom. She felt a bit flustered, as if she'd almost caught the two of them *in flagrante*, and needed something to do. It was such a sweet domestic scene of coupledom and she wished she didn't feel so sneakily – and pointlessly – envious.

'Oh, would you mind? Thanks,' Sean said. 'Paul doesn't do cats so it's no good me asking him. I won't be a sec. I hope he's making you some coffee?'

'You like him, don't you?' Paul suddenly said very quietly as she was opening the cupboard and pulling out a sachet of Sheba.

Thea felt caught out, embarrassed and rather ashamed, as if she'd been rumbled actually planning to steal someone else's partner. What was Paul about to do? Give her a firm warning to back off? She decided to pre-varicate a bit, try to get some composure back. 'Of course! Woody's a very friendly cat. What's not to like?'

She bent to pour the horribly smelly cat food into Woody's bowl. He was pushing at her hand, purring.

'Here you go, puss. Enjoy that.'

Paul laughed and clapped, then handed her a cup of coffee, saying, 'Well played, Elf, but you know I wasn't talking about the cat. I meant Sean. You have a fondness, there. I could see it.'

He didn't sound hostile about this at all, but then why would he? She was hardly a rival. Possibly he was even laughing at her.

'He's great, yes,' she admitted. 'But just as a friend, sort of thing. Well, obviously. I mean – I know and he'd know that anything else really wouldn't be an option, would it? And even if I – er, well, there are clearly other considerations. Sorry, I'm waffling.'

Paul laughed again. 'Ah, right – I see. As I'd thought. Well, there you go. Life throws some oddnesses at us all, doesn't it?'

'Now and then, yes.' She gulped at the coffee and burned her tongue, but she wanted to finish it fast and get out of there, preferably before Sean came back. Paul was obviously in a playful mood and she wouldn't put it past him to throw an arm round Sean and tell him that she had an almighty crush on him and wasn't it hilarious. Oh, how they'd laugh.

'I'd better get back. I'll go and have some breakfast and check what we're all doing today,' she said, putting her cup in the sink. Too late. Sean came back, fully dressed and tousling his damp curls into place.

Paul reached out and flicked at the front of his

hair, saying, 'That's better. It was all over the shop.'

Sean quickly side-stepped before Paul could arrange any more. 'It's only hair, mate.' He pushed it back to where it had been and gave Thea a grin.

'All décor needs arranging, even if it's about one's own person,' Paul insisted. 'And Elf, whatever it is you're planning to do today, I wouldn't try venturing beyond the beach or the pub, and certainly not in a car. The road is still pretty bad. It may thaw later, though.'

'We thought we'd barbecue some sausages down on the beach at about lunchtime,' she said, 'so if either or both of you want to come, there's plenty.'

'No cold turkey?' Paul said, giving her a sly glance from behind Sean.

'Not so far, no,' she told him. 'I'll maybe see you both later.'

'Not me, sweetie,' Paul said. 'But thank you for the invitation. I have to get back to the ancestral homestead in my trusty tractor.'

'The tractor is yours?' she said as she was just about to open the door. 'You don't exactly—'

'Look dressed for the part?' he supplied. 'I do have with me a hideous mud-coloured jacket to put over this lot' – he stroked the soft velvet nap of the jacket – 'which is on loan from my aged father. Just because everyone connected with the agricultural milieu wears clothes the colour of manure, it doesn't mean we can't be sartorially glorious beneath them. Enjoy your barbecue, my

dear, and think of me in the warm with my roast pheasant and some perfectly chambréd Burgundy.'

'Sorry about him,' Sean apologized well within Paul's
hearing as he saw Thea out through the door. 'I might
well rock up on the beach later, if that's OK?'

'Of course it is,' she told him. 'No pheasant for you
then?'

'God, no. Enough's enough over at their gaff. It's a
fabulous place and they're great folks, but it's all a bit
formal. They are more sherry in a schooner than
beer in a bottle, sort of thing. I know which one of those
I am. And thanks for taking care of Woody. He
wasn't here when I got back so I assume he slept with
you?'

'He did,' Thea informed him as she stepped out into
the cold.

Sean's eyes were sparkly with mirth. 'That must have
been very nice for him.'

'It was nice for me too.'

'Well, good. A mutually happy night then.'

Thea laughed. 'About as good as it gets for a maiden
aunt, yes.'

'So, mistletoe . . .' Elmo was asking as Thea went into
the kitchen. 'Is it only, like for *before* Christmas – or can
you still use it after?'

'"Use" it?' Rosie asked her son. 'What do you mean?
Use it for what?'

Elmo blushed and took another huge bite of toast and marmalade, gazing at the table.

'He means does it have *the powers* once Christmas Day is over. You know, are you still allowed to grab a cheeky snog or is it all over till next year?' Charlotte explained to Rosie.

'Oh. Right. I don't know. I suppose *the powers* – if you think it's got any – last while it's up. Why do you ask?'

'Oh, no reason. Just wondered,' Elmo mumbled.

'It's probably valid till Twelfth Night,' Thea said as she shoved some bread in the toaster. 'That's if it doesn't go all crumbly and fall down first.'

'I suppose if it's gone stale, then so would the *lerve.*' Charlotte was sitting at the table, putting on purple nail varnish. 'What do you think?' she said, holding up her hand to show Thea and Rosie. 'A bit tarty? Or a bit vampire?'

'A bit of both. I like it, it looks great,' Thea said. Charlotte had pretty hands, plump and soft, and with several large-scale silver rings.

Charlotte sighed. 'Bloody snow. I'm starting to feel thoroughly stir crazy, aren't you? I can't help thinking that if I hadn't taken that stupid panto job, I could be in my own flat in London now, getting ready to go out to a Boxing Day party or something. Or' – and she looked wistful – 'better yet, I could be outside Selfridges, getting crushed in a queue, waiting for the doors to open for the sale. Oh, the bliss of fighting through the hordes for a bargain handbag!' She closed her eyes, looking ecstatic at the very thought.

'Who'd fight for a handbag?' Emily came into the kitchen with Milly and Alfie. 'Sales are just ghastly scrums with nothing in them but stuff nobody wanted first time round.'

'I'd fight for a handbag if it was a knockdown price. In fact, right now I'd almost kill just for a bigger selection of nail varnish than what I've got here with me. I need to *shop*!' Charlotte declared, as if excess vehemence was all it would take to make it happen.

'You could trudge up the lane and see if the village post office is open,' Emily suggested. 'You never know what they might stock. There could be a whole rack of cosmetics to choose from.'

'Yes, and it's all so likely to be Lancôme and Chanel, isn't it?' Charlotte said, sounding a bit snappy. 'No, thanks. I'll stay in the warm. I don't want to risk too much excitement, do I? I might go mad in the shop and be tempted by tinned peaches and a sliced white loaf. But I would like to make an effort for tonight.'

'What's on tonight?' Rosie asked, rubbing at her head. 'Whatever it is, I hope it won't be loud.'

'The pub,' Thea told her. 'They're having a music thing and Dad said he's arranged to play a couple of songs.'

'And I'm going to sing a bit,' Charlotte added. 'I shall need more glitter than I've brought with me. I didn't expect to be putting on a *show*.'

'It's a village pub,' Emily pointed out from over by the sink where she was breaking eggs into a jug to make scrambled eggs for the children, 'and half the village will be too cut off by snow to attend. It's hardly going to be the Albert Hall.'

'Darling,' Charlotte said, 'a performance is a performance. An artiste always gives of their best even if it's for two pensioners – oops, no offence to any of the occupants here, I must be careful after last night – and a farting dog. The show's the thing and all that.'

'Are we all going? I'm not sure about the children. It'll be way past their bedtime,' Emily fretted.

'Oh, let them stay up,' Charlotte said, giving the bottle of nail polish a vigorous shake. 'It's only Christmas once a year and they can fall asleep on a sofa at the back. Never did my boy Louis any harm.'

'I'll stay and mind them, Emily. I don't think I can face a crowd,' Rosie volunteered.

'Well that's very sweet of you, thanks. But are you sure? I doubt that whoever gets through the snow and ice will constitute a crowd, but we shall see.'

Effectively, this was their second-to-last day here, Anna thought. They were supposed to leave in two days but the snow didn't seem to be going anywhere and the sky was looking threateningly leaden again. Surely there couldn't be more of the damn stuff up there? It had already been a record-breaking Christmas for snow in the south-west, and the snowy Cornish coast had made it into the world news reports. Now it looked as if the weather was intending to make it a record-breaking New Year as well.

Anna suddenly longed to be home again, sitting on her own squashy sofa with tea and something on the TV that involved period costumes, coquettish girls who said, 'Oh la, sir,' to would-be rakish seducers, and a shockingly bad script with delightful anachronisms to spot. She and Alec had, one day in London, spent a happy half-hour in the pub, laughing about an Elizabethan drama they'd both watched in which the heroine had flounced out of a castle room wearing a ruff and farthingale and shouting a sulky 'Whatever.' These meetings would almost certainly not happen again once they were home, unless there was a break for a while and afterwards they could become friends – but definitely *without benefits* from now on.

Anna put a couple more logs on the fire, then wandered round the sitting room, picking up more of the children's toys and putting them into the big plastic boxes that Emily had brought with her for the purpose. The Christmas trees were looking a bit depressed now, as if they too had had enough of the weather, but it was more likely to be because the house was so warm. They were shedding little spikes of pine and Alfie had already had one stuck in his tender bare foot and howled like a lost wolf cub at the pain.

'Do you think we'll be stuck here till the New Year and beyond?' Emily came in and asked. 'This could go on for ages.' She was chewing at her thumb. Anna remembered she always did that as a child and had had to have plasters put on to save the skin that she'd bitten down to blood level.

Anna knew she just wanted reassurance but it was hard to give it with any conviction, because she simply didn't know any more than anyone else what would happen. The weather forecast on the radio had said something about a cold front being 'stuck'. Not encouraging.

'Oh, it won't, Em. Don't worry.' But Anna remembered the winter of 1963 which had seemed an eternity of freezing, increasingly grubby snow.

'The children have to go back to school on the third. And I have to work. It's all right for Sam, he can file copy from here if he has to, but I've got my stupid, lazy January late clients to deal with and I'm not feeling particularly . . .' She stopped and went to the window.

'You do look a bit pale,' Anna said, going to look out at the view next to her. 'Are you ill?'

'No. I'm not ill. I'm fine.'

Anna gave her a sharp look. 'Pale but fine. Right. What does Sam think?'

'There's nothing *to* think,' Emily said firmly. 'Look, that snowman from last night has still got his hat on. You'd think it would have blown away, wouldn't you? That's a sign the weather's completely static.'

'So you haven't told him yet.'

'There's nothing to tell. Leave it, Mum, please.' She pointed at the bird table, still determined to avoid whatever subject she thought Anna was raising. 'Look, at least someone's getting the benefit of the weather. Elmo's been topping up the bird table. He's such a love when he's not being Silent Teen.' Some feisty robins and a couple of starlings were bickering over scraps of bread and bacon rinds out on the terrace table.

'He is a good boy.'

'Boys are so easy, definitely easier than girls,' Emily said, half to herself.

'Girls aren't difficult, they just question things a lot and that's to be encouraged. But it's not good to stereotype them, to think ahead about how you reckon they'll be. Milly is a delight – she's bright and funny and moody and imaginative. Who wouldn't want that in a daughter? She's a lot like you were.'

'Really? I hope she doesn't get all anxious like me. I wouldn't wish that on anyone.'

'She'll be fine. Right now she's really looking forward to the lunch barbecue. Thea's got her in the kitchen, teaching her and Alfie how to fry onions.'

'She's brilliant with them. I wish she had her own.' Emily's eyes filled with tears. 'You know yesterday was her baby's due date?'

'Oh, poor girl. I'd guessed it must be around now,

because it was eleven weeks when she lost it, but she hadn't actually said. I wonder if she thought about it? She didn't let on.'

'She doesn't. She just gets on with things. And yes, she did think about it.'

The kitchen door opened and Alec came in, wafting with him the scent of frying onions.

Emily went even paler. 'Oh God, that smell!' she said, rushing from the room.

'Ah – so I wasn't wrong,' Anna murmured.

SIXTEEN

After being on the ground for several days now, the snow no longer looked so pure, fresh and sparkly. The novelty of it had thoroughly worn off and Thea longed to see greenery and earth and stone. She felt as if she were being thoroughly ungrateful to nature, but so much white – and now shabby white – was getting on her nerves and she was beginning to understand Emily's anxiety about being stuck in one place for eternity. She went out to the garden to pick up the paper hat that had fallen from the snowman's head and was now lying soggy and ripped on ground that was jagged and scuffed by so many footprints. The white was tinged with mud, greyed from the salty sea air, and looked like sheets that had been slept in for far too long by somebody fevered and grubby. She wouldn't want Milly and Alfie rolling about in it now, as they had so joyfully done a few days before.

'The grass under that will be wrecked.' Sean came out from the Stables, carrying bags of bird food to top up the terrace feeders. 'Paul tells me that walking about on snowy grass makes it go all black in the shapes of the footprints. He could be wrong, though – I don't see why it's any worse than walking on it when it's wet.'

'Sorry,' Thea said. 'There was a bit of a snowman event and we scuffed it all up a lot. I expect the snow's all packed tight on it.'

'Oh, I don't mind. Grass recovers fast enough and I can always re-seed in the spring. Or I can work out which footprints are yours and put a special frame over them to treasure them for all eternity as reminders of your stay.'

'You're completely barking, you know that?' she told him.

'I know. But I really don't care about the grass, because the snowman – well, it had to be done, didn't it? After all' – and he smiled at her as he poured peanuts into the feeder – 'we made ours, didn't we? Only fair the rest of your family should get a go at one.'

'We completely did.' It felt like ages ago now. Those mad moments on the moonlit beach.

'I think it's still there,' he said. 'We can check it later, yes?'

Thea felt a bit awkward, wondering if Paul had said anything to Sean. But why would he?

'We can.' She ran her hand along the low terrace wall,

gathering up snow in her gloves to make a ball and then chucking it at the snowman. One of his pebble eyes fell out.

'Hey, you've hurt him!' Sean said. 'You have to put that back or his vision will be all skewed.'

'OK!' she said, laughing as she skidded down the steps and went to restore the poor thing's sight.

'Sean?' she said, watching him concentrating on pouring seed into one of the bird-food containers. 'What happens if we're stuck here after tomorrow?'

He turned and looked at her. 'The snow, you mean? You'll have to stay here for ever, I guess.'

'But haven't you got new clients coming in for New Year?'

'Not this time. We advertised a bit late so most people had got themselves sorted. If you have to stay on, it's fine. In fact . . .' and he came down the steps and stood close to her. 'I'd really like it if you did.'

'There are a lot of us,' Thea said.

'I didn't mean all of you,' he replied, 'though of course I know that if *you* can't go, neither can they. If it's the weather that's keeping you, that is.' He turned away, stamping across the snow-chunked lawn. 'I'm making a mess of what I'm saying, aren't I?'

She laughed, feeling quite elated by what he'd said but confused at the same time. 'You are, a bit! But thanks – it's good to know we won't have to go and camp in the woods or beg the pub landlord to give us a cupboard to sleep in.'

'No, it won't come to that,' Sean said, 'but this morning's forecast does say we're in for a change soon – winds and so on. That usually means warmer weather. Unless it's from the east, of course.'

'Charlotte will be thrilled. She's feeling trapped and missing shops,' Thea told him.

'Which one's Charlotte?'

'The red-haired, rather plump one, Dad's – er, friend. She's a mistake who shouldn't be here but her lift home got snowed in so she ended up staying.'

'A mistake?'

'Yes. Alec is the other one. He's my mother's mistake.' Thea felt she'd said too much, but at the same time Sean seemed to be finding the information entertaining, so what did it matter, in the big scheme of things?

'Wow, your family is quite something,' he said, looking rather admiring. 'You cover pretty much all the bases between you, don't you?'

'Do we? What other base is there?'

'Well, there's you.'

She grinned. 'I've got the maiden aunt slot, that's all. Nothing special about me.'

'Oh, there is, Elf, there is. What time's the barbie? I might go down to the beach early, pretty soon, and collect up some wood to make an extra fire. Call it being a good landlord going the extra hospitable mile.

Do you fancy coming along and giving me a hand?'

'I do. Yes.'

'I'll see you in ten? By the cliff gate?'

'Date.'

Sean went back to the Stables and Thea stayed in the garden for a few minutes looking out to sea. In the distance she could see a ship making its slow way across the horizon. It was a dark one, all squared off, probably stacked with containers. Would it be colder out there on the sea than it was here on the land, or warmer? If she were Emily, she'd be imagining the crew having to be careful on an icy deck. Emily would be seeing them slipping, sliding towards the rail, falling, tumbling beneath the rail and into the freezing sea. Thea felt quite sorry for her, always seeing the danger side of things, and she wondered if that was something to do with fearing the worst for your children, once you'd got them.

Maybe she should have been less breezy and confident herself, when she'd been pregnant, then it would have been less of a horrendous shock when it all went wrong. She didn't lack imagination herself, but apart from the mild superstition of not wanting to tell anyone until she'd had her first scan, she had assumed – being young and healthy and pretty damn fit – that the baby would stay cosily inside her until it was 'cooked' and at the right time to come out. 'Some of them just don't stick,' the midwife had told her after she'd come crying to her, looking for reasons, *any* reasons, as to why the miscarriage had happened. Was it something she'd done? Something heavy she'd lifted? Benji tugging just that bit too hard on his lead and wrenching something? 'Chances are, you'll be perfectly all right next time,' she'd been told. But would there be a next time? Thea did hope so.

She went back towards the house to get more warm clothes. If she was going to be spending a long time on the beach she'd need the furry hat and possibly warmer socks. She could hear sounds of a ping-pong game going on in the barn and remembered that there'd been talk of a table-tennis tournament, but somehow it had been forgotten. All the same, someone had remembered and was giving it a go. As she passed the open door, she briefly looked in and saw Elmo playing against the girl who had come to the house with Maria on their first morning. Delia? Daisy? Definitely Daisy. They were both laughing and racing to hit the ball, giving it plenty of competitive effort. She watched for a few minutes until Daisy won a point and they stopped for a second to change servers.

'Who's winning?' she asked.

'I am,' Elmo told her, looking pleased with himself.

'Only just,' Daisy said. 'Ready?' She served and aced him.

'No *wayyy*!' he said, laughing at her. 'Right, this is war . . .'

Thea left them to it, pleased he'd made Daisy a friend. Someone for everyone, she thought. Almost.

She didn't like the expression on his face. Sam was looking angry, hostile, challenging.

'Were you going to tell me?' He faced Emily in the bedroom. He was holding the pregnancy test kit box and pointing it at her like a dagger. 'Or did you think you'd let me hang on till I started wondering if you'd been eating all the pies?'

'Of course I was going to tell you.' Emily sat on the bed, folding children's clothes that she had just taken out of the tumble dryer. They were still warm. She held them soft in her hands, imagining feeling the shapes of her children's limbs in the sleeves of jumpers. 'You seriously thought I wouldn't?'

'I don't know. You've kept it bloody quiet. When you were pregnant with the other two you couldn't wait to say something. One day overdue and you were bouncing around like a kid waiting for . . . well, Christmas. I don't get it. Surely you didn't think I wouldn't be happy about it? That I'd not want to know?'

Emily flicked her finger against her thumb, trying to stay calm and logical and also not to cry. She didn't want to cry. He didn't like her easy tears and associated them with angling for her own way. Right now, she didn't even know what kind of 'own way' she wanted. He didn't say anything about pregnancy: she wished he'd express *something* so she had a clue how to feel.

In the background, from downstairs, she could hear the sound of Mike's guitar. He was singing one of his favourites, Pink Floyd's 'Arnold Layne'. He'd sung it to her when she was little and she associated the song with lying snugly in bed, being gently lulled to sleep. It had been quite a strange feeling years later to realize it was a song about a man who stole – and wore – women's underwear. But that, as Charlotte would probably say, was hippie parents for you: none of that ordinary Golden Slumbers lullaby stuff.

'I didn't know what to say,' she said eventually. 'It's just as much a surprise to me as it is to you. I blame that food poisoning last month. The Pill doesn't like episodes like that.'

'The dodgy prawns? I remember.' He grinned. 'You said you'd never eat another prawn in your life.'

'You're cross.'

'I'm not. Of course I'm not. But I wish you hadn't kept it a secret. I hate to think you've been worrying alone all this time.'

'You are cross. So am I.'

'But what's the point of that?' At last Sam came and sat beside her. 'It's not so terrible, is it? It'll work out.'

She wiped her eyes with one of Alfie's vests. As always, Sam handed her a bunch of tissues and she blew her nose.

'How can it work out, Sam? Do you mean I should

have a termination? Or not? And if not, what about my job and the children and . . . well, everything? And I feel bad about Thea. She wanted hers so much and now look, I've suddenly got one, far too easily and carelessly, and she hasn't.'

Sam gave her a puzzled look. 'You mean *you* don't want it?'

'Well, of course I do. But it's so difficult. Three of them?'

'Yeah. Three of them. Your folks managed it, didn't they? If they'd gone by your thinking, you wouldn't even be here.'

'You can't manage three – you get flaky enough with the childcare for these two. And we both know I have to hang on to my job. It's a lot more secure than yours.'

'We do know that.' He nodded his head. 'But there's maternity leave and so on. It'll work out. And anyway, by then, as Del Boy would say, we'll all be millionaires.'

She laughed and at last looked up at him. 'So we're having a baby, then?'

He hugged her close and kissed her. 'Looks like we are, doesn't it?'

Alec was very quiet and had cut himself off a bit from the rest of them. All morning he'd been in a corner of the smaller sitting room, in an armchair by the window either staring out of it in the kind of way that made Anna think he wasn't really focusing on anything, or he was reading a four-day-old *Guardian* but never turning a page. Anna herself was busy in the kitchen. She'd cooked onions, chopped up tomatoes and counted out plenty of buns to put the sausages in. Charlotte had gone on kitchen strike, citing her newly varnished nails, and was lying on a sofa watching *The Great Escape* on TV and claiming that a friend of her mother's had once slept with Steve McQueen. That had been yet another thing that made Anna feel her age, and it annoyed her. She didn't normally think anything of being in possession of a Freedom Pass because she was already full of a lifetime of good times and fun. She must, she resolved for the New Year, learn to ignore such remarks or at least not read anything into them.

Anna went to check the fires and found that Alec hadn't even noticed that the one close to him had almost gone out. If she were being ridiculously fanciful, she'd imagine him on a polar expedition, showing signs of being the first one to crack and silently pondering that long walk out into the snow.

'Are you OK?' she asked as she carefully offered the fire some more kindling and smaller logs in a plea to get it restarted. 'You're very quiet.'

'I just checked the website and there are no trains,' he said, looking glum.

'Well, there weren't going to be any today, were there? So what does it matter?' She sounded, even to herself, a bit aggressive here. 'Sorry, I meant, well – it's Boxing

Day. You couldn't escape yet even if there wasn't any snow.'

'The line's blocked, apparently. There's a warning for when the trains start running again. It could be months.' He sighed. Clutching his book and leaning back in the chair, he briefly reminded Anna of some swoony, consumptive Victorian heroine. She managed – just – not to laugh.

'You're being a bit dramatic, aren't you? Of course it won't be months. It wasn't even that long when the line got broken by the floods, and this is nothing like so bad. Are you so fed up with us all?' She went and sat on the arm of the chair and stroked his hair. It was quite long and soft and felt like a young boy's hair. She removed her hand quickly.

'That was nice,' he said, giving her a wan smile. The consumptive look again, she thought.

'You're just bored,' she told him, feeling a bit impatient. 'If you're short of something to do, you could go and empty the dishwasher. It's just finished its cycle.' Even to herself she sounded like a mum chivvying a lumpen teenager but she wasn't going to apologize for that.

'Oh. OK then. Sorry – have I been lazy? Suki always thought I was. She said it was my mum's fault for doing everything for me. But now Suki does everything for *our* kids. You can't win.'

He looked even more gloomy, which made Anna

315

want to slap his wrists. There could be no surer sign, if any more were needed, that they were no longer possible as a relationship. He wasn't that much younger than she was, only about fifteen years, she wasn't quite sure, but today he seemed like a young sullen lad in need of coaxing into cheerfulness. She'd done all that and had no wish to start again.

'Look, this weather can't last much longer. You'll be out of here soon enough,' she told him, crossing her fingers and hoping she was right. She was as fed up with being incarcerated as any of them but she and Thea seemed to be the only ones making the best of it – apart from Milly and Alfie, who loved it – and trying to gee the others up. 'You'll be on the train home in a day or two.'

'Mum wants me to pick her up in Southampton on Thursday. She doesn't believe I might not make it.'

'What happened to her cruise?' The fire was reluctantly spitting into life and Anna went and prodded it a bit more, moving logs to let air through.

'Norovirus,' he said. 'Went right through the ship, crew and passengers, she says. They're docked in the Solent and they've got to stay there till Thursday, even the well ones, till the health people clear them. Mum hasn't got it, which is lucky, or it might kill her off.'

'So you heard quite a bit from her then?' Anna pictured Muriel on board, sweeping through the ship's smartest dining room in one of her voluminous butterfly-sleeved ensembles, obliviously swishing glasses and cutlery from the tables of those she passed. She wouldn't give house room to a nasty intruder like norovirus. Her immune system would trip it up on a heap of defending bacteria.

'Email. I told her I was staying with you and she said what a coincidence that you knew me; she assumed I was a friend of one of your children.' They smiled at each other for a moment and she knew that he knew that whatever it was they'd had was now over.

'Thank you,' she said, leaning down to kiss his cheek.

'What, no mistletoe?' he said, looking a bit flustered.

'No. No need for it now, is there?'

'I suppose not. But thanks for what?'

'For a very good time I never expected to have. Don't ever think I didn't enjoy it. But . . .'

'I know. I was sure there'd be a "but".'

'She's right, your mother.'

'She didn't say anything.'

'She did, you know. That thing she said about my children. It was just a nudge – something we do. I'd probably do the same if it were my children, even when they're pushing fifty, like you are.'

There was a rustle and a bustle and Charlotte whirled in wearing a sleeveless taffeta dress studded with diamanté around the low neckline. The skirt was a tulip shape, although Anna, if she were being as catty as she was ashamed to be feeling, would say it was a tulip in very full bloom rather than one demurely half-open.

'Shall I wear this?' Charlotte said. 'Not too much, is it?'

Anna took a sly look at Alec; his face had livened up at the sight of Charlotte and several pounds of on-show flesh. Well, it was good, she thought, that at last something had cheered him up.

'For a barbecue on the beach?' Anna said. 'Well, it's very nice and you do look lovely in it, but could I suggest a warm cardie?'

'Aw, aren't they sweet? They're holding hands.' Sean, sitting beside Thea close to the fire they'd made at the foot of the sandy hill, was looking at Sam and Emily standing close together by the barbecue. Mike and Alec were poking sausages around the flames with spatulas, and Charlotte – now wearing trousers and a huge baggy jumper – was squidging ketchup onto Milly's hot dog.

'She's pregnant,' Thea murmured, hardly knowing where the words had come from.

'Is she? The hand-holding one? Is she the one who's got the two little children?'

'Yes, that's Emily.' Thea felt a bit choked. She didn't even know for sure if she was right, but the statement had come from somewhere almost primeval. There was a softness to Emily today. There'd been a jumpy, cold worriedness to her till now.

'I could be wrong,' she backtracked, 'but I don't think I am.'

'Oh. OK. Well, that's good, isn't it?' Sean asked. 'Tell you what, shall we go and look at the rock pools over there? I want to see what's survived the cold.'

He was being tactful, well able to tell that she was getting emotional.

'Yes. I'm up for that, so long as the warmth from the fire that we've got on us doesn't disappear too quickly. I'm liking being here and being able to look at the sea while not completely freezing.'

He got up, then reached for her hand and pulled her up, and as they walked away from the others, he didn't let go of it. She wondered what the others – if they saw – would make of that.

'Can we come?' Milly and Alfie rushed up beside them. 'Where are you going?'

'To look at a rock pool over there,' Sean said. 'And yes, of course you can come.'

Milly, still clutching her hot dog, took a big bite of it and ran ahead of them and Alfie followed.

'They are cute, aren't they?' Sean said.

'Very. I love being their auntie.'

'The maiden aunt,' he said, laughing at her, then he looked serious. 'But something you said, the other night . . .'

'I know. I said I was supposed to be having a baby. It

would have, or more likely *could* have been born on Christmas Day.'

'My sister had IVF.'

'Did she? Did it work?'

'Yes, eventually. She's got twins.'

'Wow, hard work.'

'Where did you get yours from?'

'My what?' She felt puzzled.

'Was it a clinic? Or . . . Sorry, forget I asked!' He laughed. 'I just like to know stuff. I'll have to learn not to intrude on the house-guests. Curiosity and cats, all that. None of my business.'

'Sean, did your mummy never tell you how babies are made?' She stopped walking and faced him.

'Eh? Well, of course she did. Actually, scrub that – no, she didn't. I found out the usual way, from the school playground and mucky books. Sorry, I just thought—'

'That I might have gone the IVF route? No, I went the person-I-live-with route. Sorry, *lived*. Definitely in the past.'

'Oh. A man.'

'Yes, a man – you know, like lots of people do.'

'Come *on*!' Milly shouted. 'Are we there yet?' She was standing on the edge of where the rocks began. The sea had washed them clean and Thea, fed up with the endless snow, loved how the subtle stripes and whorls of the rock formation gleamed.

'Look at the patterns,' she said to Sean, as they caught

up with the children. She was stroking the rock's rough surface through her gloves.

'If it wasn't for the contrast with all that snow we'd probably just see these as "brown" and nothing else,' he said, tracing his finger along a grey faultline.

Sean found the rock pool and showed the children the tiny, near-transparent shrimps swimming about. 'I was hoping for a starfish to show you but there aren't any in here just now, just lots of shells,' he told them. 'Look carefully.' He pulled one shell out and prodded it gently, and a tiny crab came out.

Milly squealed. 'It's living in there!'

'It is. Lots of things live in shells, not just the owners of the shells. It's like having visitors.'

'Visitors like we are?' she asked him.

'Like you are.'

'Can I take the shell and show Mummy?' Alfie asked.

'Yes, but we must put the crab back in the water so he can find somewhere else to hide. He won't like being out in the open.'

'Will he get cold?' Alfie asked, looking worried.

'In the air, yes, but look.' Sean bent down and dabbled his hand in the pool. 'Feel this – it's warmer than out here, isn't it?'

The children took off their gloves and splashed about for a second and then Sean let them dry their hands on his jacket. Then they took a few shells each and ran off.

'You're very good with them,' Thea told him.

'I come from a big family,' he said. 'And I'd like some kids myself too.' He looked a bit embarrassed as if this was a tricky revelation. Perhaps it was, she thought. How much harder must it be for a gay man of possibly limited means to become a father than it was for a gay woman? The goodwill of even the most generous of surrogates must be hard to rely on.

'Perhaps you will, somehow,' she said, feeling it was a rather lame comment.

'The man you spoke of,' Sean said. 'Was he just a . . . donor?'

Thea took a deep breath so she could say the whole lot in one go. 'No. He was an actual old-fashioned fiancé. We'd been going to get married. And then I became pregnant and at eleven weeks I lost it and I was really, really upset and sad about it, but then he said that surely it was just as well really as he didn't want children. And on that horrible, heartless comment I knew that we were absolutely and totally over. And that's it. See? That's why I'm now the maiden aunt.'

'And not gay.'

'Gay! Me? No – why?'

Sean laughed. 'Oh wow, have I ever got my wires crossed. I just thought . . .'

'You thought I was gay? But why?' She felt utterly mystified. And then light dawned. 'It's my hair, isn't it? Oh, for goodness' sake, you surely don't think every woman with short spiky hair is a devout reader of *Diva* magazine, do you?'

He shrugged. 'Not exactly. It was just a couple of other things. Sorry. Or not sorry, because it doesn't matter either way, does it? And yet it does. Yay.' As they walked back to the others, he kept laughing quietly to himself. Thea didn't know what to think. Nothing, probably. After all, essentially nothing had changed. She might not be gay, but of course Sean still was.

Thea was the last one off the beach. She volunteered to make sure the fire died down properly and to cover it with plenty of sand so some twilight surfer wouldn't come bouncing along and burn themselves on the embers. Sean went off to do some much put-off VAT returns and the others climbed back up the path, most of them heading for a bit of a snooze before the evening at the pub.

Emily had gone up to the house as soon as she'd eaten. She did look very happy, Thea thought, and was glad that she felt no envy, only the pleasure of looking forward to another niece or nephew. She was good at being an aunt, even if she never did get to be a mother. If she had to, she'd make the good aunt thing be enough.

There had been a subtle change in the air temperature, she sensed, as she walked back up the path to the house. It felt softer, just that tiny bit warmer. The snow was still there but it was gleaming wet and quieter underfoot now, not so much the treacherous crisp ice that had been there for the last few days. Maybe a thaw really was coming.

Up at the top of the path she could see a light on in the barn. There was no sound of table tennis being played so she went to see if there was someone there or if the light needed to be switched off.

There was a slight noise and she walked as silently as she could to the door, scared she might be about to startle an owl, just as she and Sean had the other night when he'd been up that ladder, but no – this wasn't an owl. She had a very swift look, then immediately tiptoed away towards the back door of the house. Elmo was in the barn, kissing Daisy, both of them completely oblivious to anything but each other. And on the ping-pong table was a little sprig of mistletoe.

SEVENTEEN

Cold turkey. It was a shame the term had such negative connotations. In Mike's opinion, not a lot could beat it. 'Cold turkey, chips and peas and the rest of the red cabbage and all the leftover cold bread sauce and last bits of pickles and relishes. Food from the heavens. Even reheated sprouts taste brilliant,' he declared as they all sat down in the kitchen for an early supper.

'I'll have a bit more of that Stilton with my chips,' Charlotte said, heading for the fridge. 'It'll make my voice all husky for later.'

'I can do you an omelette, if you like,' Anna offered. 'There's plenty in the fridge to go in it.'

'I could do an omelette myself,' Charlotte said, looking at Anna with suspicion.

Anna shrugged. 'Just being a good host,' she said. 'I wasn't going to spike it with arsenic. Not this time, anyway.'

Charlotte flew back across the kitchen and hugged Anna, almost crushing her into her ample bust. Anna made a 'help' mime from her squashed position and Elmo splorted with laughter.

'I'm so sorry, Anna. That was horribly rude of me. Truth is,' Charlotte began, 'truth is, I'm a bit nervous. I always am before facing my public, though you'd think I'd be well over it after all these years. It makes me defensive and bad-tempered.' She kissed a very surprised Anna loudly and firmly on her cheek, leaving a big scarlet lipstick heart shape. 'You've been a star, you know that? I came in here all mouthy and bad and you took me in. And all I've done is take and be greedy.'

'I wouldn't say that,' Anna conceded, escaping to a chair on the far side of the table, out of range of any more demonstrations of affection. 'You've been a dab hand with the potato peeler.'

'No, trust me,' Charlotte said, looking briefly at Alec. 'I've been very greedy.'

'Have you been at the wine, Chazz?' Mike asked.

'No more than usual, darling,' Charlotte purred at him. 'Just a little livener for later, to put me in the mood.'

'You always seem to be in the mood,' Rosie said, rather unexpectedly but not without good humour.

'That's me, sweetie,' Charlotte said. 'Life's too short not to grasp every opportunity, isn't it?'

Mike watched as Charlotte reached into her jumper

and adjusted her bra strap, showing as she did so a soft creamy expanse of breast. A few weeks ago, barely even that, he'd have found the gesture madly stimulating but at the moment he was simply reminded of Les Dawson, dressed as a gossipy woman in an overall and adjusting his bosom before passing on a titbit of scandal to a neighbour over the fence. He now preferred the grace with which Anna glided round the place. He'd almost forgotten – only almost, thank goodness – how elegantly she moved. She'd done a lot of ballet in her youth, she'd told him years before when they'd first met in a teepee while watching Bob Dylan at the Isle of Wight festival, and she had never lost the poise. Over these few Christmas days Mike had realized he'd never get tired of watching her simply walking around the place. Whatever had they been thinking of? And was she on the same page as he was about this? He very much hoped so.

Thea wasn't sure what to wear. It was only the village pub they were going to but she wanted to make an effort. She was tired of being bundled up in jeans and jumpers and layers of scarves. She had a dress that would work – dark blue, simple, warm and not over-the-top fancy, with a strange looped-up hem in places which made it look quite wacky – but it wouldn't really go with the sheepskin boots she'd be needing to tramp over the snow to the Fisherman's Arms. She decided she'd take the medium-heeled ankle boots she'd brought with her in a separate bag, in the hope that the simple act of changing from one pair to another in the loo wouldn't mark her out as an overdressed up-country emmet. It wasn't Sean she was dressing up for, definitely not. He wouldn't notice anyway, although he did seem quite . . . what was the word . . . *fond* of her. Twice, she recalled, he'd even had a go at kissing her under that damn mistletoe, but it had all been just a fun, polite thing, the same as the way she kissed Jenny at home and her other female friends hello and good-bye. Nothing more than general affection. Shame really, but that was the way things went sometimes.

Emily came into her room as she was applying mascara. 'I'm not coming tonight,' she told Thea. 'Rosie offered to babysit but I think I'll just have an early night. If we can ever get out of the village, we'll be going home tomorrow and it's such a long, tiring way when half the world is on the road with you. It'll be jams all the way, won't it?'

'Probably. I wonder if we will get to go, though?' Thea said, fumbling through her make-up bag for the right lipstick. She did wonder why she bothered with it – the stuff never seemed to stay on. She wondered what Charlotte's trick was; her mouth seemed to be permanently a deep rich scarlet. 'Like a baboon's arse' her mother had said, just after Charlotte had arrived.

'I need to get home.' Emily sat on Thea's bed. 'Is there no one who can clear a road in this county? Where are the snowploughs?'

She was sounding frightened, Thea thought. 'Even if there are any, they can't do every country track, Em. But it'll be fine. I had a feeling earlier that it's starting to melt. Another couple of degrees up and it'll be gone in hours, and then we'll have a mass of mud to complain about instead.'

'I wouldn't complain. I'd just be grateful. You and that Sean were very lovely with the children on the beach earlier. He's OK, isn't he?'

'He is.' Thea smiled at Emily by way of the mirror. 'And if things were different . . .'

'How different?'

'He's gay.'

'He so isn't. And he likes you. He was holding your hand. Sweet.' Emily chuckled.

'No, he is. He and Paul . . .'

'Paul? No, no, no, you're wrong. I bet you fifty quid.' Emily was adamant. 'And you can't argue with a—' She stopped abruptly.

'Pregnant woman?' Thea risked it.

'How did you know? Did Mum say something?' Emily frowned. 'It's too early days to tell anyone.'

'No, she didn't say anything. It was just a feeling. And something about you. And the fact you keep refusing wine – I'll admit that was a bit suss.'

'You don't mind? At the risk of sounding like Charlotte, the word "greedy" does come to mind.'

'The words "lucky cow" come to my mind but that's only envy, not actual jealousy. I think it's brilliant.'

'It was a mistake.'

'Yeah, and? Mistakes can be great things. And besides, you've got the maiden aunt to help out with the other two if you need her.'

Emily's eyes filled with their usual easy tears. 'Thanks, Thea. You're a lot more than I deserve.'

Thea's instinct about the temperature rise had been spot on. As they all walked up the lane to the pub, lit by the boot-room torch, the snow underfoot was now definitely slushy, soft as a sorbet. Snow dripped from the trees, and every now and then a whoosh of the stuff fell into the road. Some landed on Elmo's head and he brushed it off impatiently, saying, 'Oh man, my *hair*,' and tweaking at it furiously.

'That's new,' Rosie commented to Thea. 'He's never given a flying one about his hair before now. I'd only just got used to the constant whiff of Lynx. Next it'll be hair products and a ton of bathroom clutter.'

Thea thought she wouldn't mention seeing Elmo kissing Daisy. A teenager was entitled to conduct his first romances without parental gloating and questions. 'He's quite a looker. He'll get a lot of attention,' she told Rosie.

'Do you think so? Hard to tell, me being his biased mother. Am I going to get a stream of minxy young girls in the house, making me feel old and fat?'

'Yes. That goes with the territory,' Anna joined in. 'But they'll be lovely young things, and just as you get used to them and decide they're part of the family, the two of them will break up and you'll be asking "Where is Lucy/Sophie/Chantelle?" and Elmo will just shrug and bring in a new one. My top tip is never learn their names – that way you can't send them into a sulk by calling them by the wrong one.'

The pub was busy, full of people taking refuge from the remains of Christmas and looking thrilled to have come out in the snow to find the world still functioning. The clientele was a mixture of locals in what Paul would call 'dung-coloured' clothes, and holiday-makers and families from up-country in woolly hats and ski jackets. There were a lot of bright, new Christmas scarves and Thea felt a bit overdressed in her blue frock and arty necklace of multi-coloured chunky stones, but not as bizarre as Charlotte who almost struck the main bar to silence when she changed her boots for strappy high silver shoes and took off her coat to reveal her sparkly taffeta dress, fishnet-clad legs and a lot of exposed flesh.

A small stage had been set up in a corner of the bar, complete with a drum kit and amplifiers and micro-phones, but the music hadn't begun yet. There were several guitar cases propped alongside various tables, and Mike commented that it looked like a popular gig. 'Who'd think, out in the wilds here, in the snow? I thought it would be a couple of folkie geezers and maybe one of those fey, wispy girl singers who don't bother with consonants.'

Mike and Charlotte went to talk to the barman who seemed to be in charge of the running order, and Thea – from the big corner table they'd bagged – looked quickly round the bar in case Sean was there. He'd said he would be, and as it was her last night, she really wanted to make the most of seeing him, even if he turned up with Paul. She did like both of them, after all. And it could well be the last time ever that she'd see them. Maybe they'd stay in touch via Facebook or email, or maybe by this time next month Sean would have forgotten she was ever there and have moved on to being charming, funny and just that little bit flirtatious with a new house-guest. The thought was quite painful. What an idiot she was, she told herself. Sean was so firmly *not* on the availability list that she shouldn't even be thinking of him this way. And yet – when Emily had been so sure she was wrong, she'd felt a little spark of something that felt like hope. Perhaps she had been wrong to believe he was gay? She didn't think so, but it was definitely a bet she'd be happy to lose.

Mike came back with a tray of drinks for everyone and Charlotte followed, laughing.

'What's so funny?' Anna asked. 'Are you going to share it?'

'I shouldn't laugh,' Charlotte said, sitting down. 'But it is so damn typical.'

'What is?'

'This gig. It's a true SOBs one. I've just had a look at who else is playing and you couldn't get a more typical open-mic night line-up.'

'What is SOBs? Is someone crying? Have they been told they can't play or something?' Rosie looked puzzled. 'I thought anyone could, if they fancied it, even if they're rubbish.'

'Oh yes they can,' Mike said. 'There's no quality control at things like this. You take your chance and if you've got the balls to do it, then good luck.'

The first act started up, a girl with a pink Fender Stratocaster, long blonde hair, a very short green skirt and lime tights with yellow stripes.

'Bit of a Kermit look, that,' Charlotte whispered as the girl tuned up and nodded to her goth friend on drums who started softly with brushes on the snare drum. The hum of conversation in the room dropped as she started to sing, fairly badly, David Bowie's 'Starman'. Mike winced a couple of times as she didn't quite hit the notes but the audience joined in the singing and it really didn't matter that this wasn't a top-rate act.

No sign of Sean. Thea felt disappointed as two more guitar-based acts, both men old enough to be able to play their instruments really competently, sang – one of them specializing in Bob Dylan and the other with a strange and slightly creepy take on very old Cliff Richard songs, performed as if they were a bit punk.

'See what I mean about SOBs?' Charlotte said as the second one finished.

'Not really. You still haven't told us what it means,' Anna pointed out.

'Sad Old Bastards,' she said, rather too loudly. She was on the far side of two large glasses of wine now and several people turned to look at her. 'It's from a song I heard, about going into any pub, any bar and there are sad old bastards with guitars. I saw it on YouTube, a really funny song about gigs like this by a bloke called Terence Blacker. You should have a look at it.' She pointed a purple-nailed finger at Mike. 'Well, not just you, sweetie. I didn't mean you. You're not a sad old bastard.'

Alec was smirking, trying not to laugh openly. Thea looked at her father's face. He seemed to be considering a reply that would be exactly the right one but just then the barman waved across the room and said, 'You're on, mate.' So instead he got up, took his guitar from its case and said, 'This sad old bastard is off to do his thing. Give me a bit of a cheer at the end, won't you?'

'You just *had* to say that, didn't you?' Anna rounded on Charlotte the moment Mike was out of earshot. 'If you had to come out with it, couldn't you at least have waited?'

'Sorry! I didn't mean Mike, honestly. But you've got to admit, some of the others are SOBs, all pony-tails and biker jackets, thinking every young chick in the place will want to shag them.'

Mike started playing, and Thea felt massively proud of him. He was playing an acoustic guitar, which most of the others weren't, and he sang 'Arnold Layne' again, which went down well with the older ones who knew it and with the younger ones who enjoyed the wry comedy of it, and ended with Willie Nelson's 'You Were Always on My Mind', which had Anna wiping a tear or two away. At the end he called Charlotte over to do her bit.

'They haven't rehearsed much. This could all go horribly wrong,' Jimi said to Thea, grinning wickedly.

'Oh, don't say that.' Thea crossed her fingers. 'Charlotte will only manage to make it Dad's fault, not hers, if it does.'

'What with him being a Sad Old Bastard,' Anna said crossly, taking a large gulp of her wine. 'Honestly, what did he ever see in her?'

'She'll be brilliant,' Alec said, gazing at Charlotte with a look of devotion.

Charlotte, arranging herself on the front of the stage and moving the microphone up its stand to the right position for her, took her time to start singing, and just as Mike started on the opening notes, she casually hitched up her skirt to adjust a suspender, to great cheers from the men in the audience.

'I think that might be a bit of a clue,' Thea said to her mother.

Anna laughed. 'Well, if she has to resort to being that obvious to pull the blokes, then you can only feel sorry for her.'

'It's only a bit of performance art,' Alec said.

'You keep defending her.' Anna suddenly turned on him. 'What's got into you?'

Jimi leaned close to Thea and whispered, 'Maybe it's more a case of him getting into Charlotte.'

Thea recalled the afternoon of Christmas Eve when she'd seen Alec and Charlotte giggling on the landing, having not been to the carol service. Jimi could well be right but, as with Elmo and Daisy, it wasn't for her to say anything. Their business and all that.

Charlotte, ready at last, launched into 'The Lady Is a Tramp'.

'Says it all, doesn't it?' Anna said with a giggle.

Emily watched her children sleeping. Milly was spread out like a star and had kicked her duvet off and chucked her toy owl out of bed but Alfie was cuddled down, all curled up and holding the arm of his teddy bear.

Sam came into the room behind her and put his arm round her shoulders. 'Beautiful, aren't they?'

'When they're asleep, yes,' she said, snuggling close to him.

'No, all the time. Sometimes I look at them when they're running around and I think, Hey, aren't we brilliant to have made these fabulous creatures?'

'And now another one,' she whispered, not quite trusting that he'd still be happy about this.

'The bonus package,' he said. 'Don't worry so much. We'll just go along with it, yes?'

They left the room and pulled the door halfway shut, then went into their own room. Emily walked over to look out of the window. Melted snow was dripping from the roof and the snowman out in the garden had fallen sideways.

'It's really melting now,' she said, 'which is good – but suppose it freezes in the early hours? It'll be even worse than just snow – it'll be treacherous.'

Sam picked up his phone and flicked at it, then showed her the screen. 'Look – the weather for tomorrow. Sunny and five degrees, going up to six or seven later. That doesn't spell ice to me. We'll be able to get away.'

'Oh, good. I can't wait to be home.'

'She's not bad. But your dad's better.' Sean appeared as if from nowhere and startled Thea.

'I thought you weren't coming,' she said, then wished she hadn't. It sounded as if she'd been waiting for him all evening, which of course she had, but she'd prefer him not to know that.

'I had to talk to someone in the other bar about some repairs to the house. We're hoping to get the barn done up like a proper games room later in the new year.'

'We'. There was that little reminder. Oh well.

'Good plan, though it seems to work OK as it is.' She thought of Daisy and Elmo in their clinch by the table-tennis table. So sweet for them. It would definitely have made their Christmas.

Anna leaned across and said, 'We're heading back to the house now. Are you coming with us?'

Thea hesitated. 'Er, maybe.'

'Oh, don't go yet,' Sean protested. 'I'll walk back with you later.'

'OK, I'll stay for a bit. That all right with you, Mum?'

Anna laughed. 'You're way too grown up to have to ask me!' she said. 'Stay and enjoy yourself – last night and all that.'

'There are lots of mums who would have reminded you that it's a long drive tomorrow and to get a good night's sleep,' Sean joked.

'Hippie parents don't do that,' Thea said. 'My mother's very keen on the live it while you've got it philosophy.'

'She's not wrong.' Sean took hold of her hand and she felt confused all over again, then he let go and said,

'Sorry. I've been madly flirting with you and I really shouldn't.'

'No. I guess not.'

'You must think I do this with all the house-guests.'

'I do. I think it's a top technique for getting repeat business. They must be clamouring to rebook just so they can be charmed all over again by your devastating smile and your undivided attention. Little do they know just how divided it is and that you play the same game once a fortnight.'

'Bang to rights, Elf. You got me,' he said, giving her a strange little grin. 'But you couldn't be more wrong.'

Was he playing with her? She was beginning to feel that this was bordering on the unkind. He must know she liked him.

'Is Paul coming tonight?' She thought maybe she should remind him that he wasn't exactly single.

Sean looked surprised. 'No. I know he did say he might, but then he remembered he had to be somewhere else. He's taken the children to the pantomime in Truro.'

'Children? Is he a maiden uncle, the equivalent of me?' she asked.

'Do you even *get* maiden uncles? Oh yes, you do. They're called bachelor uncles, aren't they? Preferably rich gay ones who make wonderful godparents and will introduce their charges to fine wines and teach them how to behave in restaurants without making idiots of themselves.'

'And take the children to the pantomime,' she finished for him.

'Ha – yes. But not in Paul's case. It's his own children.'

Thea was silent for a moment. 'He has children? Are you sure?'

Sean laughed. 'Of course I'm sure! He and Sarah have three of them. Aged between about seven and twelve, give or take.'

'Sarah?' Thea felt she was being spectacularly dim.

'His wife. Has he not mentioned her? He never stops going on about her. They're still like love's young dream, those two.'

'But I assumed . . .'

'Oh, you thought he was a bit on the camp side, did you?' Sean said. 'Most people do. Not at all. He's just a metrosexual sort who got used to putting on a bit of an act back in the advertising business days. He said it gave clients confidence in his arty side. He once told me that nobody trusts someone who sounds like a golf-playing lawyer to choose wallpaper and the right sofa for a set. So there you go. Another drink?'

'Er, yes, please. A small white wine would be lovely.'

While Sean was at the bar, Thea collected her thoughts and came to some heartening conclusions. But it was a bit late now, wasn't it? She was going home tomorrow. And he'd let go of her hand and apologized.

For a while she listened to the music in the background, the last of Charlotte's Sad Old Bastards singing the Rolling Stones' 'Wild Horses' in a voice that managed to make it sound – appropriately enough – as if he were actually neighing.

When Sean came back with the drinks, Thea took a deep breath and said, 'I've been such an idiot.'

'Aw, have you? What have you done?'

'I made . . . assumptions.'

'You said. About Paul.'

'Yes. And about – er, you.'

'Me? What assumptions?'

'That you and Paul were a couple.'

Sean spluttered into his beer. 'Ha! I can't wait to tell him – that is so funny!'

'No, it isn't!' She clouted him hard on his arm. 'All the signs were there. You said he was your partner.'

'Only businesswise! Jeez! Even if I *were* gay, I wouldn't fancy Paul. I'd go for someone more in the Johnny Depp line. Paul's a bit George Clooney for me, sorry to disappoint him and all that.' He couldn't seem to stop laughing. 'Oh, Thea, you are so funny. I've been coming on to you since the minute you arrived and you obviously didn't even notice.'

'But then you thought *I* was gay,' she reminded him.

'Paul knew I liked you. But then yesterday morning,

when he was having a go at matchmaking, he told me that you said that in other circumstances you'd maybe quite like me. He thought you were hinting that you weren't playing on the usual team, so . . .'

'We're both idiots then.'

He turned and looked at her. 'Seems as if we are. What shall we do about it?'

EIGHTEEN

'So – have you all had a Merry Christmas then?' Maria had done an hour or two already, helping Emily and Rosie to dismantle their Christmas decorations and pack them away, and helping Mike and Jimi to clear out the fridge and deal with leftover food. There was no turkey left and Charlotte had suggested they put the carcase out in a hedge for a passing fox to take.

'An unusual Christmas, yes, thank you. A good one, I think so. Definitely mostly merry,' Anna told Maria.

Charlotte and Alec had gone. Charlotte's friend had turned up early in his Mini and was going to drop both of them off at Truro station so they could travel back to London together on the train. Outside was now mostly clear of snow, apart from where it had piled up in drifts, and the snowman in the garden was reduced to a lopsided heap of slush.

'You didn't need all the rooms after all then?' Maria said.

'Oh, we did – we were definitely a full house,' Anna told her.

'Well, one of them hadn't been slept in,' Maria said. 'I've just been in to do the beds in the two who've gone and only one has even been touched.'

Mike and Anna looked at each other. 'Bloody hell,' Anna said, 'and there was me feeling sorry for Alec.'

'And me for Charlotte. I've been feeling guilty about her.'

'She doesn't surprise me.'

'Nor me,' Mike admitted, 'but I'm surprised at yours. He seemed far too wet for instant shenanigans.'

'Clearly not,' Anna said. 'The influence of Christmas mistletoe, I expect.' Then: 'We didn't do the fireworks, did we?' she asked suddenly.

Mike looked at her. 'I rather thought we did.' He looked sad. 'And I didn't think it was just me.'

'No, literally fireworks. They're still in the car.'

'Save them for New Year's Eve then, at home?'

'Good idea.'

They'd all gone home and no one (apart from Charlotte) had seen Thea coming in through the back door in the blue dress she'd worn to the pub. She had tried to whiz up the stairs to shower and change without anyone seeing her, but Charlotte was on the first-floor landing, dragging her case on wheels out of her room.

'Ah – the stop-out! So you got Sean then,' she said with a naughty grin. 'I knew you would in the end. Had to be done.' She hugged her. 'Bye, Thea, and good luck. And thanks for not being a cow to me. I might have been, in the circs, if it had been me.'

'No, you wouldn't. It is Christmas, after all – season of goodwill and all that.'

'Season of good *men*,' Charlotte said with a wink as Alec, trailing his own case, came out of the room after her.

'You saw us, didn't you?' Charlotte went on. 'Under the mistletoe that night.'

'I did,' Thea admitted. 'But not everything I see has to be broadcast to the wider world.'

'That's a freakin' good philosophy for life, that.' Charlotte gave her deep, throaty laugh. 'But probably a bit late for me to take to.'

'I'm so glad you could stay on.' Sean put the cushions on the terrace bench and pulled Thea down beside him. It was really warm with the sun shining directly on them, and the sea was twinkly beneath the hillside. The snow had melted and exposed the daffodils, some of them almost in flower. The Siamese was sniffing at the plants as if he'd forgotten – with the snow – that they'd ever existed.

'I have to be back at school on the fifth,' Thea told him, snuggling close, 'but I'm free till then.'

'And I have to be in London for a week or two after that, so . . .'

'We've got a while then. Good.' Sean would be coming back with her in her car, staying at her house, and he'd bring Woody as well. What would Mr and Mrs Over-the-Road make of Sean, she wondered. His surfer-dude look was a long way from the neat and buttoned-up appearance of Rich. They'd liked Rich – thought he was a dependable sort, although Mrs OTR had once said she wasn't sure about the poodle and why didn't he get a nice Labrador. Now they'd have something to tut about. Thea going off for a nice innocent family Christmas and coming back with a luscious man? That was quite some Christmas present. And Mrs OTR could sleep easy too, knowing Thea wasn't about to waltz back and make a play for her precious Robbie.

The much-reduced mistletoe (it seemed everyone had taken a piece of it) was now attached to the top of the bird table in the middle of the lawn.

'Should we have burned it, do you think? Isn't that what you're meant to do with Christmas greenery?' Thea asked, watching as a robin pecked at the berries. How strange that it wasn't poisonous to birds, only to mammals.

'We can burn the tree or the holly instead. It's all to do with the midwinter passing, the triumph of light over dark in the battle of the seasons. So long as something evergreen gets burned we'll be in with a chance for good fortune.'

'I'm glad it's out here for the birds,' she said. 'That way, it's got the best chance of being reproduced somewhere else. Spread the joy.'

'Exactly. Now it can go and be lucky for someone else. It's been pretty damn lucky for us, hasn't it?' Sean said, pulling Thea closer to him.

'It has,' she said.

ABOUT THE AUTHOR

Judy Astley became the author of witty, contemporary novels after several years as a dressmaker, illustrator, painter and parent. Her own Christmases are a mad mixture of ever-increasing family, too much food and a panic-stricken last-minute hurtle round the shops for presents. She has usually managed to pay off the resulting expense by the time the next lot of Christmas cards come on the market. Judy lives in London and Cornwall.